Rose's Garden

~ Rose's Garden

a novel by CARRIE BROWN

Carrie Brown

Algonquin Books of Chapel Hill   *1998*

Published by
Algonquin Books of Chapel Hill
Post Office Box 2225
Chapel Hill, North Carolina 27515-2225

a division of
Workman Publishing
708 Broadway
New York, New York 10003

*This is a work of fiction. While, as in all fiction, the literary perceptions and
insights are based on experience, all names, characters, places, and incidents are
either products of the author's imagination or are used fictitiously. No reference
to any real person is intended or should be inferred.*

Library of Congress Cataloging-in-Publication Data
Brown, Carrie.
    Rose's garden : a novel / by Carrie Brown.
        p.   cm.
    ISBN 1-56512-174-0 (hardcover)
    I. Title.
    PS3552.R68528R67   1998
    813'.54—dc21   97-41082
                                                          CIP

10 9 8 7 6 5 4 3 2 1
FIRST EDITION

For John
and in memory of
Arthur Milne McCully,
G. Gernon Brown Jr., and
Carrie Frances Brown

Why do you make me leave the house

And think for a breath it is you I see

At the end of the alley of bending boughs

Where so often at dusk you used to be

—THOMAS HARDY, "The Going"

Rose's Garden

One

THE ANGEL APPEARED on Paradise Hill the night of the fall equinox, light and dark dividing evenly over the world. As the sun set that September evening behind the horizon of Conrad Morrisey's garden, the moon rose over the far side of the hill, and a musical wind took up among the trees. The lindens' heart-shaped leaves spun, reversing to silver; the alders shivered. Next door, May Brown's washing stiffened and snapped on the line, a wild arcade of sheets and white gloves. The soft-feathered homing pigeons in Conrad's loft stepped side to side, testing their wings in the gathering wind.

It was the sound of the rain that woke Conrad, who had been asleep in his easy chair by the French doors.

The room was dark, warm, close, the seasonal air of slow twilights draining quietly over fields of tall grass heavy with seed. Conrad felt the weight of the water, the weight of the mountains, the weight of the clouds themselves, pressing close. He looked out the window into the dark rain and then, turning slowly, crossed the soft carpet, a meadow of wildflowers sewn within a border of flaming euonymus, each leaf stitched by his wife, Rose, in the days when her hands had been young and strong and clever.

Switching on the brass-bracketed light above the case for his phonograph records, Conrad fumbled through them, selected one, and slipped it from its cardboard sheath, soft as cotton with use. He leaned over the phonograph, the needle poised above Schumann's "Vanitas Vanitatum," the wind breathing deeply around his house. But before the stylus could fall, releasing the cello's first note, Conrad was arrested by an owl's deadly, fluting cry.

He thought, of course, of his pigeons, their soft, black eyes, the gentle throbbing of their breasts in his hand, the silken feathers laid over the milky blue skin. Setting the needle down on its rest, he hesitated, and in the pause he heard the owl again.

It happened so quickly—this decision to step outside, into the rain, into the storm, to defend his flock. It happened quickly, but in that moment, everything about Conrad's life changed.

For he knew the angel standing there in his garden, its features running with rain, its sleeves outspread, its flexed wings rippling the air. And because he knew the angel, Conrad thought that now he would be escorted up to heaven, would be handed step-by-step through the storm clouds that twisted overhead like a hornet's nest. And he was glad.

BUT WHEN MORNING came, with its baffling silence and smooth tide of gray mist falling over the grass gone wild and the late summer flowers, the garden was empty. Conrad had seen a miracle, and now it was gone. Or was it? The night before, a door had been flung open, and all the windows. Now papers lifted from the desk, sailed to the floor. The curtains filled with air. A set of wind chimes —blue-and-white china windmills that Rose had hung by the French doors—tinkled and shook. Conrad was surrounded by strange urgings, voiceless expectation, rivers of wind.

New grass grew over his wife's grave, and her silence in the house was immeasurable. But Conrad knew that something had changed. He had thought he was alone on Paradise Hill, alone as a man could be. But now, he could feel it—a change in the air. The wind was bringing something toward him, a gift or a burden. He wasn't sure which.

Rising from his chair by the window, Conrad was suddenly terrified; what he knew and what he thought he knew were all mixed up, everything strange and familiar at once. If Rose had been there, if Rose had been alive still, he would have rushed to her, would have buried his face in the shifting folds of her nightgown, would have whispered what he'd seen.

But he was by himself, seventy-five years old, a new widower in an untidy house on Paradise Hill, a low-lying, bowl-shaped ridge at the base of New England's greatest mountain range.

Standing outside in the diamond of grass on the highest terrace of his garden, Conrad considered himself, head to toe. He'd been tall once but was shrinking now from six feet. Awkwardly thin until he married Rose, he was burgeoning around the waist after a lifetime of helpless indulgence at her table. His hands dangled from his cuffs, two rough spades. His blue eyes were clouded. His hair, silky and white, lay childishly over his forehead and grew long over his collar.

He gazed out over the descending terraces before him, their lush folds and exuberant meadows freshened by the previous night's rain. Beyond and below the neglected acres of his garden lay the land through which the river ran. On the far side of the river, the mountains began their coiling ascent.

Though he'd let it go since Rose's death, the garden was lovely this morning; the flower heads glowed and sparkled, rain caught in their petals. And yet, since last night, since the angel, all the earth—even this familiar view—was unknown to him. He had wandered into foreign territory, a place where he could be taken by surprise.

He wanted—no, *needed*, he realized—to talk to someone. It had been too long, four months since Rose's death. And he wanted now to show someone where the angel had stood the night before, the place in the sky where it had vanished.

Standing there in his garden, the sun just rising, he saw May Brown next door, worrying over her late summer lilies, slapped down by the night's rain. She was holding her hat to her head against the wind, which toyed with it, tugging it and tipping the brim.

Conrad burst through the hedge that separated their gardens, took May around the waist, and ushered her along, his fingers pinching her elbow. He led her to the very spot and stopped, breathing hard. A fine sweat had broken out on his forehead. He pointed. "I saw an angel last night, May," he told her. "Right here. In the storm."

He saw May look him over, wary as a rabbit.

"Right there?" she asked, patting her ear as if she might have misunderstood, looking skyward and squinting, glancing back in the direction from which she had come, toward the bowed passage through the hedge. "In the rain?" she asked doubtfully.

"Yes!" he said, dropping her arm.

But it was all over her face. Disbelief. Fear. Even sympathy. He cast around on the ground for something the angel might have left behind, some evidence—a curved feather big as a ship's hull, a burning footprint, still smoldering. But there was nothing. Just the splintered stalks and clotted beds of the vegetable garden, an overturned bushel basket, fallen fruit. It didn't look like much, especially after the storm, he acknowledged, though in general the garden had astonished him that summer: pumpkins the size of boulders, the tomatoes garnet red and surprisingly heavy, crooked squash and striped gourds dense as stones.

May brushed delicately at her sleeve as though something had landed there. Conrad stared at her, saw her face fall softly. She lifted her hand as if she might press his arm, but then withdrew it and looked away, knotting her hands together beneath her apron.

"Well. That's something," she said. "Always something, I suppose. Must be going." And she left him.

Conrad stared after her a moment and then turned away, running his hands through his hair. He looked out over the terraces of his garden, down Paradise Hill to the silver arch of the river and, beyond, the rising mountains.

He and Rose had taken advantage of the intrinsic sense of expectation that clung to their house, with its high dormers like surprised eyes, by planting rows of Japanese maples across the lowest terrace, the grassy paths between them ending in a hazy vanishing point. Low-lying fingers of mist rose now from the ground on these ghost roads, snaking between banks of shrubs and conifers. Spiderwebs descended like sets on a stage, hung in the tree branches, threaded with drops of water. The bright, wavering air gave the impression of something drawing near, proceeding down the avenues of maples, emerging from between the fine curtain of the willows' leaves.

Rose had designed each of the four terraces below the house: one for the herbs and roses, another for the perennials, another for the vegetables, and a fourth, closest to the house, with a grape arbor, a ring of fruit trees, and a quiet diamond of grass, a circular pool like a blind eye at its center. Conrad remembered Rose as she had been her final fall—a frail, gray-haired old woman in a chair in the middle of the garden, a scarf around her head, a notebook on her lap, paper bags of bulbs arrayed at her feet. He had buried each bulb according to her plan.

In the field beneath the lowest terrace was Conrad's pigeon loft, a miniaturized two-story affair designed for him by his father-in-law, Lemuel Sparks, and modeled after a Belgian senator's loft that Lemuel had admired. Painted white, with louvered sliding doors opening to the roost compartments and a wide landing board running between the stories, it had an orderly, European appearance. Lemuel had roofed it in curved terra-cotta tiles, though they had cost him a fortune, and Rose had surrounded the loft with dwarf fig trees and plantings of shrubs that in the summer attracted migrating swarms of monarch butterflies.

Conrad glanced toward May's house now, saw she had abandoned the bundle of stakes for her sodden lilies. He imagined her standing behind her window curtain, watching him. Sighing, he headed over the grass toward the stone steps that led down to the pigeon loft.

Pearl, his rare frillback, was standing by the door to the first compartment. He reached in and took her in his hands, put his cheek to the whorl of white feathers at her crest, ran his finger over the curling dorsal coverts, which lay over her back in an elaborate cape. She dipped her head, rubbed it against his chin.

The other pigeons, alert at his presence, had gathered at the screens that separated them from the landing board. They fixed their round eyes on him. Conrad regarded his birds, their speechless expectation. If he opened their cages now, he knew, they would step to the lip of the landing board and spread their wings. In less than a minute they would be tuning their bodies to all the mysterious emanations of home, the signals that distinguished this place from any other. They might go near or far, down Paradise Hill to follow the serpentine curls of the river and through the orchard rows that flowed down to its banks. They might climb through the laurel and dogwood into fragrant pine woods, might fly in a banner over the lowest of the mountains' foothills. But they would, Conrad knew, no matter how far they went, find their way back by memory, remembrance itself distilled into a hundred different essences—sight, sound, smell—a penumbra of the familiar, all the resonances of the heart.

Conrad put Pearl back into her roost compartment, stood before her, and watched her neat motions. He did not consider himself a hysterical man, a man inclined to delusions or hallucinations. He understood that at seventy-five, and without Rose to take care of him, he wasn't likely to live so very much longer, a truth that, in his grief, he found comforting. And he believed it best to walk into whatever future he had left with his eyes wide open, gathering to him what he knew of himself and his life. But now an angel had chosen to make itself part of that life, had chosen to touch down like a spark at the end of a wire. What did it mean? And what would Rose have done?

She would have told anyone who'd listen. She would have celebrated. She would have told her friends.

But Conrad didn't really have any friends, he realized, not more than a couple anyway. He'd always just had Rose. That had seemed enough.

He returned to the house now, climbing the steps from one terrace to the next. Inside, he sat down at the dining room table, its lacquered surface holding the indistinct shape of his own reflection. He considered his story. Something unlikely, something unbelievable, something wonderful or terrible or even some mixed-up combination of the two—something he hadn't ever thought of, couldn't have imagined—had happened to him. He had become a stranger visiting his own life, and the sensation made him want to put himself at the heart of this mystery, claim it before it claimed him.

If you don't have many friends, he reasoned, you have to start with strangers. You never know who a stranger *really* is anyway, Rose always said. Anyone might be Jesus Christ, or an angel in disguise, testing the content of souls.

And so after some consideration—May Brown's skepticism

firmly in his mind—Conrad got up, found paper and a pen in the clutter of Rose's kitchen desk, and then sat down again at the dining room table to write a careful letter to the editor of the local newspaper, the *Laurel Aegis*.

He shook out his sleeve and bent low to the page, tongue exploring his lower lip. It would be a testimony and an invitation, he thought: Here is what I saw.

THE PREVIOUS AFTERNOON had been one of the worst he could remember, his most intense spell of unrelieved grief since the night Rose's body had been carried away to the funeral home. The needle of the barometer had twitched uncertainly. All day he had paced inside the house, sometimes bursting into fits of weeping that would overtake him from his knees up, doubling him over. Afterward he drew a shaky breath, stared around him as though he had been away on a long voyage. He thought he sensed a vibration in the air outside, a subtle intercession. Something was eddying down the garden's paths, winding through the leaves, unfurling. Coming closer.

That night, he'd pulled his easy chair in front of the French doors facing the garden, held them ajar against the hot wind with a sack of sugar. He'd fallen asleep by degrees, sinking into it. In the night sky, advancing clouds pared away the moon above him. The garden filled with pools of ink. Shadows tall as trees stepped forward.

He'd woken to the sound of rain and a sensation of terrible haste. His heart was racing. He sat for a moment, listening to the rain, and then turned to the cabinet at the other end of the room. He put the Schumann record on the phonograph, his beloved folk songs, and leaned over to blow dust from the needle.

And then he'd heard that owl. He'd returned to the French

doors and looked out through the streaked glass. The garden had become a sea of dark crests and lime-colored breakers, the wind lashing at the white flags of the leaves.

Rose would have called this his Summer of Neglect. He'd left the vegetables to rot on the vine; he'd allowed the flowers to fall, unstaked; he'd watched, hardly even noticing, as the leaves of the roses were eaten away by black spot. He thought he knew that if *he* had been the one to die, Rose would have looked after the garden anyway. It might have been her most beautiful garden, in fact, just as now, despite her absence, the flowers themselves seemed to be responding to some distant urging from her, some expectation. And now, he thought, an owl would take one of his pigeons, a storm would ruin the garden. Don't let it go to waste, Connie— that's what Rose would have said.

So he had moved then like an obedient child, relieved to be of use, happy to be busy, pleased at what they had wrought by day's end in their garden—a border weeded, the lilies staked, rocks piled for a wall and studded with sea pinks and sempervivums, beard-tongue and sunrose. She would have taken her finger and touched it to his brow, polishing the shining leaves of the bay tree with his sweat, filling her apron with branches of rosemary and lavender, with figs and persimmons.

Get your hat, he told himself now, and he did, pulling it down over his eyes against the sheets of rain.

The pigeons were safe, no owl in sight. Conrad adjusted the louvers that Lemuel had built for him along the north side of the loft, which protected the birds from slanting rains while still allowing fresh air into the roost. "Oh, you'll ride it out," he told Pearl, touching her crest with a finger. "Think of your ancestors on the ark."

In the vegetable garden, though he could hardly see, he'd

knelt among the furrows running with water, tried to heel the soft, resisting pumpkin toward the basket, failed, and left it to see to the beans instead, huge and wormy now and pocked with ash rot but yielding easily to his grasp. A tomato caved apart in his hand. The tent for the yellow squash swayed and collapsed in the darkness of the night storm. Conrad had been frightened. Heads of cabbage dissolved at their root; the leaves turned swampy and slick. Above him, branches had broken with sharp cracks and sailed toward the earth, denting the soft, black ground. Leaves like bats' wings had flown toward him and plastered themselves to his back.

Crawling down the rows, inching his way through the darkness and the rain, Conrad had tried to find something he could take inside, something he could keep. All summer, wandering the house, he had suffered spells of inchoate rage, his house full of fragile surfaces, things poised at the lip of ruin—Rose's porcelains and her Swiss figurines, plates lined up on the mantel, tiny glass animals threading a path to a spun glass ark on the sideboard, chips of soft sea glass on the kitchen windowsill—all of it acquiring a thin garment of dust. He had looked around for something to throw but had seen nothing that wouldn't do some damage, wouldn't cause Rose, even in her death, some pain to see shattered.

Now, the wind bearing down around him, he came forward on his hands and knees through the mud, toward the oak tree that sheltered the northern end of the garden, bathing the spinach and tender late lettuces in afternoon shade.

And at last he got his hands around something, a stone or a root. He'd pulled, bent his shoulders, thrown his weight into it. But whatever it was did not yield to his hand. He cursed, rain cascading over his hat brim. And he swore—at it, at *him,* not a lopped root nor the thick knee of the oak tree but the long shin of what looked like an angel, the thing that said it *was* an angel, the thing with the voice that said, "Rise up."

For there it had stood among the trunks of the trees, soaring up from the earth into the flooding night sky like a magnificent statue, its mouth gaped to the rain, its feet turned briefly to clay, its wings shuddering.

Yet this was not a heavenly angel, with a pure expression and an innocent brow, a harp borne at its hip. It did not look like an angel whose likeness might hang on a wall in the Vatican Museums. This was someone Conrad knew—an angel with a rutted, Abraham Lincoln face.

It had not been what he might have expected, what he thought anyone, even a grieving widower, had a right to expect. If he'd ever imagined such a thing, it would have been along lines somewhat holier, more picturesque—the eyelid of heaven itself, lifted to issue forth a swirling cloud of steam. And in that widening eye of light, a heavenly cavalcade of angels might have streamed down from on high, ferocious expectation on their faces, their gowns billowing behind them like a white afterlife, holy and endless, smoke blown down from heaven's fires.

Conrad had raised his eyes and taken in the angel's towering form. It held its head nobly, a carved figurehead against the rushing black clouds. Its wings had rippled, an expanse of sailcloth behind its back. The pinfeathers crackled; the flesh had seized.

Oh, Jesus. Death becomes me now, Conrad thought, kneeling in the mud, his hands wrapped around the angel's foot. Dust to dust, mud to mud. I'm fit. It's over. And he'd lain there, had begun in relief to weep, thinking he would see his Rose again, thinking he had not been left alone to suffer so long after all, that he would take the wild Rose into his arms now, hold her gray head, her soft cheek, against his own. Here it was, in the devastated empire of her garden—the deep voice of his heavenly escort. So he had raised his face.

And there had stood *Lemuel,* his father-in-law, dead fifteen years now, his bony hands dangling from the vaporous sleeves of his robe, his gentle manner and wandering eye regarding him.

"Rise up," Lemuel said, but Conrad could not. He cast his eyes down, looked into the dirt. "You've come for me," he whispered. And it was not a question.

But Lemuel didn't answer, and Conrad was frightened then at the sensation in the air above him, streamers of wind and night wrapping themselves around the angel, around Lemuel.

"You've come for me!" Conrad had cried, insisting, lifting up his arms. "I can't stay here forever!"

"You don't have forever," Lemuel had answered, and Conrad understood then that he was not leaving. Lemuel's appearance that night was not a deliverance but a sentence. Not a route of escape but a path that would return him to where he began, back through old age, middle age, adolescence, childhood, birth, each stage a notch on a diving plumb line.

"Please! Lemuel! Where is Rose?" he had cried, struggling to his feet. "Can't you do something? Show her to me!"

But Lemuel had turned aside and averted his eyes, casting them upward to the roiling sky, to the black-and-purple geysers of cloud. His voice was distant when he replied; his answer was not an answer. "Go home, Conrad," Lemuel told him.

Lemuel's form had shivered, then contracted itself like a cloud.

"Wait!" Conrad cried. "Go home? What do you mean? What else?"

"Isn't this enough?" Lemuel said, and he had extended his wings then. They were surprisingly large, and Conrad saw an impatience to the gesture, Lemuel's strength boiling up inside of him, a flood ready to be unleashed. "Watch!" Lemuel cried.

Conrad had ducked as an enormous, invisible mass hovered over him. The trees themselves bent down in the wind that lifted Lemuel. Conrad saw the lights of his house flicker, the hexagonal enclosure of Rose's herb knots, the reflecting pool, the filigreed grape arbor encircling the house, the gilded trim of the eaves, the elaborate green framework of his garden falling into itself with a breath like a collapsing tent—all of it illuminated in a sudden burst of phosphorescent light. His world had grown small in that instant, a faraway place.

"She loved you," Lemuel called, his voice snatched and carried away. "Rose loves you, Conrad."

And then he was gone.

Conrad had come to his knees, covered his face with his hands. The rain pelted against his back, hard, like gravel thrown at him, like some pain—or some awakening joy—meant to spur him on. All around him the garden's vines were hauled in; the heads of the flowers were knocked from their stems and flung into the dark distance. The roosting crows left in a long train, one after another, flying through the rain. Seed cases held a moment, then exploded and were drowned. Leaves were stripped from branches, torn apart.

And as Conrad lay there alone, a disheveling hand hesitated over Paradise Hill, taking down bowers and scaffolds, bearing away the anemone and achillea, the lamb's ears and the leopard's bane, the speedwell and Jacob's ladder, ending the summer and beginning the fall.

HE COULDN'T PUT all that in a letter to the editor, he knew, but he tried to be exact anyway; it seemed important to be accurate. He brushed at the page before him, scattering erasings. He tried to be humble, admitting that he did not know, did not understand why he had been given this vision, but that he was—*grateful* was the word he settled on, a word Rose would have liked. And because it seemed important to share not just the story but also the place it-self, he finished his letter by saying he would welcome visitors. Anyone who wanted to see where it had happened. Between the hours of—four and six sounded convenient, he thought. Any day of the week.

His letter completed, Conrad set down his pen, stared off into space, and allowed himself a few minutes of speculation: You gather what believers you can, he decided. You gather them for whatever they might make of what happened to you. You tell the story. You see what happens. You watch how everything stays the same, apparently the same.

Except, except—now there was this; now it was not just the fu-ture that looked different, but the past, too.

The memory of the angel in his garden, the vision that had overtaken him, worked away inside him. He had wanted one more moment, one more moment with Rose, one chance to say not what he had said—"How could you leave me here?"—but this: How will I ever find you now? He would have given anything for an answer. Sold his soul.

And she'd said something, there at the end. What had it been? He rubbed his head, tried—unsuccessfully again—to bring her be-fore him, to reel back the months. She'd said something, turning her eyes toward him.

But now *this,* he thought—this *apparition.* This was not exactly what he'd asked for, was it? He'd wanted *her,* not Lemuel. And yet he had the feeling that she *had* been there, standing some distance away perhaps, invisible but present in the way the wind brings dis-tant places near for a moment, a scent borne from far away.

He sat quietly at his table, his letter under his hand. His whole life was reeling back to him, both known and unknown at once. Now the whole world quivered with suggestion, with a thousand rippling meanings and surprises, announcing itself not just for what it was but for what he, you, anybody, might make of it.

AFTERWARD, THINKING IT over, Conrad thought he should have been prepared for it. For an angel, or something like it. For his father-in-law finally capable of real flight, not just its imagined ecstasy. Standing on his rooftop, his pigeons gripping his out-stretched arms, their wings raised in expectation, Lemuel had be-lieved in the rewards of concentration, of desire, even of faith. And the spectacular behavior of the garden this summer, despite Con-rad's neglect—this heroic display, flowers larger than ever and more brilliant and numerous—all this, surely, had been the gar-den's way of making itself ready to host a miracle.

So he should have been prepared, Conrad thought, should have been ready. Another man might have been ready. But he had not.

Since Rose's death four months before, he had spent most mornings with his pigeons, many of them offspring from Lemuel's original flock. He swept and scrubbed the loft, coddled his birds, brewed up herbal teas on the little camp stove, and dosed the pi-geons, drop by drop, their warmth spreading over his lap as he held them. He felt among their feathers for boils and lumps, watching for the swollen beaks of birds suffering from mycoplas-mosis, the inflamed eyes of those with ornithosis. He knew he had neglected his birds during Rose's last weeks, and so he worked carefully now, afraid of overlooking something.

He had walked to and fro, a pigeon on his shoulder, its throaty warbling in his ear. He remembered Lemuel pacing on the grav-eled rooftop of his own house in Brooklyn, conversing with his birds, nodding assent or disagreement.

The summer afternoons he had spent dozing in his easy chair, the one Rose called Sleepy Hollow for its comforting, deep curves.

From time to time he came upon articles of her clothing—a shoe, the pink blazer she'd worn when she'd been a volunteer at the hospital, a skirt with its elastic waistband—and took them on his lap. He sat, the minor weight of her cardigan resting over his shoulders, and attended to his own heartbeat. He took her purse down from the hook on the kitchen door and held it, his fingers resting over the clasp.

He spent his evenings sitting in the arbor with a pigeon on his lap, or laid out on the grass on the middle terrace, feeling the earth tug at the center of his body.

He could not cook at all—he had never learned and never imagined that he might have to—and so he'd been, in those early weeks after Rose's death, still and watchful around food, as if he were a pool of water inhabited by a hungry, muscled carp. He would lunge, with a ferocity that surprised him, at the pears that dripped from the trees. But though he could feel the sweet nectar drain down his chin, he had lost all sense of taste. Late at night, unable to sleep for the hunger in his belly, he would pull the ribbed chain to the light in the pantry, stand before the jars of roseate pickled beets and spiced apples, pale cucumbers and marmalade with its shavings of ginger, all put up by Rose her last autumn. He would select one jar, unscrew the lid, and plunge his fingers in, withdrawing them and skimming them across his lips. Nothing. The fruits were as scentless and tasteless as river stones. It had made him weep.

But one afternoon, two or three weeks after Rose's death and months before the angel came, he was standing listlessly behind the lace curtains in the dining room, staring out the window. His eyes traveled up and down the empty street, up and down and back across his small lawn, and then stopped at the sight of a small basket resting on the top step of his front porch.

The meditative sawing of grasshoppers' wings ceased when he opened the door and stepped outside. Conrad saw an unfamiliar little terrier, white, with black, pointed ears like two cocked dunce caps, veer sharply across the deserted road before his house and disappear around the corner. He'd scanned the street again and then picked up the basket and brought it inside.

He'd laid it on the kitchen table, where a long bar of sunlight fell across it. A residual heat rose from the woven lid, shimmering in the air; Conrad had been momentarily dizzy. Some scent, sweetly familiar yet belonging to a place so far back in his memory that he could not place it, rose to his nostrils. If a swarm of butterflies had risen when he opened the lid, if honeybees had built their wax paper combs inside, he would not have been surprised. The inside of his cheeks clenched; his eyes watered.

It had been his first real meal since Rose's death: a veal stew with tiny pearl onions and pink peppercorns; a half-dozen corn muffins, studded with a confetti of hot peppers in pink and green. There were sausages, brown and glistening, in an earthenware jar. A faceted glass bottle held wine. He ate two pieces of the chocolate cake, dense and rich and flavored with coffee, and then he pushed back from the table, his hands over his middle, tears running down his face.

This was Rose's cooking, yet with something slightly altered about it—some herb he did not recognize in the sausages, rum in the cake. But he had known, even as he raised the lid of the basket, that its contents would restore to him the flavor and essence of sustenance, the pleasure of Rose's table, which had made him, throughout his marriage, nearly faint with gratitude. He had known that the meal to follow would be good—he could smell it, and if he could smell it, he knew, he could taste it. And it had been so delicious, so satisfying; it had reached in and placed a kind palm over the wound in his heart. Who, what kindly neighbor, could have done this?

That night, the night of the veal stew, for the first time in weeks and weeks, he had slept for almost six hours straight, sunk down into the chair by the window where he had made his bed since Rose had died. From far away he heard the sound of a dog baying. The yellow moon had sailed past the window over the bowl of Paradise Hill like a child's toy pulled on a string. Next door, May Brown, who was afraid of the dark, knelt under her orange porch light to clean her deep freeze, scraping bitter ice crystals into the ash bucket. Her radio, set on the windowsill and turned to face the evening so she could hear it out on the porch, had been tuned to a comedy show. Conrad fell asleep under the comforting tide of audience laughter rising and falling under his window.

Two

THOUGH LEMUEL CAME to be the man Conrad loved most in the world, their friendship did not begin auspiciously. It began, Conrad considered, as so many men's friendships do—though he had been just a child at the time—with what those who raise pigeons call *la guerra,* with war, the battle waged for fun and profit among pigeon fanciers. Mumblers, they call themselves, to describe their vague and limited attention as boys in school, more interested in the wheeling flight of birds outside the window than in the crabbed and distant writing on the blackboard. The teacher would ask them a question and they'd mumble a reply, for they hadn't, in truth, been paying any attention at all. They'd been looking out the window at the spokes of light thrown from a bird's wing.

Conrad was just a child, eleven years old. He first came to know Lemuel Sparks without ever meeting him, without ever laying eyes on the man, for Lemuel had been poaching Conrad's pigeons —and quite successfully, too—for some months before Conrad finally met him face-to-face or even knew his name.

All he knew was that someone was stealing his birds, though the thefts were executed fairly, according to the rules of the sport. Week after week his pigeons were hooked down one after the other into someone else's flock, birds so expertly trained and organized that they rose together like a puff of smoke and then fell in unison, movie footage reversing itself in fast motion. It was an old trick: a perfectly synchronized flock would surround a lone bird, usually young and probably poorly fed, and draw it down in a captivating embrace to a foreign roost. Conrad had seen it happen, watching from his fire escape, his heart sinking. Whoever this poacher was, Conrad understood the man knew what he was doing.

And as the rules required, Conrad paid up at the pigeon exchange on Marion Street, one quarter a bird. By the time he arrived at the exchange after school, his loss having festered in his heart all day, his opponent would already have brought in the band from his latest captive. It always seemed particularly cruel to Conrad that he could lose not only a pigeon but his dignity and a quarter, too. Soberly, Conrad would hand the money over to Frank Pittilio, Marion Street's proprietor, who enjoyed the joke of keeping Lemuel's identity a secret.

"Lost another one, I see," Mr. Pittilio would say when Conrad placed his coin in the man's hand. "Your personal *nemico* has just been here. He's knocking down your birds just as easy as taking candy from a baby. Aww, Conrad! Don't look so sad! You should be happy he takes only one at a time." And then Mr. Pittilio would laugh, put Conrad's change in an envelope, slide the envelope back into a drawer, pat it shut.

"I want my birds back," Conrad would demand, red faced. That was the rule; he paid the price of losing, and his pigeons would be returned to him.

"All in good time, little man. All in good time," Mr. Pittilio would reply, laughing, leaning closer. "He's waiting for the good fight. A worthy opponent."

Conrad would leave then, defeated. He'd stand at the window of the pigeon exchange a moment, looking in at the birds, the homers in yellow, white, and isabella, that color of spun honey, the low light of the setting sun illuminating their feathers. And then he'd go home, back to his fire escape, back to his flock diminished by yet one more bird.

Conrad knew that his experience with pigeons was limited by his youth and his wallet. He bought cheap birds, small racing homers Mr. Pittilio was willing to let go for a song, and kept them on the fire escape in orange crates.

"Street filth," his father would mutter. "Going to catch a disease from those."

But he had an ally in his mother. He'd find her sometimes, still in her housedress, leaning on the radiator with the broom in her hand, watching the pigeons in their crates, making little kissing noises at the glass. "It's something, what he can do with them," she'd say to her husband. "Let him be. It's harmless."

At night, when she smoothed the child's blankets, tucked them in, she'd stroke his head. "They won't be too cold out there? We shouldn't bring them in?" she'd ask.

"No," the boy would say, smiling. "They're meant to be outside, Mama. They're used to it."

"So cold," she'd say softly, shivering a little, shaking her head. And then she'd kiss him good night. "Sleep well, little bird boy."

Though he loved his mother's touch, Conrad fancied himself a daring flight guy. That's what they called themselves, Conrad knew, those pigeon fanciers willing to take risks with their birds, willing to let them duel in the air. But Conrad was, in truth, cautious, even as a child. The only risk he took was stealing grain—a handful at a time, sifted into his pocket from the sagging bags on the floor of the Marion Street Pigeon Exchange. The stolen grain on his palm, he taught his pigeons to loft up into the late afternoon sky and then butterfly down for their meal. He would sit cross-legged on his fire escape, looking out over the low roofs and chimney pots of Brooklyn, the fading sun and black funeral wreaths of smoke hanging low over the city. And he imagined himself a magician, drawing doves from his hat, the ladies in the audience exclaiming at the beautiful sight, at his most marvelous gifts. Sending his pigeons wheeling up into the sky, he imagined he could make a lightning bolt spear from his fingertips, make the thunder crash with a clap of his hands. He thought he could darken the sun itself.

And how he hated that man, that man stealing his birds.

"Ad ultimo sangue, ad ultimo sangue," Mr. Pittilio would say, backing off, laughing and waving his hands at Conrad's furious assault as he rushed into the exchange after school, ignoring the men at the stoop smirking at him and drinking their coffee. "It's a caution, Conrad! Remember! He could be stringing them up by the neck. I happen to know he's taking good care of them. He pities you, poor boy."

At last, though, it was too much for Conrad. It was autumn. The high and gusty winds were playing roulette with his pigeons. Sitting on the fire escape after school one afternoon, he looked up and confused his few remaining pigeons with the falling leaves blown topsy-turvy over the rooftops and through the streets. The strange, indirect light of approaching weather gave everything a sad and sinister veneer. The world was lost to him that day, and he felt sentimental about his defeat. He knew he was a child, just eleven years old, and he knew he was being bested by a wiser and more experienced flight guy, a man who was enjoying the terrible game of bleeding him dry, one bird at a time. His nameless enemy had won his birds, fair and square. Conrad had paid him the money, a quarter for every one he'd lost—child's wages. His enemy had Conrad's pigeons *and* his money. Sooner or later, if he was a gentleman, he'd give the birds back. But meanwhile, Conrad had nothing.

He had not a cent to his name that particular day. He kicked through the gutters for a penny or a glinting nickel, to no avail. He lifted his mother's pocketbook from the hook in the hall, took it to the bathroom, and locked the door. He unfolded the faded bills from her little change purse but couldn't bring himself to steal from her. He importuned Mrs. Findley, his neighbor, for an odd job, with no luck. And *il nemico,* his nameless enemy, had added another pigeon to his roost.

"I want to meet him," Conrad told Mr. Pittilio, banging his fist at last upon the counter at the Marion Street Pigeon Exchange, tears in his eyes. "I want to meet this man who is ruining me."

"Ah," said Mr. Pittilio, softening. "Such dramatic words for such a small boy." And he came out from behind the counter to kneel in front of Conrad, cuff his shoulder, take his chin in his hand. "It's only *di buona guerra.* It's just a game," he said gently.

But Conrad burst into tears then, for all his birds now lost, for all the feed he'd held out hopefully in the palm of his hand for a pigeon who would never return, for all the ways in which he felt he would never grow up, never become a man, never take something for himself and fight to the death to keep it. Mr. Pittilio knelt, put his arms around the boy. Conrad smelled the cigar smoke in his hair, in his collar with its frayed edge. Conrad felt him tremble.

"Come on," Mr. Pittilio said, rising painfully, his knees cracking. "Can you be a little late for supper? It's time we went to shake down Mr. Lemuel Sparks. It's time he gave you your birds back."

Mr. Lemuel Sparks. That's his name, Conrad thought as he wiped his hands across his face, across his pants. He combed his fingers through his hair, tucked in his shirt, sucked air into his cheeks. He trotted along beside Mr. Pittilio, who, after locking the door to the pigeon exchange, cocking his head at the birds, lit himself a cigar and clapped his hat on his head. He nodded good evening to the proprietors of stores they passed, men in aprons leaning in door frames with their arms crossed over their chest. Conrad imagined them whispering, laughing; he imagined they knew where he and Mr. Pittilio were headed, were relishing the scene they could see pictured in their mind: little one tilting at Goliath, little one come to beg his birds back. Mr. Lemuel Sparks. Conrad thought he could see him, looming from his rooftop among the chimney pots belching devil's fire. He was afraid.

Mr. Pittilio walked fast, like a tree blown over in the wind. Conrad hurried to keep up as they raced down one street after another, leaves blowing at their feet, thronging the gutters and toppling over one another in haste.

"Ever seen a really big loft?" Mr. Pittilio asked, the cigar clenched between his teeth, smoke and his own words trailing behind him in an acid wind.

"Just Mr. Polanski's," Conrad said, panting with his effort to keep up. "He took me up there once."

Mr. Pittilio laughed. "Well, get ready," he said. "This one will take your breath away. It's a whole Holy Roman city up there. Another world altogether."

At Modena Street Mr. Pittilio turned, and they walked to the last house. A huge barbed wire fence threaded with vines stood at the dead end before a scrub line of ailanthus and maple trees and the deep gully in which the train tracks ran. The house was a wide, four-story brownstone, with a short flight of concrete stairs leading to the second story. At the bottom of the pitted steps Mr. Pittilio paused, neatly clipped off the lit end of his cigar with the toe of his shoe, and folded the sodden remainder into a piece of stained newspaper, returning the whole mess to his pocket. He squinted up toward the roof.

"Look up there," he said, stepping backward and putting a hand to Conrad's shoulder to draw him back. Conrad craned his neck and looked. On the roof behind a brick balustrade he could see the jagged roofline of a pigeon loft, its peaks and dormers jutting up into the purpling evening sky.

"Listen," Mr. Pittilio said.

As they stood there, the sound of Lemuel's pigeons became audible, a distant cooing. The sun was sinking directly behind the brownstone. Conrad squinted into the sun, wondering over the proportions of what he judged must have been an enormous loft, a veritable empire. And then the tall, dark silhouette of a man in a hat and jacket passed slowly into the sun's glowing circle. Conrad looked up at Mr. Pittilio, who glanced down at Conrad and nodded. And then they heard the sound of the train, its warning whistle. The ground shook under their feet. And as its siren split the air, Conrad saw his enemy's pigeons rise from the roof in a cloud of white, a twister rotating furiously into the mouth of the sky, a hurricane that unraveled at its spire and opened like a white flower, sparks shooting into the dark. And then they were gone.

Mr. Pittilio craned back, nearly fell trying to follow the ascent of the birds. He gave a low whistle. "'Their faces were all living flame;'" he intoned soberly; "'their wings were gold; and for the rest—'" Mr. Pittilio shut his eyes, "'—and for the rest, their white was so intense, no snow can match the white they showed.'" He looked down at Conrad and smiled. "Dante," he said reverently. "The *Paradiso*. My father knew the whole thing. You know it?"

"No," Conrad said humbly, though he saw what Mr. Pittilio meant, the poetry of it all.

"Here's the rest," Mr. Pittilio said. "'When they climbed down into that flowering Rose, from rank to rank, they shared that peace and ardor which they had gained, with wings that fanned their sides.'" He paused, sighing.

Conrad looked up at the sky. The pigeons were gone.

"Come on," Mr. Pittilio said, and knocked at the door.

And that was Conrad's first look at her. At Rose. She opened the door, and for a moment Conrad thought he was seeing things. She looked to be his own age, but somehow older. Hers was a face he thought he'd seen in his art book at school—the same long nose and high, sad forehead he'd seen in that portrait, the perfectly shaped eye and pursed mouth. She was wearing, incongruously, a makeshift toga, with a headband of scarlet leaves threaded with ivy wreathing her long, yellow hair.

"Yes?" she said, drawing out the syllable. And then she swept into a low, formal bow. "Enter," she said.

They stepped into the hall, and Mr. Pittilio stifled a chuckle. Conrad stole a glance at him.

"Miss Rose Sparks," Mr. Pittilio said. "This is Conrad Morrisey. Conrad, meet Rose, leading lady."

And Conrad was smitten. There, at that very moment, the reed-like Rose in a toga of sheets, the leaves askew upon her head, he fell in love. Yet it was not just desire, its first vague and alarming stirrings, that he felt. It was something else, too, some feeling of stewardship, as though from that point forward things would be more complicated than he could ever have imagined. From that point forward, he understood, poised between disbelief and faith, he would have some role to play in determining whether Rose had a happy life.

When she died, so many years later, Conrad saw that her eyes remained open, staring just past his shoulder. As had been the case their whole lives, she saw something there that he could not see, saw the miraculous and the ordinary all mixed up together, some space populated by strangers in conversation, their heads close together, their words intimate and knowing. A moment before her death, as he'd held her hands, she'd said something, and he'd put his ear to her mouth, trying—and failing—to catch the whispered voice.

But that evening so long ago, when they were both just children: Rose, the young Rose. She smiled at Conrad, and he thought he might faint, for the overpowering recognition was so strong he could practically reach out his hand and touch it, touch the shape of what stood between them.

"I'm a priestess," she said, as if that explained her ridiculous costume. "Hello, Mr. Pittilio."

"And where's the high priest himself?" Mr. Pittilio asked, laughing.

Rose stopped, struck a pose of infinite patience. "Up there," she said, wagging a shoulder toward the ceiling. "Performing his errands of mercy. And now—" She began to drift archly down the hall, her arms floating, toward a lighted room at the end, from which came the aroma of supper being cooked. Suddenly she turned.

"You're the bird boy?" she asked.

Conrad nodded.

She smiled again, and a blush rose through her whole face. She drew nearer and peered at Conrad as if there were something under his skin that would explain his presence there. "He's got a surprise for you," she said, poking a finger at Conrad's chest where his heart thudded. "Wait a minute."

She ran down the hall and disappeared, returning a moment later, followed by a tall woman wearing a pale pink duster and wiping her hands on a dish towel. Her face was Rose's face, Conrad saw, matured into adulthood, but with the same classical shape. Her body carried the same long, tapered waist, the same swaying hips.

"Frank," she said warmly, extending her hand. "Lemuel's up on the roof." She turned to Conrad. "You'll forgive him, won't you? We've been waiting for you."

Conrad did not understand what she meant, nor their mutual tone of conspiracy, but he sensed there in that household an agreement that life was meant to be lived in search of miraculousness, in service to a human effort to contrive wonder and delight among the unforgiving surfaces of daily living. While his own household lived within the modest confines of a certain unavoidable drudgery, with a resolution to stand fast against occasional hunger, against certain disappointment, the parties of Mr. Lemuel Sparks's household were trained on a different sort of existence, one in which the whole matter of being was an exercise in determined joyousness. It took only one evening, that first evening, for Conrad to know that he wanted, though it felt disloyal, to stay there forever, exploring the darkened rooms that opened off the hallway, tasting the supper laid upon the table. He wanted to be initiated into Mr. Lemuel Sparks's fantastic world of wings and light up on the roof. As much as he was afraid of this man, he wanted to belong there.

"I'm just finishing supper," the woman said, and Conrad judged her at that moment to be Mrs. Sparks. "We'll join you up there in a minute." She smiled, glancing from one to the other. "Go on, go on up. He'll be delighted."

Rose hopped on one foot, her toga slipping off her shoulder.

"Get your coat, Rose," her mother said, shooing Mr. Pittilio and Conrad with her hands toward the staircase, its heavy newel carved with a globe of the earth balanced in the arching tails of three fish.

They climbed the stairs. Above them Conrad could see the doors of four rooms opening to a center hall, and within those rooms, an occasional fire burning against the chill of early fall, the tassled sleeve of a canopy over a bed, a slipper chair with articles of clothing strewn across it. At the first landing, two small boys a few years younger than Conrad lay on the floor, shooting marbles across a richly colored rug. A tattered toy lion mounted on wheels, its lead dangling, carried a rider in the form of a small monkey with a wizened face and clasped hands. The three—boys and monkey—looked up as Conrad and Mr. Pittilio passed. The boys smiled. "Gotcha," said one.

"Good evening, John, James," Mr. Pittilio said. "Melchior," he added, nodding to the monkey. And to Conrad, to his astonished gaze, he remarked, "Strange little creature, that one." The boys waved, flicking their hair out of their eyes. Conrad stared at the monkey, who stared back with black, iridescent eyes.

Conrad followed Mr. Pittilio up to the next landing, each step more and more crowded with teetering stacks of books, and then at last through a door on the top floor, which led to a narrow staircase.

A cold wind filtered down through that stairwell. The stairs rose into a small glass house with a steeply pitched roof, more ornate than an ordinary street vestibule and opening to the sky instead of the sidewalk, its faceted glass obscuring the pearly light. Conrad breathed in the cool air, with its aftertaste of cinder and wood smoke, its underlying flavor of the East River, rushing darkly between its banks a few blocks away.

When they stood in the glass house at last, Conrad looked out onto the roof, trying to see through the bevels. Everything was muted, softened. He seemed to be looking through a thick mist, the blue and purple shades of evening chalky behind the thick glass.

"Ready?" Mr. Pittilio asked, standing aside, looking down at Conrad.

Conrad nodded.

"Close your eyes, then," Mr. Pittilio said. And he placed his hands upon Conrad's shoulders and turned him toward the door. Conrad felt the fresh air from the opened door, heard the sounds of the rooftop come into sudden, sharp focus. Mr. Pittilio steered him a few paces onto the roof. Conrad could feel the gravel beneath his shoes. He could feel someone looking at him.

"Lemuel Sparks," Mr. Pittilio said then. "Mr. Conrad Morrisey." And he gave Conrad a push.

CONRAD HAD MADE it his business in life to transform the ordinary object into something treasured, something beautiful. He was, though he came to it accidentally, a gilder, a person who layers the blemished surfaces of the world with gold, a veneer fragile and vulnerable as a decomposing leaf.

Educated as an engineer, Conrad had made his home in northern New Hampshire, where his first job—blasting a tunnel through a mountain called the Sleeping Giant—had brought him. But early in his career, early enough to make an abrupt about-face, he had been fortunate to discover a method and formula for gilding that had placed him far and away above other craftsmen of the same pursuit.

The magic of alchemy. It had started with their house, his and Rose's house, which, with its gingerbread trim, called for embellishment, Rose had said, flinging her arms wide the first day they saw it. It called for gold, like Hansel and Gretel's sugar house in the wood. And so, experimenting during those first few years in their house, Conrad had stumbled across the technique that would eventually allow him to earn a living for the rest of his life.

He could, through his craft, make time stop, or at least delay its passage. For though gold is a soft alloy in general, it is, he knew, a mighty metal in all other ways, the path of entire civilizations diverting to its source. And he had in his time gilded some strange things, things that made him wonder about their owners—the unembarrassed man with the collection of plaster phalluses, or the woman with her dead dog's collar and tags. But there had been plenty of common objects, too—baby booties and golf balls. He had gilded capitol domes and church spires, weather vanes and the masts of boats. Sealing the plain old world in shimmering layers of gold, he had paused, from time to time, in satisfaction and amazement.

And sometimes he thought that it was at that moment, that first moment on Lemuel Sparks's roof, that he was given his calling.

For when he first opened his eyes on that rooftop, Mr. Pittilio's fingers trailing from his shoulder, it was to an assault of light: broad trapezoids and bars of it, the planes of space become mirrored surfaces, hard, reflective plates that caught and refracted light in a mighty sport. And so when he first saw Lemuel Sparks and raised his arm to shield his eyes from the light, it was because he meant to protect himself. He could not be equal to the gift Lemuel was about to make.

He had known then, though he knew it more now, that this was an extraordinary moment in his life. Now, considering the angel in his garden, he thought that perhaps he had been too aware of the plain and humble matter of the world, the imperfect form that lay beneath the gold veneer. After all, he thought, if you flood something with gold, with light, perhaps it really *is* different. It isn't anymore the dull, humble thing it once was. It is transformed, something sacred, something beautiful.

And that was why, now, he had chosen to believe that his angel was in fact what it said it was: not a hallucination, not a grieving man's worshipful vision, but a miracle. Conrad had never been a man who expected more in the face of life's abundance. He had expected less, expected that what was good and satisfying would last a lucky moment and then drain away like water vanishing down a whirlpool. It wasn't that he was unappreciative or morose. But low expectations were reasonable, he thought. Rose might have saved herself some pain, he'd always felt, if she'd just expected less. It's wanting too much, he used to think, that leads a man to disappointment.

But now Conrad felt he had no expectations left, small or large. His life had become, in the breathtaking instant between Rose's life and death, in the terrible privilege of staying on behind her, a scale in which all things weighed equally, or weighed nothing at all, a solemn time in which he was simply waiting. So though he suspected that he might have failed in the past to appreciate the nature of what Rose would have called *grace,* or Lemuel, *magic,* he was willing, now, to believe. He had stepped, he decided, whether accidentally or not, into the path of a miracle.

SO HE STOOD there that autumn evening on Mr. Lemuel Sparks's roof, the setting sun firing up that miniature world in the sky. The tin chimney baffles, the many-angled copper roof of Lemuel's pigeon loft, the carpet of glinting stone beneath his feet—all of it was aflame in the sun's final frenzy of illumination, that last moment of day's light. Lemuel stood before Conrad, his hat in his hands, his hair blowing over his eyes. "Mr. Pittilio," he said, "you have an extraordinary sense of timing."

"My young friend," he said, turning to Conrad, "I have a surprise for you."

Mr. Pittilio sat down on a battered wooden folding chair, withdrew his cigar from his pocket, relit the crushed end of it, and inhaled deeply, squinting. Lemuel turned and strode toward his loft, the hundred or so birds there stepping lightly back and forth at their gates. He motioned for Conrad to follow him to the far end, to a larger enclosure where a dozen homers, Conrad's homers, jostled together.

"Here are your birds," he said. "I've kept them together. They fly well together now. The problem, of course, is that now they unfortunately believe *this* is their home." He frowned, as if a solution to this problem had so far escaped him. He moved to the door and regarded the pigeons. They did not feel to Conrad as though they belonged to him anymore.

"It isn't your fault I was able to capture them so easily," Lemuel said then gently, turning to Conrad and taking in his crestfallen face. "The first one was an accident, after all. Frank identified your band for me, told me of your circumstances. I didn't understand at first, but after some thought I realized what a gift I had here, we have here. So I continued taking them, just to see if I could. And now it all seems clear." He smiled broadly, delighted. "We have been brought together in a most auspicious way. I hope you will accept my offer."

Conrad tried to think. All he could understand of Lemuel's words, however, was that Lemuel intended to keep Conrad's birds on his own roof. Conrad could not imagine how this was to his own benefit in any way. But at that moment, Rose stepped out onto the roof under a Chinese parasol. She wore a coat over the toga, its white hem trailing beneath the coat like a nightgown.

"Did the bird boy say yes?" she asked her father, coming to stand beside him and looking at Conrad's birds, now Lemuel's birds.

"Well, the bird boy, as you call him"—Lemuel turned to smile at Rose—"has not said anything yet." He replaced his hat on his head. "Perhaps I need to be plain, my friend, Mr. Conrad Bird Boy Morrisey. What I am proposing here is a quid pro quo. A fire escape and an uneven diet is no way to train a flock. I, on the other hand, have plenty of space and can provide an excellent diet. What I lack is sufficient time. My work now requires me to leave the country for some time, and there is no one to look after my birds. A boy like yourself has time in immoderate quantities." He smiled indulgently. "If you'll agree to help maintain my loft in my absence— this absence and others to come—I will lease to you, in exchange, sufficient roost space for as many birds as you can buy or breed yourself." He waited a moment, then continued. "I'll throw grain into the bargain, just to tempt you."

Conrad looked around and took in, for the first time, the extent of Lemuel's creation. This loft was not the patched and cobbled affair of so many Brooklyn pigeon lofts, constructed from odds and ends, bits and pieces, salvaged lengths of chicken wire and boards hammered together. Lemuel's loft was the work of a master architect, which Lemuel indeed was—a restorer of religious properties, in fact. The loft was a series of turrets perhaps ten feet high and capped in copper, each turret linked by a short hyphen. At a height of perhaps seven feet ran the landing board, to which each separate box had an entrance. The whole effect was a bit medieval, Conrad thought—like a walled city. And yet it was familiar in character, painted the same clean white of New England's farm buildings, with their unornamented lines and breezy aspect. He had seen such things from the car window, when he and his parents would take a drive out beyond the city, the three of them sitting silently in the car, looking out over the calm and sunny landscape. And at the base of each turret of the loft, in hexagonal boxes, Lemuel had planted shrubs, their shapely spires fluting upward.

Conrad imagined that seeing Lemuel's loft from above, from a passing airplane, perhaps, or a dirigible, it would seem a chimera, something that bloomed in the mind's eye as a fleeting vision, a trick of light, a small white town rising from the black and gaping spaces of the city, with its looming walls and shadowy crevices.

"Oh, say yes, Conrad Morrisey," Rose breathed in his ear, twirling her parasol.

"Say yes!" Mr. Pittilio agreed, laughing, drawing on his cigar, wreathed in smoke.

Conrad looked at Lemuel. At his brave confidence. And though something in him whispered then that it was not so easy as they imagined, could not be so effortlessly contrived, that something other than the simple contract they suggested awaited him up there on that rooftop, he understood that his choice had already been made.

"Yes," he said simply. "All right." And then he laughed.

Three

NOLAN PEAK, EDITOR of the *Laurel Aegis,* his Adam's apple juggling his bow tie, looked up at the battered tin ceiling in his office, looked down at Conrad's wrinkled and splattered trousers. He was taking note, Conrad decided, standing there before Peak, his hat in his hand—of something. Of the troubling disarray of widowers, perhaps.

But Conrad had always felt untidy around Peak, a result of the man's own suspicious fastidiousness. A bachelor—in his early fifties now, Conrad guessed—Peak was encumbered with a terrifying mother. Bennett Peak, now folded over onto herself with crippling osteoporosis, could still be seen from time to time inching her way down Main Street toward her son's office, an amphibian craning its short neck, preparing to berate Nolan for what she saw as his constitutional foolishness. Most people in town had seen her take Nolan apart publicly once or twice, and Conrad thought it excited in them a vague feeling of protectiveness—alongside their annoyance—over this beleaguered man.

Bennett, who had run the paper herself for many years after her husband's death, had made enemies of even the mildest of Laurel's citizens, insulting them in her weekly editorials for crimes of mediocrity, sentimentality, triviality—anything that struck her as weak minded. She believed that the chief of police and at least one city council member at any given time were involved in some underhanded miscarriage of justice. It was no small irony, Conrad thought, that a woman who now endured a backbone twisted into a terrible question mark should have been so fixed on what she perceived as "spineless" behavior among her neighbors.

But it was not Nolan's way to court controversy. He was a meticulous man, terrified of making an error. He believed secretly, Conrad suspected, that any public notice was an affront to individual privacy, that the newspaper itself, ghosted over by his mother's vengeful presence, was an invidious force, and that he needed to be careful indeed where he trained its feeble light. Consequently the *Laurel Aegis* was, under his guidance, the world's dullest newspaper, weighted down with long columns of pointless and uninteresting information, bland and unappetizing recipes, the tedious minutes of various board and committee meetings, long strings of school sports scores, and police reports so scrupulously devoid of detail and fact—by the time Nolan was done with them—as to be almost uninterpretable and therefore strangely alarming. Rose, whose context for criminal behavior was New York City, enjoyed the police reports enormously. Rose's favorite, which she mailed to Lemuel, had been an item that read, in its entirety, "Suspect discovered with evidence. Seized with difficulty."

"Makes it sound like a boa constrictor," she'd said, cutting it out with her sewing scissors. "What *sort* of evidence do you suppose it was?"

Conrad quite liked Nolan's weekly column, though. There, a different man emerged than the thin and nattily attired Nolan, his wrist under his watch raw from eczema, his whole self reeking of some powerful antiseptic ointment. The writer of this column, called "From Peak's Beak" and accompanied by a tiny, postage-stamp-sized photograph of Nolan in a Tyrolean hat, was instead a devout, gentle, and wonderfully observant chronicler of the area's native birds, capable of a surprisingly lyrical bent. He kept track of annual migration patterns, published suet recipes and construction diagrams for bluebird nesting boxes, and shamelessly endorsed new bird-related products for sale at Supplee's hardware store. And only in his column did Nolan voice an opinion that might be considered vaguely inflammatory. Once, he had taken the owner of Laurel's seniors' home sharply to task for forbidding tenants to install bird feeders, which were thought to encourage nests, a hindrance to the efficacy of the building's gutters.

"Imagine," Nolan had implored, "a world without birds, their music silenced. Such a world might not be worth inhabiting."

Conrad, who felt sympathetic to this particular cause, had taken pains to ask Nolan about it when he saw him one day at Eddie's, the local lunch spot on River Road. Nolan was sitting hunched over his meal, as usual, and Conrad had stopped at his table on his way out the door. "Peak," he said. "Good column about those gutters. What's happened?"

"Nothing," Nolan said, looking up, spoon in midair. And then he added ominously, "Yet."

Now, standing in Nolan's office before the man himself, Conrad shifted uncomfortably on his feet and glanced around at the walls and the gallery of photographs hung there. There was Nolan, his hat tipped childishly to the back of his head, standing beside the colossal leg of an elephant, his hand tentatively on the great animal's dusty, scabrous knee. That must have been taken at that circus that came to the fairgrounds one year; Conrad remembered that for an extra dollar, you could have your portrait taken with the elephant, or beside a clown who would pinch your cheek, or with your arm around the lady acrobat with the star-shaped spangles on her breasts. In the photograph, Nolan's expression was faintly reverent, like a cleric on holiday in Athens, leaning against a wall of the Acropolis.

In another picture, Nolan wielded an oversize pair of prop scissors, gesticulating with them toward the ribbon before the doors of the natatorium up on the hill. You could see two half-moons of dark stain beneath Nolan's armpits. At the extreme edge of the gathering, which had been arranged in a semicircle for the photo, stood Bennett, all in black, with a faintly mocking expression on her face, her hands clenched on two metal crutches.

There was also a picture of Nolan sitting obediently on Santa's knee in the town bandstand, his legs thrust out before him, and another of Nolan in the uniform of the high school baseball team, surrounded by the team players, most of whom towered above him.

There were plenty of photos, Conrad reflected, plenty of evidence that Nolan Peak had been in Laurel for a long time, doing his bit at charity affairs, serving in his role as one of the town's few functionaries. But he looked so miserable in most of the pictures, Conrad thought—except for that one with the elephant.

Conrad glanced down at Nolan's desk. His eye fell on a tiny hourglass, its pale sand trickling downward in a needle-thin stream. He looked up, startled. Was his visit now being *timed*?

All of a sudden, Conrad felt himself hugely annoyed. There was something about Nolan that made you want to lean over and shake the man by the shoulder, nudge him to sit upright, make him take a fresh look around.

"He always looks as if he's got an anvil on his back," Conrad had told Rose once, after passing Nolan on the street one day. "I just wish he'd stand up straight, for God's sake."

Rose, who had been in her greenhouse repotting her scented geraniums, had turned around to look at Conrad, lifting her eyebrows at him and suppressing a smile. "Is that right?" she said slowly.

Conrad, who had been slouching against the soapstone sink,

stared back at her. When she failed to turn away, looking at him with a funny expression as though she might laugh, he had grown uncomfortable. He straightened up suddenly, wiped his hand on his pants leg. "Well," he said at last. He waved at her vaguely. "I'll be with the birds."

After his retirement from the gilding business, Conrad had lunched more frequently at Eddie's. Its stated name, on a sign above the door, was the Four Leaf Clover Cafe, but everyone knew it as Eddie's. Eddie Vaughan, missing half a leg from a shrapnel injury in World War II, had returned from combat and taken his limping place at his wife's side. After her death, he continued to man the small kitchen with no help whatsoever, and the quality of the food, which had been the stuff of legend in Kate's time, seriously declined. The only things Eddie could prepare with any confidence were ice cream, turned the old-fashioned way in a hand crank on the back stoop, and soup, which appealed to his innate sense of frugality. Each day, Eddie posted on a board by the side of the road the day's ice cream flavor and the soup, though after a while the soup was always posted as VEG BEEF, as its ingredients became less well defined, including in greater or lesser quantities some vegetables, some meat, and whatever else struck Eddie's fancy.

He had a regular group of devotees who took three meals a day there. Conrad liked the place, despite the food and the surroundings. The kitchen was grimy, and sitting at the counter, you could see into the back room, where a military cot with a rumple of blankets was pushed up next to the dishwasher with its comforting tumult of suds. Eddie concocted ice cream flavors that Rose said were the inspiration of a lunatic—pineapple, corn, and green onion—but Conrad had a secret taste for the black walnut, which Eddie served with a shot of rum.

Sometimes Conrad took Rose along with him for lunch there. Eddie would always come out from behind the counter on these occasions, a soiled dishcloth folded over his arm. He would stop at their table, bow painfully from the waist, take Rose's hand and bring it to his lips. "Give her anything she wants," he would say to Conrad, staring at Rose's face.

Once, surprised at Eddie's serious expression during this exchange, Conrad had waited until Eddie had left them before leaning over the table and saying to Rose, "He doesn't just mean lunch. What does he mean?"

Rose hadn't looked up from her menu. "I think he's just trying to show me his gratitude," she said.

"Gratitude? What for?"

Rose sighed. Still without looking up, she said, "Conrad, I've told you. Their girl. The one who works out in the cemetery gardens now."

Conrad thought a moment. "The one who's not quite right"— he knocked against his temple—"in the head. With a funny name."

"Hero," said Rose, still looking at her menu. "From the myth, of Hero and Leander. It was Kate's favorite name."

"That's it." Conrad looked down at his menu, too, but after a minute he raised his head and glanced at his wife again. "Why is he grateful to you?" he asked finally.

Rose made a noise of impatience. "I help her in the gardens out there sometimes. I've told you that." She hesitated, softened. "I feel sorry for her. Something about her—I don't know—reminds me of myself when I was her age—"

"Well, that's good of you." Conrad realized he'd interrupted her. But he remembered meeting this girl Hero now; it had been at one of Rose's garden club meetings. Conrad had been carrying a tray of lemonade glasses down the hall when the bell had rung. He had turned—slowly, so as not to upset the tray—to answer the door, but Rose had come flying down the hall past him and admitted a young woman in an inappropriately formal lilac dress, with long gauzy panels like bats' wings sewn into them; she had greeted Rose with a smile of immense shyness and beauty. But she was not what Conrad would have called a pretty girl. There was something too angular about her face, and her eyes and hair were strangely pale, he thought. She had the look—well, it was exactly the look of a deer caught in the headlights of an oncoming car, Conrad had thought at the time, startled by the realization that, as often as he'd heard the expression, he'd never actually seen anyone who fit the description quite as well as this girl. Hero had the look of something that has come to know the taste of its own wound.

"I'm so glad you came," Rose had said, looking into Hero's face. She had taken her gently by the hand, stepping outside to the porch to draw her inside. They had passed down the hall together, Hero looking at the floor, a small smile still playing around her mouth. She had not looked at Conrad at all. But Rose, holding Hero gently by the arm, had glanced up at Conrad and given him a quick smile into which he thought he could read triumph.

Later, helping Rose clear away the glasses and the tea things, he had listened to her babble on about the meeting.

"And I was so pleased that Hero came," she had exclaimed at last. "She didn't say anything, just sat there with us, but I think she actually enjoyed it. She's done the most amazing things with the cemetery gardens, Connie. You should see the white-and-silver garden she built by the fountain—white agapanthus and Michaelmas daisies, white honesty, white veronica—" Rose stopped, looked out over her own gardens. She and Conrad had just finished building the third terrace, and the first roses there, pink and richly yellow, were in bloom. "She has a strange feel for it, for knowing what will work," Rose mused aloud. "I just wish I could get her to talk."

"She doesn't talk?" Conrad asked, picking up a tray.

"Well, of course, she *does*, but she clearly doesn't like to. She's terribly shy. You know, Eddie and Kate had her hospitalized for a number of years at that place in Grant's Falls until it closed down. There were awful stories about it. Don't you remember? People strapped to their beds, and their hands burned with cigarettes if they wet themselves or something."

"Is she that bad?" Conrad felt momentarily disgusted.

"Oh, no. Of course not."

"Well, what's the matter with her then?"

Rose shrugged, then picked up a teacup and ran her finger around the fragile brim. A low fluting noise left the cup, a soft treble. "The world is—too much with her," she said after a moment, and she turned away from Conrad. "She's fragile. I don't know."

But Rose had clearly adopted the girl. From time to time she would bring home some bit of news about her—that she had trained the clematis 'Nelly Moser', with the dark crimson slash on each sepal, over the gates of the cemetery. Rose said the sight had made Havelock Eddison, the town's grim benefactor, who had made a fortune mining Bloodroot Mountain for iron ore, weep with pleasure at its beauty. She had successfully budded two of the magnificent heirloom roses by Mrs. Ashforth's grave and started six new bushes by the gardener's cottage. She had rooted several shoots of prize rhododendrons in an agar jelly.

But to Conrad, Hero was just another in Rose's collection of damaged souls: the sour-smelling drifters who came to the door appealing for grace and were served Earl Grey and sponge cake from Rose's good china; the blind, raving souls in the hospital's permanent wing whom Rose organized early each spring to pot up bowls of paperwhite narcissus for the town's schoolteachers, and late each fall to bury tulip bulbs in the beds by the hospital gates; the shut-ins and crippled children and unfortunates for whom Rose had such ready sympathy. Sometimes, shopping in the Smile Market with Rose, he would return to their cart, having fetched some item from another aisle, to find Rose standing with her hands being held by an old crone with watery eyes, who would disengage herself as soon as she saw Conrad and scuttle away.

"Who was that?" Conrad would ask.

"Oh, that's Nellie Anderson," Rose would say. "She cleans at the Congregational church."

Conrad did not think of himself as a jealous man; but the broad range of Rose's tolerance and sympathy had the twin effect of making him feel unkind by comparison—he was frankly disgusted by and sometimes afraid of the people Rose embraced with such tenderness—and also angry with her, as if because she was so liberal with her attentions, he himself was suffering as a result. He knew that wasn't true. But nonetheless he found over the years that he didn't like to inquire much about any of her pets, as he called them—though only to himself, for he had used the word with Rose once to shocking effect: he had thought she might slap him, and she had refused to speak to him for three days, a vigil of neglect that she made look maddeningly easy. Hero, though she had come along relatively late in Rose's life, had fallen immediately into the category of people Conrad knew he was happier knowing nothing about. It wasn't that he was unkind, he thought. It was that he couldn't bear imagining even for an instant how terrible it must be to stand in their shoes. With her averted face and wide hands and foolish dress, Hero had made him feel, just in that one instant in his front hall, as though nothing he could do would ever be enough.

NOLAN ATE LUNCH at Eddie's every day, Conrad knew. He sat alone at a table by the window, looking out through the curtains at the river from time to time in a suspicious way. He took in his food dutifully, alternating spoonfuls of ice cream and soup. Watching Nolan eat was like watching a dying man reluctantly take in just enough food to satisfy his doctor. Conrad, who considered his own kitchen and Rose's parade of succulent roasts, fragile pastries, and glistening vegetables fresh from the garden an almost erotic nerve center, wondered how anyone could like food so little. He himself was helpless in front of a warmed plate, placed before him by Rose with the flick of a clean towel. Though she herself seemed to exist mostly on air, she liked to sit across the table from Conrad and watch. "How is it?" she'd ask, and Conrad, forking in new pink beets, roasted crisp and bathed in butter and thyme, or shepherd's pie under a cloud of mashed potatoes, or angel food cake, iced with dark chocolate, would groan, reach across the table for her hand, kiss her knuckles.

What's the point? he had wondered, watching Nolan chew. You could shoot yourself in the head and it would be over quicker.

Now, standing before Nolan in his office, his letter in Nolan's limp grasp, Conrad wound his hat brim between his fingers, watched Nolan's bow tie go up and down, up and down, and waited.

"Can't print this," Nolan said at last to Conrad's shuffling stance. "Won't. Don't print stuff like this. Angels. Ghosts. What-not. Whatever you saw—nonsense."

He folded Conrad's letter neatly, set it on the desk, and flattened his palm over it as though it were an insect. He pulled at his collar. "I wouldn't mention this to anyone else, if I were you," he added, leaning forward slightly. "Good day." And he swiveled around in his chair.

I've been dismissed, Conrad thought, and glanced at the hourglass. The sand had run out.

Betty Barteleme, the walleyed gatekeeper at Peak's newspaper, lowered her glasses when Conrad came back into the front office. He lingered there, trying to find the words to say what he felt. Nonsense? he thought. What does he know?

Miss Barteleme sniffed, waved her letter opener at Conrad. "Go on home now, Conrad Morrisey," she said through her nose as Conrad stood there, gazing at her, thinking. "You've bothered Mr. Peak enough already for one day. Go on home before I take a broom to you and your feathers." But then, as if remembering Conrad's recent loss, she softened. "There's no point in waiting. He's not going to see you again this morning. He's a very busy man. Very, very busy." She leaned over and patted his arm. "Go on." And she waved the letter opener toward the door.

Conrad looked down, brushed at his trousers, saw a feather drift across the floor toward Miss Barteleme's dimpled ankle, turning over on itself like a tumbleweed. Miss Barteleme, of the fat, powder white Pan-Cake cheeks and penciled eyebrows and two-tone pantsuit—sizing her up, Conrad imagined that she now fancied she herself had a way with words, as if the talent for it were contagious. She guarded Nolan Peak like a little flat-faced dog, irksome and loyal. Now here was Conrad, squared off in a wordless confrontation with this officious woman who acted as though any business of the paper's readers was entirely irrelevant—even a hindrance—to the higher purpose of her beloved Peak's mysterious mission.

Well, you two deserve each other, Conrad thought.

He looked away from Miss Barteleme, past the browning arms of a philodendron draped over the doorsill, and into the newsroom with its clutter of desks. Kenny Toronto was sitting in a swivel chair by the window, eating an egg sandwich; a beagle looked out at Conrad from under Toronto's desk.

Conrad raised his hand in reply when Toronto looked up and gave him a smile. Conrad liked Toronto. He'd given up a promising career in the minor leagues for a local girl who didn't want to leave home, but he had remained a happy man with a handsome demeanor, apparently without regretting that he had never pursued what might have been a lucrative and exciting career. He covered high school and recreational-league sports for the paper with what appeared to be genuine enthusiasm. Toronto's house was also an unofficial sanctuary for wounded birds and animals—most people in town knew they could bring him a felled hawk with a broken wing, or an orphaned fawn, or a trapped raccoon with a shattered paw—not to mention a host of outlaw dogs and torn-up barn cats. Conrad himself had taken creatures to him from time to time. Once, Conrad had found a turkey vulture dragging a crumpled wing along the ground near the river. The creature had been enraged and wild with pain; Conrad had smothered it in a blanket and still taken sixteen stitches in his forearm. After several months of nursing, the vulture had developed a fierce affection for Toronto, refusing to leave and lurking in a darkly appreciative way in the trees around the cages Toronto had built behind his house, coming to feed from Toronto's hand when he called to it. Stella, Toronto's wife, raised chickens and peacocks and had once nursed a bobcat cub to adulthood.

Conrad nodded to Toronto now, but another meaningful sniff from Miss Barteleme set him to shouldering into his jacket, and he began his retreat, leaving his letter behind on Peak's desk, where he imagined it would soon enough end up in the trash. The frustration of it gave Conrad a hopeless feeling. It wasn't even so much a letter as an invitation, he thought, an invitation for all to visit his garden, regard the ground, take from the sight of it whatever they wished. And for free, of course. He wouldn't charge, the way some blessed with evidence of whatever you want to call it—grace in the form of weeping virgins and statues blemished on the hands and feet in the middle of the night—have seen fit to do. Of course, there was no evidence of anything in his garden now. Nothing to see. It occurred to him that perhaps that was a problem; he wouldn't want anyone to be disappointed.

He stood at the door to the *Aegis,* ready to go, his hat in his hand, gripping the knob. He looked into the street, at the weak gray light that drained from the heavy bank of clouds overhead. The mica in the sidewalk glittered, winked. Miss Barteleme glowered behind him, a tissue protruding from her sleeve. For a moment, Conrad imagined her, Miss Betty Barteleme, dropping slowly to her plump knees, rendered silent for once, her mouth in a gentle O, awestruck.

But then the telephone rang. Miss Barteleme threw Conrad a glance and turned to lift the receiver.

And in the opportunity created by the ringing phone, Conrad saw that he could make one more effort on his own behalf, one more appeal. Giving up now was just—what would Rose have said?—fainthearted. No man who's seen an angel ought to be fainthearted.

Miss Barteleme waved the letter opener at him as he brushed past, her eyes and mouth popping protest.

Conrad stepped around the corner of the hall and then stopped, for Nolan had someone with him. Conrad looked through the glass partition. Nolan's back was to him, but Toronto stood before Nolan's desk. He looked up, caught Conrad's eye, and then quickly averted his gaze.

"Look at this," Conrad heard Nolan say.

Conrad paused, strained to overhear. He watched Toronto, realizing that Nolan expected a laugh, for it was Conrad's letter Toronto was now holding.

But Toronto read quietly, his lips moving slightly, standing before Nolan's desk. Conrad watched his face, not knowing what to expect.

"Well," Toronto said at last. He did not look up from the page. And then, with an athlete's agile grace, and before Nolan could say anything further, Toronto stepped out of the office, closing the door behind him. In the hall he stopped, looked up, and met Conrad's eyes. Conrad glanced into Nolan's office, saw him, dismayed, rearrange his collar, swivel around, and open his mouth to call after Toronto, "Kenny, don't get any—" And then Nolan saw Conrad and froze.

Just then, having disentangled herself from the phone, Miss Barteleme came after Conrad, huffing and puffing, affronted. "Mr. *Morrisey*," she said. "Time to *go*."

Conrad allowed himself then to be taken by the arm and escorted to the door, but not without casting a look back over his shoulder toward Toronto, who put up his hand, a small wave.

Maybe there's hope, Conrad thought. But then, surprised, he thought, That man really has the kindest face I've ever seen.

STANDING ON THE street before the plate glass window of the *Aegis*'s office, Conrad glanced into people's faces. Laurel was a small town, not more than nine hundred people, and he recognized, at least vaguely, many of the passersby. But now every old man he saw reminded him of Lemuel, hawklike and proud, his mane of white hair and soft beard folding tentlike around his long face, making him look like an exotic Jacobin pigeon, its eyes peering through its feathered ruff. Every woman, small and slender, was, for a second, Rose. He put his hand against the door frame, steadied himself against the sensation that he had been uncoupled from his life. That he no longer knew anyone. That he was surrounded by strangers. Someone, a woman he did not recognize, passed him and nodded. "Good morning," she said, her voice pleasant, sympathetic. Conrad stared after her.

He had no plans, no destination. He stepped off Main Street and walked down the hill to River Road. Behind him the town resolved into the small inverted bowl of its streets and roofs. On the far side of the river rose the coarse foothills of the Sleeping Giant, the last of the low-lying crests of the White Mountains. To reach Laurel from the south, one had to pierce the slumbering body of rock through its low granite heart. The mountain's brow, nose and chin, rising chest, sweeping legs, and protruding feet looked unmistakably like an enormous man laid down heavily upon the sloping fields.

Conrad had been hired as a junior member of the engineering team some months after the tunnel project had begun. He remembered the moment when blasting had broken through the far side of the mountain, when a jagged hole of light had penetrated the dark rock. And he remembered, too, the feeling he'd had when he and Rose first arrived in Laurel. Surrounded on three sides by mountains and cinched in by the belt loop of the Mad River, which cut a gorge through Mt. Abraham and was continually fed by the rainwater washing down its granite slopes, Laurel felt comfortingly invulnerable. The low, rock-strewn grasslands to the west were given over mostly to dairy farms and, farther north toward Lake Champlain, to orchardists, who planted their hillsides with rising and falling Vs of trees, which gave the land a sprightly buoyancy.

Conrad had imagined that they had severed time itself when they arrived that first day in the town square. He saw how mountains rose up around them on three sides, how the forests and dappled orchards on the fourth side made a maze as dense and elaborate as any grown to thwart a fairy tale's sorcerer. Nuclear missiles, airborne diseases, even the insidious contagion of society's most perverse tendencies, would fall away against the town's natural geographic baffles.

Parking their car and walking across the velvet grass to the ornate bandstand in the center of the square, they had looked around, pleased. A Victorian affair with ornate trim capping the hexagonal roof like the fringe on an old-fashioned surrey, the bandstand was used in summer for a concert series and, occasionally, for a blood-donation clinic. Then, nurses would mount the short flight of steps to the varnished floor within, their white tunics fluttering, a Red Cross banner tied to the posts and flapping mightily. A steady trickle of people, who arrived with their sleeves rolled past their elbows, would be admitted under the pink lights and given juice in white paper cones, their dark blood draining into pint bags.

For the town's bicentennial celebration, Harrison Supplee, who owned the hardware store and took it upon himself to orchestrate most civic events, had asked Conrad if he wouldn't see whether he might do something with the bandstand. "Spruce it up, you know," he'd said vaguely, as the two of them had stood there one morning surveying it. Conrad, whose gilding business was by then an unqualified success, had looked it over, pronounced it sound, and spent the spring and summer evenings preceding the festivities gilding the interior framework of the bandstand. The delicately arched rafters and soaring cross ties had been painted with gold leaf, endowing the construction with a weightless grace. Rose said it looked as though you could pluck off a piece and it would melt in your mouth like sugar.

Those long evenings, as the sky grew dark, purple martins and bats had crossed the square, and Conrad had painted away happily in the glare of a utility light. The twin lamps by the hotel's green awning had glowed yellow. Single blue lights burned in the rear rooms of stores fronting the square, throwing window displays— an old-fashioned mannequin, the shining, curved armatures of plumbing fixtures, the dark spines of books—into exaggerated relief. From a distance, it appeared as though Conrad were a man on a boat, riding the dark surface of a still lake.

But that first day, sitting on the rounded benches within the bandstand, he and Rose had looked out at the square—the needle hands of the clock on the granite wall of the bank moving slowly around, the cordial progress of slight traffic, the flapping canopy over the doors of the hotel, the white spire of the Congregational church glinting in the sun. Rose had gripped his arm. "Oh, we'll be happy here," she'd said. "I can feel it."

Now, arriving at the bottom of the hill at River Road, Conrad stopped at the bulwark by the water and stared out over the Mad River, its surface strangely flat and colorless between eroding concrete banks. Once he had seen a great blue heron down here. It had been a strange sight, like a man from the past who wanders through some complicated fold of time to arrive in the present, incongruously dressed, vulnerable, ugly of feature. Conrad, who usually had his binoculars with him when he went for a walk, had pulled them out and put them to his eyes, the world rearing up into close focus inside a tiny circle. Looking through his field glasses, he always felt that he had left his place on the ground, was balanced aloft like a bird, his eyes trained on the bulging and convex dimensions of the world. He had fixed on the heron, alighted on an old truck tire half-submerged near the bank. After a minute it had unfolded its wings and flapped away slowly upriver, as though saddened by the changed reality of what it had found.

Staring out over the river now, Conrad suffered a moment of terrible disorientation. Leaning over, he put out his hand toward the water, but no reflection met his palm, no answering shape rose to meet his flesh. One of his eyes, his left, had begun troubling him; his vision would fade in and out. Was it this that accounted for the fact that he seemed so insubstantial now, too insubstantial to have a reflection? Trembling, reaching into his pocket, he pulled out a handful of coins, leaned over the water again, and let them trickle from his palm. The surface of the water scattered reassuringly as though under a quick shower of rain.

But the moment when he felt himself to have disappeared, and the unalterable descent of the coins, recalled to him another moment when he had hung above the world, terrified and uncertain.

IT WAS THE largest, most ambitious gilding job Conrad had ever undertaken. Earlier that year he had gilded a set of enormous gates woven with prancing horses and wild sea froth and wheeling planets at a Du Pont estate in Pennsylvania; it was the first job on which he had tested his new technology: a carbon-core brush used to electronically deposit plating solutions—water-soluble mixtures of zinc, nickel, cadmium, lead, tin, and, of course, gold—on virtually any surface. His employer had been so pleased with Conrad's meticulous results that he had recommended him for the bank job in Connecticut. After consulting with various engineers, Conrad had decided that the work was best done safely at ground level on thin shells, which could then be hoisted by helicopter and adhered to the original dome. And it would only take about thirty-eight ounces of gold.

The day the shells were to be fitted in place, Conrad joined the contracting crew as they ascended through the building and swung in harnesses to the lip of the dome itself, where the men were to catch and steady the new pieces as they hovered above. Conrad himself was just along for the ride, as he put it.

"I just want to see it all fall into place," he explained as they attached the belt to him.

But as Conrad and another man stepped to the trapeze and attached themselves to the safety cables, the harness at one end of the trapeze snapped, a noise like the report of a starter's gun, hollow and pointless. Conrad clung to the cable, the breath itself shocked from him; his partner, suspended in his safety belt, dropped away and caught with a jerk, hanging against the edge of the building like a man pretending flight in a theater performance, strung up awkwardly on guylines.

It was very quiet. Even the drone of the helicopters seemed to fade away in that moment. The sun, tilting toward noon, roared white and soundless above them. The city lay spread out below, its streets crawling with traffic. Conrad noticed, though he could not have said why, a woman in a lilac coat walking slowly around an empty fountain in the park, with an insect's creeping pace.

The dangling man hung perhaps twenty feet from Conrad. When the sound of the man's weeping reached Conrad, he was surprised. The man's grief sounded like a child's, a fretful child shedding tears in some distant, private place where he did not expect to be discovered. Conrad looked down, caught his breath again, and noticed with a perverse clarity the action unfolding below, as the people gathered there became alerted to the men's plight.

They were rescued in short order, the other man hauled up and poured upon the floor, his bowels and stomach having released their contents. He could not be pried from the floor and made to stand. Conrad knelt beside him, the floor spinning under his knees, breathing hard, breathing in the stench. Afterward he had wanted only to get away, be alone, had excused himself with a vague wave and taken himself to the diner across the street from the bank, the bell jangling loudly above his head as he pushed open the door with a shaking hand. Seated in a booth, wedged into its corner, he had eaten and eaten—a roast beef sandwich with gravy and potatoes, and then another; two pieces of apple pie; and then a piece of Boston cream pie. He finally had to force himself to stop. He wiped his mouth shakily, then he reached for his wallet and, frightened, discovered it gone, as though everything that established him as a certain person had fled from him in that moment when he hung in the sky, as though he had been emptied, turned upside down and shaken, stripped of all possessions, identity, and substance.

When he returned home two days later, the job having been completed without further incident, he let himself in through the front door. The radio in the kitchen was slightly mistuned, an unsettling static interrupting the voices. He felt a sudden alarm and called for Rose.

But she was upstairs, seated at her dressing table, applying her makeup, the long blue bars of the afternoon light falling through the curtains and over the floor. Rose belonged to an amateur theater troupe, a group of seven women who called themselves the Pleiades. They performed publicly once a year, a charity event held in Conrad and Rose's garden on the upper terrace, the tree branches hung with paper lanterns. But they met weekly for rehearsals, to sew their costumes, and to simply talk, these seven women who revolved around one another in perfect order, no need for a sun at their center. Their performances were, for their respective families and for the town itself, events of signal importance. Two Chinese screens from Rose's childhood home in Brooklyn formed the wings of the stage, the women disrobing there between scenes, their white spreading backsides and heavy breasts briefly exposed to the chill as they shed gowns for togas, armor for pantaloons, hurriedly shaking their feet free of clothing. Rose always hired a band to play on the front steps—a tambourine player, a fiddler, two trumpeters, and a pianist, who sat down at the old black upright, which had been wheeled out to the porch. A cranberry goblet of champagne trembled on top of the piano; a bouquet of roses in a silver tumbler dropped petals on his hands.

Sometimes before their weekly meeting Rose would sit at her dressing table, her hair brushed back from her face and caught in a net, and make up her face, just as an experiment. Conrad never failed to be startled by Rose in full costume, but the effect of her transformation into someone he did not know seemed even more complete when it was partial, just the woman herself, her dressing gown slipped to her shoulders, her bare feet hooked over the rung of her chair, her new face staring back at itself in the silvery mirror. This was how he came upon her that afternoon, her face flecked with green shadows, her mouth painted into a tiny bow.

"Connie!" Rose spun in her seat, pleased, as Conrad entered the room. She turned her strange face to her husband. "You're early!" She held out her arms. Conrad crossed the room, kissed her mouth delicately. He stood back and regarded her face.

"Who are you?" he asked, taking a seat at the foot of the bed.

"I thought maybe Lady Macbeth," Rose said, turning back to the mirror. "The green is ominous, isn't it?" She lifted one eyebrow with a finger, turned back to him. "I missed you," she said. "It went all right?"

Conrad looked at her through the gray cast of the mirror. He wished that she were not, at that moment, made up. He wanted to see her face as it was at night before they went to bed, freshly washed, a faint sheen of night cream glowing on her cheekbones, the satin ribbon of her nightgown tied in a loose bow.

Rose stared at him when he failed to answer her. "What is it?"

Conrad heard the alarm in her voice but could not think exactly what to tell her.

"Rose," he said finally, "I almost died."

"Oh, my dear!" She came and sat by him on the bed, her hand on his thigh, and listened quietly.

When he finished, he raised his hands to her. "I couldn't get enough to eat afterward," he said helplessly. "I went to a diner and had lunch, a place nearby. And I'd lost my wallet somehow. I couldn't even pay for it."

Rose put her arms around him. "It was a gift," she said quietly at last. She caught his hands and held them to her cheek. "I'm so grateful."

A MOVEMENT ON the far side of the river recalled Conrad to where he was. He put his hands on the stone bulwark, felt its gritty surface. This close, the river smelled sour, and Conrad realized that he, too, reeked of neglect, abuse. He needed a hot shower, a haircut, a proper lunch with someone across the table for company. He couldn't remember the last time he'd had any of those things. No wonder Peak had thrown him out. I need to make an effort, he thought. See someone I know.

And suddenly the thought of the Smile Market, Lenore's voluble presence behind the cash register, the delivery boy's looselipped grin, made him hungry for company, for food. He had not eaten much lately. The last mysterious basket had been delivered to his front porch a week ago—a curry so spicy it had made his eyes water, rich with currants and almonds and crimped shavings of carrot. It had come with a wax paper packet of thin, crisp breads and a little tin of chocolate truffles. Conrad had eaten the truffles in the dark of the arbor that night, as if he couldn't wait, couldn't get enough; he'd eaten all of them in a single sitting, a pair of

Rose's shoes in his lap, one hand fitted inside, nestled against the sole. When he'd finished, he had set her shoes down on the soft floor of the arbor, pointed them toward the horizon, the mountains now framed by the broad palms of the grape leaves. He had sat in the twilight, watching the shoes, until a rabbit had crept from the underbrush, inched forward, and touched its nose to the empty toe of Rose's shoe. Conrad had held his breath against the grief.

WHEN HE STEPPED up to the cash register at the Smile Market, carrying eggs and a box of cinnamon rolls, a net bag of oranges under his arm, Lenore snapped open the cash drawer, sized him up, and said, "Well, you don't look any different."

Conrad startled, imagined May Brown on the phone to Lenore, hooding her eyes, looking out her kitchen window through the small dangling parachutists of her spider plant. "Lenore?" she must have said. "It's me. May. You'll never guess. Conrad Morrisey saw an angel last night. He showed me the exact place."

Conrad looked at Lenore suspiciously. Just what, exactly, had May Brown told her?

"Heard you had a visitation," Lenore said, lowering her voice.

Conrad nodded at her, mute. His appetite for telling his story had waned in the face of this other, more urgent appetite, forkful upon forkful. He saw, for a moment, Nolan's dismissive expression, Toronto's careful silence. And May Brown's closed-up face, her eyes darting away. I *should* have kept it to myself, he thought.

But Lenore continued, quietly. "My aunt saw them, too," she said, packing Conrad's eggs sideways in his bag. Conrad glanced at her face, was distracted by the bracelets on her arm, the charms dancing there, her freckled skin like a pigeon's breast, mottled beneath the secondary feathers. One of the charms, a little pair of pewter shoes laced with a ribbon, held his eye.

"Ever since she was a little girl," Lenore went on. Conrad looked up at her. "Said she always saw them in the fig tree, talking and laughing and eating figs. They told her she would die painlessly and so she never had to worry. And she never did, after that." Lenore took Conrad's bills, smoothed them in her hands, turned them faceup. "And do you know what?"

"What?" Conrad asked, leaning toward her.

"She did die painlessly. Fell asleep at eighty-five years old in the waiting room, waiting on the dentist, and never woke up. Never had to have her tooth pulled, either." Lenore handed him his bag.

Conrad felt disappointed. He had thought Lenore would tell him something more persuasive, more—uplifting. Something about how the woman's life had been changed.

"What was it like?" Lenore asked. "May Brown said you showed her the place where it landed."

"It wasn't like martians," Conrad said, offended suddenly. "It didn't land. *He* didn't land."

"It was a he," Lenore said, nodding, as though that confirmed it. "It always is."

"It is?"

"Seems like it. My aunt's always were. You know—" She paused to inspect her hands, her white fingers splayed, her many rings bunched nearly to her knuckles. "I used to go out to that tree sometimes, stand underneath the branches. I'd had a little brother who'd died. I used to stand there, thinking about him and missing him. I thought maybe the angels, my aunt's angels would, you know, sense me there, and come down and give me some comfort. Show me my brother again." She stopped and looked at Conrad. He was startled to see tears in her eyes. "He was just a little boy," she said, staring at him as though she were seeing not Conrad but the child, a boy in a white nightgown sweating under a fan that revolved slowly in a darkened room, insects gathering thick at the window screen.

"You're lucky," Lenore whispered. "Very lucky." She straightened her back, looked hard at Conrad. "Rose would be happy," she said.

Just then, another customer stepped up behind Conrad, a young man with a ponytail, a bunch of cellophane-wrapped roses in his arms. Lenore glanced at him, smiled.

"Have a good day," she said then to Conrad. "And don't be a stranger."

Four

AT HOME, CONRAD tied Rose's apron around his waist and
fried himself three eggs, prodding them with a spatula and listening to the snap and spark of butter in the pan. He considered
Lenore's surprising confession, the image of angels in a fig tree,
fitted in among the crooks of the branches, passing the soft fruit
from hand to hand, their robes tucked up around their knees. Her
story had seemed so unextraordinary, he thought—as though angels were perhaps always present, and it was all a question of looking up at the right moment and seeing them picking their teeth,
spitting out skins.

His eggs set, he put the plate on a tray, along with the box of
cinnamon rolls and two oranges, and went outside to the garden.
He pulled a chair over to the stone wall at the edge of the highest
terrace and set the tray down. As he ate he looked out over the gardens. The perennial borders, which Rose had orchestrated for a
long season of bloom, had seemed to pause earlier that summer at
five feet. Now, though, they were heaving themselves upward,
seven feet, eight in places, the lilies blown open, the hardy amaryl-
lis strong as Doric columns, the heads of the alliums persevering
into August, as enormous and round as moons.

Everything that summer was, in fact, twice, three times its usual
size. Though the season was sloping toward September, the garden still seemed to be horned everywhere with new buds, overlaid
with yellow pollen, vines laying a multitude of tiny forked feet
along the tree trunks and up over the eaves of the house, explod-

ing into blossom. Conrad reached for an orange, held it in his hand. Wiping his mouth with his sleeve, he gazed around him. Even when Rose was alive, he thought, the garden had never seemed so lush. In a way, it seemed to be thriving *because* of his neglect. As he stood up now and looked down the hillside, he felt that he was witnessing an incantation, a strange magic in the milky sap that ran through the leaves, some advance work taking place in the very cells of the trees and flowers, their membranes swelling with bubbles of water, with sweet air, with lively anticipation.

Swarms of bees, wide as the wingspans of planes, tilted back and forth in the indistinct light that fell from the overcast sky. Agitated flocks of birds disturbed the lindens, shaking loose fistfuls of leaves and clouds of the trees' winged pellets, which spun to earth. The garden seemed to be burning with a green fire, with a spongy, condensing verdancy.

Yet when he left the highest terrace and began descending the steps, a conjurer's quiet fell over the grass. The crowds of flowers, blossoms that had multiplied that summer by tens and hundreds, slowly folded their petal hands over their bristling black eyes, a thousand averted gazes.

Full of the hush of bewilderment, in grief over Rose's death and his own inconceivable lingering on without her, Conrad walked across the soft grass. At his approach the swallows fell silent in the trees. His face was brushed by the thousands of tiny new leaves, pale as moonlight, that overran the paths. Pollen rained upon his shoulders, a shower of gold.

Beneath his feet new shoots were coming up everywhere, even raising the flagstones of the terraces. He stood beneath the impossible hollyhocks, giants towering dreamily over his head. He reached toward the sunflowers, which wagged their heads high above him, wide and darkly yellow, crowded against the gray sky.

He stood beside the treillage for the wisteria, tangled with explosions of curling vine, beryl green as Fourth of July Catherine wheels. The sky seemed to darken even further, as though the rain would begin at any moment, and the ground—the boiling, violent, joyful, terrifying ground of Rose's garden—faded into dimness. The preposterous activity at his feet, new growth shouldering up through the dirt, green and yellow and white and furled tight, lost its clarity. The surface of the earth fell into shadow deep as a pool of water.

Conrad walked among the pear trees, his shirt unbuttoned now against a strange heat that had risen into his cheeks. His old man's soft belly lay draped over his belt, a low breeze brushing the fine white hair there. He stepped carefully, laying his hands, which were mapped with an unfamiliar continent of age spots, on the golden fruits. This was to be an endless summer, he felt, pausing in the Concord grape arbor, the dusky fruits there grown so thick and heavy they rested on his head and shoulders like a dripping bishop's wig. This was a summer that reached its high bright equinox and then, with a heroic thrust, drove on, drove up and over the tight white glass ceiling of the August sky.

This was the most painful season of his life, he thought, coming to his knees in the fragrant beds, cupping the flowers in his hands. It was the most beautiful and the most painful. And it seemed that it would never end.

BACK INSIDE THE house, Conrad surveyed the mess he had been living in, the litter of clothing, the pile of unwashed dishes. It was as if the garden itself, in its long, exhausting season of bloom, had issued an opiate that filtered into the rooms of the house, made him feel sluggish and drugged. Cleaning wasn't his strong suit, but it hadn't really been Rose's either; she had liked a sense of industry about her. Conrad had thought it a trait inherited from Lemuel, who always seemed to be trailing things untidily from his pockets, paper scraps and lengths of twine. There was something faintly necromantic about Lemuel's disorder—Rose's, too. It was as if in their various experiments with plants or instruments they were always on the addictive brink of discovery. Lemuel had once invented an electrical contraption for altering the angle of the interior shutters' slats so as to provide Rose's night-blooming cereus with a perpetual, false darkness, day shortened to an arctic winter, brief and bright. Adele, though, had asked him to take it down after Melchior, the monkey, had become entangled in the pulleys and nearly hanged himself in the mechanism's ropes.

Conrad walked from room to room. The mess of the last four months seemed so deep that his resolve to put things in order failed before it. This was just purgatory, he felt, staring out the window at his garden. It was a long hesitation that would end in the first killing freeze. And then the garden would collapse under its own preposterous weight, overgrown fruits and flowers, barbed seed heads big as grapefruit and freckled pods thick as a man's finger, all of it cut down. And when that day came, he thought, he would fling out his own arms, would open his mouth, would agree to be taken. He wanted to be taken. Lemuel *should* have taken him. What did he mean, leaving him here all alone?

Sitting in the kitchen, he emptied Rose's sewing basket, took out each spool of bright thread, lined them up like a battery of soldiers, the pins and needles a sparkling pile of arms laid down, surrendered. One day, he told himself, the clematis would unwind its arms from around the windows, where its plate-faced blossoms pushed up against the glass and stared at him. The grandiflora 'Queen Elizabeth', with its pink vigorous ruff, would tremble at the touch and drop its multitude of petals. The poppies would fall, the phlox would scatter, and the air, now choked with drifting clouds of seed, white thistles with black, driving tips like arrows, would, at last, empty.

WHEN HE CONSIDERED how he might spend the rest of his day, he was overwhelmed by the mass of empty hours ahead of him. He was used to Rose with her brimming agenda. For four months he hadn't even pretended to be useful. Now, though, since the angel, he felt vaguely that he ought to try. Pacing restlessly, he walked into the living room, glanced out the front window at the street to see if another basket might have been left for him. The eggs and the Smile Market's cinnamon rolls had helped, but something in him yearned for the strange familiarity of those baskets, their contents always hot, their effect on him like Rose herself—calming, sweet, and filling. But the step was empty and Conrad felt disappointed. He turned away from the window. He wanted his pigeons, wanted their company.

Putting on his hat now, mindful of the sky, which stretched tight and gray above him, he went back outside, brushing away the astral heads of the cleome and the clouds of sweet autumn clematis that crowded the path. Rose would have been amazed at all this, he thought. Even Rose, who was always prepared to be delighted by her garden, would have been amazed—and something cut at his heart then, a little blade like the sharp knife Rose used for grafting. She's missing all this, he thought.

But as he passed the vegetable garden, he saw a shape flutter there behind the fence. He stopped, his heart seizing as though a finger had reached in and touched the rictus of the chambers. Again, something caught his eye, a white shape, like a hand raised at a distant window.

But when he approached the garden, he saw that it was only the bows of sheeting used for the peas, some strands unwound now and lifting in the wind. Rose had sat in a chair carried out to the garden to do this, one of her last tasks, and Conrad had stood beside her, tearing an old sheet into narrow strips, cutting the lengths for her.

He paused now to close the gate, stood beneath the wrought iron letters that curved in an arc above his head: SO LONG AS MEN CAN BREATHE, OR EYES CAN SEE, SO LONG LIVES THIS, AND THIS GIVES LIFE TO THEE. Shakespeare, Lemuel's choice; he had thought it would please Rose. Lemuel himself had performed the ironwork, and Conrad had gilded the arched filaments, entwined with curling stem and heavy fruit, which were mounted atop the gateposts.

It had been a gift to her, this addition to the garden, meant to make her happy, meant to rouse her. The whole of that summer, the first after Adele Sparks's death, Rose had seemed unnaturally exhausted. One Saturday afternoon, when he happened to glance from an upstairs window, Conrad had seen Rose trundling the wheelbarrow over the grass; and he had cried out her name when suddenly, with no warning, she had simply dropped to her knees, brought her forehead to her hands, still gripping the handles. He had not moved from the window, though. Frozen there, his fingertips against the glass, Conrad had willed her to rise, to move, to pick up where she had left off. And after a minute she had, leaning into the weight of the wheelbarrow and disappearing behind her toolshed. Later, finding her sitting quietly on the grass in the shade of the oak tree, her eyes closed, he had stopped at her feet. He wanted to say something to her, wanted to know that she was all right. But he could not admit to her that he had seen her from the window and had failed to come to her. By various evasions he was able to pretend to himself that it had never happened, her moment of collapse. But the truth of it—that Rose could sometimes fail, did fail, and that he did not want to know why—never really left him.

He had feared all through that June that she was veering toward one of her spells, the profound shifts in mood that forced her to her bedroom, where she might remain for days behind its locked door. He had known with a terrible certainty that it would eventually come to that. And finally, one morning, Rose simply failed to get out of bed, rolling away from him, her fingers clenched around the sheets.

And so Conrad had called Lemuel. "It's starting again," he said. "I don't know what to do."

Lemuel had come, disembarking slowly from the train with his battered valise. Meeting him at the station, Conrad had been struck by how old and lonely Lemuel looked without Adele at his side. Back at the house, the two men had paced the kitchen and dining room for a day, leaving trays at Rose's door, listening to the terrible silence there. Once, sitting on the floor on the landing outside the door, Conrad had spoken aloud, as much to himself as to her: "I wish you wouldn't do this. I don't know why you have to do this." And he had been surprised when he heard, from behind the door, Rose's voice.

"I'm sorry," she said, close by as if she had been leaning against the door, waiting for him, listening. "I'm sorry."

But she would not come out, and so Conrad and Lemuel had taken themselves to the garden, finished digging the vegetable beds and building the gate. They worked quietly, not talking very much, playing with the pigeons in the evenings, leaving trays, which went mostly untouched, at Rose's door. From time to time they glanced up to the house, to Rose's bedroom window, looking for her face behind the glass, some sign of life, some recovery of interest on her part.

At last, four days after Lemuel's arrival, Rose had come downstairs in a fresh yellow dress, her hair clean and pulled back in a long braid. Like a child apologizing for a transgression, she had wept, embraced them both, and wept again when they led her outside and showed her the gate. Conrad had been almost afraid of her, had wanted to jump when she touched him. "I'll never be good enough for all this," she'd said.

But she had always loved her gardens. On the rooftop of her family's home in Brooklyn, she had raised flowers and vegetables with a deft and gentle hand and a chemist's concern for the soil. Early on she became a purveyor of seed catalogs, and as a child she began a lively correspondence, which was to last until her death, with several nurseries, reporting on the success or failure of various plants. Once she and Conrad had married and moved to Laurel, where she could have her own real garden, not just boxes on the rooftop, she made a modest income by selling plants and dispensing advice to local gardeners, and she was often called upon by area garden clubs to deliver lectures on herbs, her specialty. The first time she'd been paid a fee for her services, she came home with a check made out in her name and handed it proudly to Conrad. "Fifteen dollars," she said, "and it was easy as pie. Just telling what I know."

The first winter Conrad had spent at the Sparkses' tending Lemuel's flock, he had helped Rose build a set of trellises along Lemuel's design, a Chinese construction of cleverly interlocking shapes that the following spring bore vines full of sweet peas and moonflowers, their white blossoms fingered with mauve and yellow. Working in coats and hats, scarves knotted around their necks, he and Rose had knelt on the rooftop. Lemuel had posted his drawings to them from Belgium, where his services as a church architect were being employed on a decaying fifteenth-century chapel, and where he was enjoying the company of a Belgian senator who kept a distinguished flock of pigeons at his country estate.

When the idea to construct the trellises had struck Rose, she had sent her father a letter requesting his assistance. And she appeared unfazed by Lemuel's meticulous instructions, which arrived a few weeks later by mail, and spread the drawings out on the rooftop, weighting them with heavy stones. An accompanying letter had given a precise list of the supplies they would need. Rose had already filled the order and carried the lathe herself to the rooftop one afternoon after school, along with a sack of three-penny nails, two small saws, and two hammers.

Conrad was up on the roof the afternoon she appeared with Lemuel's drawings rolled into a tight baton. "Here they are," she said, waving the roll at him. "I have all the stuff already. Look."

She was wearing a red boiled-wool coat, her hair braided and wound severely into two knots at the back of her head. Her eyes were very bright, but thin blue shadows ran down her temples and neck, as if she had not been eating or sleeping enough. She knelt on the rooftop and unrolled the papers, studying the lines.

"That looks complicated," Conrad commented, looking over her shoulder.

"You'll help me?" Rose glanced up at him.

Conrad looked down at her. He frowned at the drawings. He could make no sense of Lemuel's intricate lines, the puzzling shapes.

"You don't need my help," he said, surprised at the bitterness in his voice. He turned away with the push broom. "I have to do this, anyway. I have to get home." He turned back to the loft, to the pigeons stepping lightly within their boxes.

Behind him, still kneeling on the stones of the roof, Rose was silent. Conrad pushed the broom roughly over the varnished landing board, scattering feathers and seed. He stole a glance at Rose. He realized at that moment that he resented her place in that household, the privilege of her position there. He had met with Lemuel twice before his departure overseas, to learn how Lemuel expected his flock to be maintained. Lemuel had shown him how to mix and brew the herbal teas he prescribed as flight-conditioning agents, how to administer the drops. Conrad had been amazed at the refinement of Lemuel's routine with his pigeons. It made his own former system of crude crates on the fire escape look not only amateurish but cruel. Both times he had visited the Sparkses', he had passed through the house with its rich overflow of belongings, like a music box playing a tumbling waltz. He had envied the sense of enterprise there—the boys building a tower of shiny metal pieces hinged with paper clips, pots of herbs trained up coiling supports stationed on a long table before a window, Melchior busily wringing his hands and spying on him from some perch.

The first afternoon after Lemuel's departure, Conrad arrived to fulfill his duties. He sat on the roof in the chilly afternoon air, reading Lemuel's written instructions for the care of his pigeons. Finally, stiff with cold, he descended to the kitchen for boiled water for the tea. He hoped to see Rose.

Adele Sparks had set the kettle on the stove for him as he stood awkwardly beside the table, surveying the long kitchen with its battery of pots and pans suspended from a welded rack. A tank on a low bench was full of strange, undulating fish throwing a quick-silver light. A lamp was lit on the table, which was scattered with books and papers, the cutlery for the family's supper already laid out. Adele was cooking something that smelled so good it made the insides of Conrad's cheeks clench and water. She was trying to put him at ease, he knew, making conversation about the birds, asking questions about school. After a while, waiting for the water to boil, he worked up enough nerve to ask casually, "Is Rose home?"

Adele had paused a moment at the stove, her back to him. "She's not feeling very well tonight," she said quietly. And yet the way she said it made Conrad feel it was something else, something more complicated. On his way back upstairs he had passed Rose's room, the door shut, a faint light showing beneath.

Weeks later, when he glanced at Rose kneeling on the roof, her head dropped to her chest, he remembered that moment, his sense that what had been wrong with Rose that evening was something unlike the childhood illnesses he suffered through restlessly, the occasional fevers and suffocating colds, days when he would stay home from school, his mother returning to their apartment at lunchtime to check on him. Before too much more time was to pass, Conrad would begin to understand the nature of Rose's illness—if it could be called that, he thought—how it worked upon her like something clandestine, something furtive and mean, a colony of blind ants eating away at the scaffolding of her personality, rendering her mute and withdrawn, a child who lay upon her bed, her face turned to the wall, to the detailed drawing of the Acropolis pinned there, its yellowed edges curling.

Kneeling on the roof, Rose did not move, and Conrad felt suddenly alarmed, worried that his remark might have hurt her, that he might be blamed for having been unkind. What he'd said, his rebuff—"You don't need my help"—might have compounded whatever it was that troubled her, that thing that forced her to hide away sometimes for days at a stretch in her bedroom.

He returned to her side, touched Lemuel's drawings with his foot. "So. Where do you start?" he said.

Rose did not answer.

He knelt at her side. "Show me," he said.

Rose dropped her head lower on her chest.

Conrad looked at her hands, clenched white at the knuckles, gripped together. He reached out, hesitating, then touched her hand. She flinched.

"I'm sorry," he said. "I'll help you."

And when she neither moved nor answered, he reached for her hands again, began to unlace her fingers one at a time, until he held one of her hands in his own.

They did not look at each other, the two children kneeling on the rooftop, bowed under the setting sun, but Conrad felt then, holding Rose's small, cold hand, that in prying apart her fingers, in releasing them, he had taken some liberty, some liberty that brought responsibility. He had not touched anyone before, not a girl. He had not expected it to be like that.

"Here," she said then, pointing with her free hand to a line on one of the drawings. She picked up a saw, turned it so that the blade faced away from him—serious, civil, like a fencer observing the rules of the duel—and handed it to him. And when she ducked her head and lightly kissed his knuckle, releasing his hand then and turning her face aside, Conrad felt both desire and fear rising up into his mouth. It would always be hard, after that, for him to separate those feelings. It was as if the world made no allowance for a simple joy. Guarding every cave, he felt, is a serpent. For every bird I send aloft, he thought, there is the danger that it will not return.

He lifted the saw and cut where Rose told him to.

SO MANY YEARS later, leaving the vegetable garden and his reverie beneath the golden gate that overcast morning, Conrad looked down at the curved-tile roof of his loft, glowing in the weak light. He never failed, looking at the small building, to appreciate Lemuel's gifts as an architect. Conrad had sometimes thought, in fact, that he could under the right circumstances be perfectly happy living in the loft himself. Lemuel had sited Conrad's workshop area on the first story so that it overlooked the meadow and the river beyond. Conrad had furnished the room with a long table, on which he worked at his gilding equipment, and Rose had covered a small sofa and armchair for him, which he set at angles before the double doors. In a back room, where he stored grain and pigeon paraphernalia, were a camp stove and a sink.

Entering the loft, he hung his hat on the hook by the door, tucked away a barbed spray of pyracantha that had crept around the door frame, and wandered around to the open roost boxes facing the hillside. Inside he discovered one of his pigeons, a male, sitting on a nest. Conrad leaned forward and smiled in at him. The pigeon's eyes were closed, his wings drawn up close to his body. Conrad had always liked this about pigeons—that they took turns, the male and the female, incubating the eggs. It was, as Rose had pointed out, a liberated arrangement, the female taking the watch from late afternoon, through the night, until early morning, the male sitting on the nest during the day.

"I think it's a *very* nice way to do it," Rose had said, standing beside Conrad and watching the birds with him. "Very fair."

Conrad had not had any particular hand in pairing these two. Though Lemuel, who was fanatical about breeding, often mated grandfathers and granddaughters, mothers and sons, in order to ensure a fixed characteristic and reduce variations in the strain, Conrad had never felt quite right about this system. Though he dabbled some with controlled mating during the years he was establishing his flock, over time he grew faintly uncomfortable with the notion of forcing marriages among his birds. After all, they mated for life, barring catastrophe; and so, after a while, he simply allowed his pigeons to choose their own mates. Once a pair had announced itself, he helped out by moving the two birds to a shared coop, feeling pleased that nature had taken its own mysterious course.

Lemuel, on his visits north, had shaken his head over Conrad's increasingly ragtag flock, pushing his hands through the long white hair that swept back from his forehead; but Conrad had been unmoved by his disapproval.

"It's the inevitability of love, Lemuel," he had said to counter his father-in-law's exasperated exclamations over his birds. And jabbing Lemuel in the ribs with his elbow, Conrad had chided him. "How would *you* have liked to be mated off to someone you hadn't chosen?"

But Lemuel, his bearing offended and erect, had shaken his head, harrumphed like a man who has failed to impress some obtuse student and so packs up his compass and calipers, his tools and instruments of exact science, and gives up. "You're going to have rats, Connie," he said. "That's where romance will get you with pigeons. Nothing but rats."

But these two birds, rock doves, had already successfully raised a dozen or more broods, proof of the utilitarian virtue of love, generations ensuing from a spark. Conrad, who had witnessed their original mating ritual early one spring morning several years before, had been charmed by them: the male bird had put on an impressive performance, strutting and pacing around the female, his greenish purple crop swelling. The female, her eyes at half-mast, had opened her beak for the male to dip his own into hers —kissing, Rose had called it. And afterward Conrad had been touched by the birds' fastidious attention to each other, their joint efforts to feed the young peepers after birth. He referred to them as Pasquale and Evita, Rose's suggestions, after her fondness for a couple who operated a truck garden near the highway and who each summer produced mountains of chili peppers, their fantastically spirited flavors somehow disguised by their colors, disarmingly innocent, like boiled sweets. The pigeons' original names, though marked carefully in Conrad's ledger, had long since been lost to him.

"Well, well, Pasquale," he said now, looking in on the bird. "Congratulations."

Evita stood at the corner of the coop, bobbing her head against the wire mesh. Conrad reached inside and raised the door. She waited hardly a moment before taking off into the air, as if her cramped condition on the nest had made her itchy, restless to get away. Pasquale opened one eye to watch his mate leave, and then closed it again.

"Oh, it's hard work, I know," Conrad said, wiping the floor of the coop with a rag, scrubbing at a stain.

Stepping back outside the loft, Conrad walked slowly to the bench on the grass. The purple heads of late summer clover floated at his feet. Evita flew around high in the sky with the dipping flight characteristic of pouters, her wings held breathlessly wide. Conrad sighed, leaned back against the bench, and closed his eyes.

And then it occurred to him that the eggs, which hadn't been there a day or so ago, must have been conceived not long after Rose's death. He tried to count back, twenty days, twenty-one, but found he couldn't; he didn't even know what day it was. The time seemed lost to him, as though he had slept through it. And then he had to squeeze his eyes shut against the realization that the two things were so closely related—these baby peepers, now circling and circling inside the soft, damp orb of their eggs, and Rose's death.

He had been inattentive to the birds over Rose's last days. He remembered that much. At night, with the hospice volunteer seated on the slipper chair by Rose's bed, inclined toward the whispering voice, Conrad had left to hurry down to the loft, taking deep draughts of air as he descended the steps down toward the stony smell of the river. He had filled the pigeons' pans with grain and then rushed back up to the house, not bothering to sweep out the mess that had accumulated in the coops.

In their shadowy bedroom, Rose had lain in bed, her seed and flower catalogs spread out over the quilt. Her voice had been a whisper, but night after night that last week she had made him sit beside her, paper and pencil at his knee, and take down all the names of the things she wished ordered and planted after her death.

"These anemones," she said. "These lilies, 'Enchantment'"—her finger grazed the page—"for by the front fence. To the left of the beech. Don't plant them too deep. Little bleach mark on the foliage. No deeper." She tapped at the paper. "These daffodils. One hundred. For the lower terrace, by the loft. Aconitum, larkspur. You know. Fifty. Always needed blue in the border by the kitchen. Glows in the dark. Pretty."

It was, he had begun to realize, an endless list. He could have sat there for days, and she would never have run out of things she wished done, wished to do, her garden endlessly in need of dividing, rearranging, pruning, sifting; she liked that the garden often surprised her, surprised them both, some flowers migrating of their own accord to spots more suitable for them.

Once, stopping, dropping the pencil on the carpet by the bed, where it fell soundlessly, he had just watched Rose, her voice droning on quietly, whispering flower names. "Montbretia. Nice. Pretty beside the white lupines. Upper terrace. Might have to overwinter in the basement, though."

She was talking, he realized, as though she was just going away on a short trip.

"Conrad," she said at last, breathless, glancing over at him. "You're not taking it down."

"I know," he said. "I'm sorry." He stared at her, but she looked away, picked up where she had left off, her finger trailing over the pages. He retrieved the pencil from the floor but did not write.

Rose looked sidelong at him, then closed her eyes. "Conrad," she said. "Please."

"You want to work me to death?" he said, trying to laugh, but his voice cracked. "Is that it?"

And she had wept then, that soundless weeping that seemed to belong to her last days, the terrible pause between each breath, so long that Conrad sometimes held his own, waiting and willing her chest to rise convulsively again. The tears spilled out from under her eyelashes, their sparse fringe.

"I just—" she said, "I just want you to have something to do."

And Conrad had stopped at that, had looked over the slight rise under the blankets that was Rose's wasting body. To do? he thought. And suddenly the prospect of life without her beside him became horrifyingly real, as if he had been so concentrated on her illness, on fending off her pain, that he had forgotten what came next, what came afterward. He saw himself surrounded by a dizzying array of bulbs, corms, roots, tubers, and plants, vines growing over his feet, thorny tendrils creeping around his ankles, Rose's instructions swirling in his mind, the spade heavy in his hand.

EVITA HAD DISAPPEARED into the milky sky. Conrad gazed up the hillside at his garden, its tumbling, frothing mass of leaf and blossom. It seemed to sway there, a cataract of green falling from the sky itself, a voluptuary draped in silken vines and flowers. He could not see the house at all, obscured behind this rising cloud bank of green. Rose had never gone anywhere in the garden without her clippers; she was always pinching things back, ripping out woody undergrowth, pruning the shrubs and trees. But without her attentions, the garden seemed to be subduing the earth itself, wild creepers running over the paths, burrs and brambles overtaking Rose's clean squares of grass. Trumpet vines crawled up the trunks of the dwarf pear trees; purple thistles sprouted in the wildflower meadow. Conrad felt, looking up at it, that the garden was moving toward him, engulfing him. Not burying him exactly, but winding him all around in a cocoon of fragrant green, the arms of vines coiling up his legs and trunk, laying little leaf hands over his mouth, silencing him. A fog rose—columns of vapor, the wavering architecture of air. Thunderheads gathered in the sky.

A man could lose himself here, Conrad thought, and realized it was true. He could enter the overgrown bowers of his garden and never appear again, hemmed in by thorns and vines, impeded by an army of flowers, an ocean of green. At any moment he could take one step from which there would be no turning back. He could be lost, even in his own place.

Five

THE DAY AFTER Rose died, Henrietta Ellis came to the door early in the morning, knocked, and let herself in without waiting for Conrad to answer.

Behind her in single file were the other members of the Pleiades. A brood of rock doves, they were dressed alike in suits of varying shades of pale gray, their hair degrees of white tending to blue. Each bore in her hands a twinkly, foil-covered platter. These women had been Rose's closest friends.

Conrad had been standing in the kitchen, holding on to the sink and looking out the window after having forced himself to drink a glass of milk. He had been trying, in the face of the terrible constriction that had seized his lungs after Rose's body was borne away, to draw a deep breath. He did not seem able to breathe properly. The sensation frightened him, and he wanted to tell someone, report it, but could not think whom to call.

Henri, tall as a ship, sailed up behind him, turned him to face her, and enfolded him in a wordless embrace. Then she pulled out a chair at the kitchen table and sat down. Each of the Pleiades came in their turn, put their casseroles and cakes upon the counter, and held Conrad close for a moment. They all smelled the same to him, of powder and lotion and something dusty—a moth wing. Their cheeks were soft, their hands gentle and trembling. The little jet buttons on their suit jackets, carved with tiny anchors or fleur-de-lis, pressed into his chest. The short stiff bangs of black netting that jutted over their hats tickled his nose. Conrad allowed them to hold him. Sighing, he drew a deep breath at last and leaned into them, into their familiar female smell and fluttering hands.

Henri pulled out the remaining chair for Conrad, patted it, and set her enormous pocketbook on the table. Conrad sat down and looked around him. He realized he looked filthy, sleepless. A derelict. He would have broken Rose's heart, looking like that. He saw Nora Johnson glance at her friends and then stand up to fill the kettle. "Tea," she said firmly.

Conrad made as if to rise, thinking to be helpful, but she put a soft, dry little palm on his shoulder. "I *know* where the cups are," she said. "I know it as well as in my own house."

"I'll bet he hasn't eaten, either," Henri said, looking up from a paper that she had withdrawn from her pocketbook.

"Toast then," Nora said. "And some of Rose's apricot jam."

Conrad looked up at her, saw her face wither and fall and then, with effort, right itself. She smiled at him. "Nothing but the best," she said, but her mouth wobbled, and tears slipped over her eyes and down her cheeks. Conrad felt his own jaw start to tremble. Nora turned away.

"Conrad," Henri said after a second, leaning forward and laying a hand on his arm. She sat back then and took off her hat, extracting the pins and laying them side by side on the table. She patted her hair, took a breath. "Conrad, you know we wouldn't intrude, but I think it's fair to say that Rose would wish us—to help you. With the arrangements. You just tell us if there's anything special you want, and we'll take care of the rest."

She reached for her pocketbook, extracted her glasses, and shook out the sheet of lilac paper before her. "We did have some— ideas," she said, looking out at Conrad from over her glasses. "Rose did."

Conrad looked at her. "We never talked about it," he said after a minute.

There was a silence at the table. Conrad looked down at his hands and then up at the ring of faces around him. He realized that they already knew that. That Rose had, in her final conversations with her friends, told them everything they needed to know, understanding that Conrad was incapable both of talking about her death beforehand and of executing anything afterward. What had she wanted? Flowers? Music?

What did *he* want? What was fitting? What would ever be fitting enough?

And then, as if in a contraction of time, he saw Rose on their wedding day, up on the roof of her parents' brownstone, Lemuel's pigeons loosened to the skies as Conrad bent Rose back to kiss her, her spine the stem of a flower in his hands, the birds flying up and away, streamers of white.

"I'd like to bring the pigeons," he said abruptly, looking around at the Pleiades. "I'd like to send the birds up."

There was another silence. Mignon French, a transplanted Southerner, round and gentle as a fantail pigeon herself, who was always given the role of the victim in the Pleiades' performances, leaned over the table and touched Conrad's arm. Her nails were pink, like little shells. "What a *lovely* notion—" she started to say.

But Henri interrupted her. "At what point—" she said, looking down through her glasses at the paper in her hand, "at what point would that be done?"

"At the end, of course," Nora said, putting a plate of toast and a glass jar of apricot jam down in front of Conrad. She handed him a napkin. "Eat," she said, wiping her hands on a dishcloth. She waved her hand in the air with a vague motion. "It would be at the very end."

Henri took a fountain pen from her pocketbook, wrote something in slow, tiny script at the bottom of the paper. "Very well," she said. She screwed the top back on her pen, set it down carefully beside her, looked at none of them in particular. "At the end."

Nora sat down again beside Conrad, folded her hands in her lap. After a minute she leaned over, put her head against his shoulder. On his other side, Grace Cobbs leaned in, too, the blue sheen of their twin permanents glowing against Conrad's white shirt. They both must have been at the hairdresser's already that morning, Conrad thought, sniffing, the two women's heads resting lightly against his arms; they smelled the same, like setting lotion. Across from him, Adele Simms and Helen Osborne and Mignon stretched out their hands for Conrad's, and Henri, too, put hers across the patchwork of laced fingers, so that for one blessed moment, as Conrad sat there, he could feel nothing but the clasp of familiar flesh, the singular sensation of being touched by a multitude of hands, that infinitely reassuring embrace by a constellation of Rose's dearest friends.

"'So part we sadly in this troublous world, To meet with joy in sweet Jerusalem.'" Henri looked up as she spoke. She was clear-eyed and strong and held Conrad's eyes in her own.

"Queen Margaret," Nora said, lifting her head, smiling. "Wasn't Rose a marvelous Margaret?"

AND SO CONRAD had brought the pigeons, keeping them in their cages in the back of his pickup truck until toward the end of the graveside service at the cemetery. He stood surrounded by the Pleiades, a dark pool of mourners casting a shadow over the tender spring grass. Escorted to the graveside, Conrad searched the crowd. He could not understand, briefly, why he did not see Rose when so much else seemed familiar.

And then, during the readings offered by each of the Pleiades, who wore a uniform shade of blue black and had feathers—the quills of blue jays and the brown spears of hawks' tails—in their hats, their lapels bursting with clusters of Rose's favorite anemone, the exquisite white 'Honorine Jobert', Conrad had simply wandered away from the gathering at the graveside.

The Pleiades had watched him go, but Henri was reading, and none of them liked to interrupt her. Conrad just walked away; he had no particular relation to this ceremony. He was just a spectator. He glanced up once at the sky, a solemn and perfect blue, and reached to loosen the knot of his tie at his neck. He felt light headed, almost disembodied, as though his hands were not attached to his wrists. He took off his suit coat, laid it on the front seat of the truck.

In the cages he'd assembled twenty of his whitest pigeons, the fantails and the ice pigeons, the Silesian croppers and the white kings, the frillbacks and the Antwerp smerles. Trying to rid his head of the cottony sensation of dullness, he slid the cages around noisily on the bed of the pickup until they were all facing the open tailgate, and then he bent over to look in at his birds. Something like sand shifted inside his head when he leaned over. But he put his finger to the cage that held Pearl. She held his eye a moment; the world, contained in her black iris, was reduced to a wavering parallelogram. And then, as Henri closed her book and Father Mortimer stepped forward to begin the prayers, Conrad opened the cages.

The pigeons flew out in a shuddering of wings, taking off toward the light, toward the high, etherizing reaches of the sky, just as the Pleiades stepped forward to link hands and bow their silver heads over the dark mouth of the grave. The birds circled up and away, aiming at some invisible passage.

All but one.

Pearl, her wings held wide in a stately attitude, drifted just above Conrad's head, caught in a perfect updraft. Conrad craned back painfully, put his hands up—did she want to come back to him? But as he did so, he felt a capful of wind strike him gently around the head, cuffing his ears. And then he heard it, a sudden, low whine, as a long, dark current of warm air leaned in across the cemetery from over the mountains. The air smelled of faraway places, of sandbars and the ocean, a foreign scent laden with spice, the smell of places Conrad knew he'd never been and would never go. He turned to face it, saw the trees turn in the powerful gust, the canopy over the grave flap. Nosegays laid to rest here and there at the heads of the departed came loose, ran across the grass, bright spots of false color. Gyres of tiny new leaves circled and spun. The hats on the heads of the Pleiades tore loose, blew away; those gathered at the graveside clutched at their lapels, at one another, afraid they would be torn apart forever and yet exhilarated, too, by the sensation of abandon the wind created in their hearts.

Conrad staggered in the sweeping, salty respirations of the wind but managed to stand his ground, his white shirt flapping. He saw his pigeons scatter as if they had been shaken from a tablecloth, their primary and secondary feathers spread wide. They were trying to find a grasp on the slippery air, the fields of their feathers separating against the fierce draft, their bodies vertical for a moment before they were blown back and away. He saw Pearl above him, braced impossibly against the wind. He put up his arms again to catch her back, show her where he was. But as he did so, he felt himself leave the ground for an instant, not flight nor falling but an instant of perfect weightlessness, as if the wind were testing its grip on him, too, testing gravity's strength, testing the intention in Conrad's heart. It was only an instant, and yet in that moment a wondrous relief came over him.

And as he held there in an inhalation of indecision, his shirt filling with the wind's powerful breath, he saw a young woman he did not immediately recognize step away from the edge of the huddled collection of mourners, their dark coats shiny as crows' oily feathers. She was small and thin, dressed in a drab overcoat; her narrow wrists emerged from the cuffs, fragile and stiff. Her light-colored hair was so pale it was nearly white. Delicate strands whipped across her face. All around her blew a brilliant confetti of leaves torn loose, the shorn red foliage of the Japanese maples and the crimped, green paper fans of the ginkgoes, the purple leaves of the copper beech and the notched feathers of the honey locust, pale and buttery.

He saw her leaning into the wind, coming toward him, her eyes lifted in recognition; and at that moment he remembered her—the smile of pleasure she'd given Rose in the hallway, her foolish dress, the way Rose had slipped an arm round the girl's waist, steered her into the sunlight at the back of the house, and shown her the view.

When his toes touched ground again, he felt his muscles weaken like water. Pearl was beating her wings steadily against the gusts, holding her own above Conrad's head. Conrad came to his knees, dazed and light headed. He saw that the mourners at the graveside were separating, the women tucked under the men's arms, teetering backward. The tent was plucked from its tethers, flew off at a tilt. Conrad saw Henri stagger away, her blue gray permanent ruffled up oddly in the back; Mignon French raced past him, taking little running steps, tears streaming down her pink cheeks. Everyone seemed to be calling to him, trying to say something. Conrad raised his arms to the wind, feeling his shirt flatten over his chest like a sail. The sky was sharp and blue, filled with the invisible landscape of the wind as it carved out canyons and valleys, angles of ascent.

And then, as if she could hold on no longer against the steady assault, Pearl veered off and away, a white speck disappearing over the bowl of the hill, toward the river and home. The cemetery was empty except for Conrad and—standing a respectful distance away, clutching the pliable body of a Lombardy poplar, which the wind bent toward the ground—a girl who understood that she'd seen a man caught for one impossible moment between heaven and earth.

IF HE CLOSED his eyes, Conrad could remember the sensation of that moment of weightlessness, and also the sight of Pearl vanishing over his head, the intimation he'd had at that instant that he might never see her again. Now, taking a seat on the bench in front of his loft, he turned away from the view of his garden and looked out over the river toward the mountains instead. Evita had vanished into the dark clouds.

He could not see the sun, though he could sense its hot, distant presence above him, obscured behind the wall of damp clouds; he judged that it must be nearly noon. Conrad felt observed, underfoot; fetching Pearl from the loft, he brought her back outside with him and sat down again, his hand curled protectively over the pigeon's back. He gazed up at the sky. The clouds seemed to have closed solidly overhead, a wall of rock. For a moment he imagined Evita breaking through them, emerging into a light so fierce and joyful that it would burn the eye, replace the gift of ordinary sight with vision, the mundane with the miraculous. As a child he had believed that if his pigeons could talk, they would tell him the truth about heaven, for he was certain they saw it each time they rose up out of the gritty, particled air of New York, disappearing over the skyline. He believed that they saw the globe of the earth rotating smoothly ahead of them, saw their own dovecotes blinking on the surface of the planet like lighthouses at the dark edge of the sea.

How did they do it? His birds' ability to navigate home, no matter how far they'd flown, no matter how disorienting the weather, provoked an amazement in Conrad that had grown over the years rather than diminished. In the late 1800s, a famous pigeon, a black hen from Philadelphia named Dinah, had been clocked at faster than a mile per minute, and Conrad's own racing homers had once flown one hundred seventy miles in just under three hours during a bad storm. This was an impressive time, Conrad knew, one that didn't allow for much correction or dillydallying. Rose had believed romantically that it was simply the pigeon's *love* of home that brought it back each time. But Conrad, unwilling to settle for that explanation, had been more persuaded by recent experiments with infrasound. A researcher at Cornell had discovered that pigeons were able to detect sound energy at eight octaves below the limits of normal human hearing; this, more than any other explanation he had ever heard for the homing pigeon's navigational abilities, made sense to Conrad. He could easily imagine that his birds lived in a universe ringing with a complex musical score unheard by human ears, a concert of the noise of movement itself, its massive displacements and adjustments like icebergs shouldering through the Arctic Ocean. It all seemed infinitely reasonable to him. It seemed, in fact, the only possible explanation for his pigeon's miraculous ability to avoid becoming lost.

Conrad stroked Pearl's feathers and looked up into the threatening sky, hunting for Evita: the clouds rolled from side to side above him as though he stood on a tilting deck, and there was no sign of the bird. He reached up and put Pearl on his shoulder. Not many of his pigeons were as easy to handle as this one. Rose used to tease him that Pearl was a little bit in love with him; and it was true that she billed and cooed at his approach, that she settled into his hands like a domesticated cat when he stroked her. She liked riding on his shoulder, too, nibbling at his ear. Rose, watching Pearl trail after Conrad one day in the garden as he worked his way down the boxwood bushes with the clippers, had put her hands on her hips and said, laughing, "That bird's not a homing pigeon; she's a bloodhound. I believe she would find you if you were lost in Manhattan."

Conrad had put down the clippers, wiped his forehead, looked up, and put out a hand to Pearl, who fluttered down and landed on his forearm. "She just knows a good thing when she sees it," he'd said, pursing his lips in a kiss to Pearl. "Don't you?"

Pearl rode easily now on his shoulder, an acrobat on the high wire, adjusting her balance to Conrad's stride. "Come on," he said to her, getting up from the bench.

Inside the loft, Conrad sat down in the cracked-leather swivel chair at his desk and began riffling through the stacks of journals and papers there, *Turvey's Dictionary and Guide for Pigeon Racing*, Levi's *The Pigeon*, years' worth of back issues of the *American Pigeon Journal* and *British Homing World*. And then, under a pile of newsletters from the Pigeon Fanciers of America, he saw Rose's notebook, the one she had written over her last few weeks, a guide to the garden, intended to help Conrad remember what tasks needed to be done throughout the year.

How had it made its way here, to his desk? He did not remember bringing it down to the loft. A man from the funeral home had found it under the sheets when Rose's body was lifted to the gurney, and he had handed it to Conrad, standing mutely at the bedside. Had he carried the notebook here that night? He couldn't remember. But, then, he didn't remember much of anything from the last four months.

Now though, shifting Pearl to his lap, he found his glasses in his pocket and fitted them to his nose. He cracked the spine of the notebook and bent it open. Rose's handwriting sloped downhill, threatening to spill off the page. It was, he realized as he turned the pages, a monumental labor for one whose strength had been so uncertain at the end that even lifting a spoon to her mouth had seemed to exhaust her.

It was all very predictable, though. He riffled through the pages and read her instructions—when to feed the fruit trees and how much; when to prune which roses; what needed to be dug up and brought to the basement to overwinter; what needed to be divided and moved.

But then, tucked into the back of the book like an afterthought, on a loose sheet, Conrad discovered a recipe for something called rose beads. He put his finger to the lines, read slowly.

"Put red or pink rose petals through the finest cutter of food grinder," she had written. "Put chopped petals in rusty iron kettle (back porch) and cover with water. Simmer until petals adhere when pressed. Form into beads." The recipe went on, arcane and complicated, more of Rose's necromantic art. Conrad squinted at her script. "Dry in the sun, pierced on hat pins," she had written, and in the margin, crookedly, she had added, "Hat pins in top right dresser drawer, under necklace box."

Conrad closed the book. Had she meant for him to *do* this? All this? Press a clove into each of the still-soft beads, as she had written, to form a puckered indentation like a flower? Thread the beads on black twine? What *for*?

He put his hand over the notebook to momentarily silence the voice within it, the expectation. And yet he could hear it, Rose's wandering tone, meditative, considering: "Beads will retain the faint attar of roses."

He sat back in his chair and thought. Well, it was as good as anything else, wasn't it? It was, as Rose had said, something to do.

Rising from his desk, Pearl stepping lightly on his shoulder, Conrad climbed the stone steps up to the rose garden and filled his hat with petals, more than he could carry. They gave easily to his grasp, falling and scattering in a path at his feet as he walked between the beds. He heard music then, like wind chimes, tinkling notes. And in the kitchen he filled the kettle, the splashing water an echo of voices—his voice, Rose's, their conversations back and forth among the rooms, up and down the stairs, calling and answering. He poured the petals into the kettle, lit the flame on the burner, stood by as the mass swirled into black.

Dust to dust, he thought, pressing the mixture between his fingers when it had cooled. And finally, squinting, he pierced the beads on the hat pins, which were just where Rose had said they would be, laid them on a tea towel, and sat down on the terrace wall, staring, the clouds gathering overhead, gaining speed. Then, clumsily, the unfamiliar needle in his fingers, he laced each rosy bead, now dried hard as a cherry stone, onto a length of black thread. And at last he held the necklace in his hands. He brought it to his nose, sniffed, detected the faint smell of roses.

He turned the necklace in his hands, marveling at Rose's strange body of knowledge, the uncertain embodiment of her here now, out of sight yet close by. Where had she come across this recipe? He closed the lid of her sewing basket slowly over the flashing silver needles, the spools of colored thread, the tiny, velvet-covered cases of pins, her thimble with the grinning face of a monkey, the curling bias tape, and tiny scissors whose handles closed neatly over the blade, the wings of a stork. He thought then of Rose herself bent over the dining room table, her basket spilled beside her, the Singer whirring, her foot pumping the pedal, her furious pace.

For several years she had sewn all the costumes for the Pleiades' performances. Conrad remembered the women closeted in his dining room, the pocket doors pulled almost shut, Rose kneeling at her friends' feet, her mouth full of pins. The sound of sporadic laughter came from the sunny room, glancing off the polished circle of the table, Adele's silver service on the sideboard, the flowering sprays of Rose's orchids nodding low on the radiator.

One day, passing down the hall, Conrad had paused, glanced in through the crack of the doors. Mignon French, round and shapely, her hair combed into a thin knot on her head, stood in her brassiere and skirt, her arms outstretched. Rose knelt at her feet, her hands busy at the green velvet hem. Conrad had seen the white accordion folds of flesh at Mignon's waist, the tumult of flesh contained in the brassiere, the wings of flesh beneath her arms—and the slim rounds of Rose's calves as she knelt in her stocking feet on the rug, her toes curled, pulling the fabric taut, running it through her hands. The other women stood around the room in their underwear and skirts, shawls or sweaters draped over their soft, bare shoulders, holding up their costumes, exclaiming to one another, touching and caressing. He had seen Rose raise the hem of Mignon's skirt, reach beneath it to tug the fabric, saw Mignon's heavy thigh, the dimpled flesh, the heavy ankle, the lifted heel. And he had started guiltily when Henri Ellis, coming downstairs from the bedroom with her arms full of folded costumes, had stepped to the landing, the floorboards creaking beneath her weight.

A long stare passed between them. And then Henri had brushed past him into the dining room, pulling the doors closed behind her.

"Cover up, girls," he heard her say. "There's a Peeping Tom in the house."

Conrad heard shuffling, what sounded like laughter. And then Rose's voice.

"What do you mean?" He winced at the tone, aggrieved, alert.

"Your husband," Henri said, her voice muffled, "is standing in the hall, feasting his eyes on all these half-naked American beauties." More giggles.

"What do you *mean?*" Rose asked again. And now her voice was sharp, clear. Conrad drew back, moved down the hall, his heart in his throat. But in a moment, Rose had slipped through the doors, closing them with a whisper behind her.

"Conrad," she said, low.

He turned, saw her strained face.

"I was just—passing through," he said.

Rose said nothing. He saw her wind the fabric in her hands.

"It was nothing, Rose," he said, trying to keep his voice low.

But after a second she had turned and gone back inside. Conrad fled out the back door.

That afternoon, after the Pleiades had left, waving gaily as they walked down the front path, he had wandered the garden, moving in a desultory way from one task to another. He had been afraid to go back inside. Finally, as dusk began to fall, he had approached the house. It had been quiet except for the cuckoo clock ticking in the hall; long, dim shadows fell over the floors. At the kitchen sink he rinsed his hands of dirt, cleaned carefully and slowly beneath his fingernails with the tines of a fork.

"Rose?"

He spoke her name into the empty kitchen, the shadowy dining room with its litter of costumes, the sewing machine black and silent. He stood at the bottom of the stairs. Listened. No sound. He climbed quietly then, the treads creaking. The door to their bedroom was slightly ajar. He stepped to it, pushed it open.

"Rose?"

She was seated at her dressing table, the two lamps with their silk-tasseled shades lit, soft and yellow. She was undressed to the waist. Her hair, loose, was brushed over her shoulders. She wore a necklace of dull beads at her throat.

"Rose?"

He stepped into the room. She did not move, nor did she take her eyes from her own face, staring back at her in the mirror. He moved closer, stood reflected like a ghost in the dark glass. Rose's eyes were black, the pupils large. Her shoulders and collarbone glowed white, sharp.

"I'm very thin, aren't I?" she asked quietly.

"Thin, yes," he said. "Not too thin, though."

Her hands floated up, cupped her tiny breasts for a moment, then dropped again to her lap.

"If I'd had children, I wouldn't be so thin."

Conrad, his heart clenching, touched her shoulders then, moved to stand square behind her.

"I like you the way you are," he said.

He felt her shoulders lift, a sigh, saw the necklace at her throat rise and fall with the breath. She closed her eyes briefly, opened them again.

"Are you hungry?" she asked. "What time is it?"

"I'm—I don't know," he said, and he felt then that everything was slipping away from him—some moment when he might have explained himself, might have prevented this, fixed it. She stood, moving away from his hands toward the door.

He looked at the bed, her shirt tossed there. "Do you want your shirt?" he said.

She turned to him briefly before walking out the door.

"I think I'll just stay like this," she said. "If you don't mind."

And in the kitchen she had made a salad, sliced the bread, turned fish in the pan, the harsh, penetrating scent of garlic making his eyes smart. She had said nothing, moving between table and stove, her bare back glowing, the beads of her spine shifting like the locked skeleton of a fish. When she sat at the table and pulled up her chair, he looked at her face, saw the tears there.

"Rose," he said, protesting. "Come on. Come on now. Put your shirt on."

"Isn't this what you like?" she said, weeping openly now. And he had pushed back his chair roughly then, raised her in his arms, held her tight against him. How could it matter so much? But he kissed her forehead, her ear, the smooth fall of her hair, over and over, and as he felt the narrow rib cage relax between his hands, he thought how easily everything could be lost—how, in a single second, everything you were sure of could disappear when you weren't looking.

CONRAD RAISED HIS eyes from the necklace he held in his hands, saw Pearl flutter down from the terrace wall and hop along the ground, pecking at the thyme that grew between the flagstones. Following her with his gaze, Conrad saw that the thin fingers of a trumpet vine had crept over his boot while he had been sitting there stringing the beads, thinking. The miniature orange horn of its blossom, a speechless mouth, curled around his ankle. Delicately he shook his leg free.

Pearl, advancing over the flagstones, vanished into the low fog that rolled gently toward them, and Conrad realized that the afternoon had slipped away while he had been making the rose beads. The silence of the garden rested heavily around him, though behind it he heard the occasional distinct click of an insect's voice, as if occurring behind a curtain, or the sudden ruffle of leaves as a bird rose from the undergrowth in alarm. He looked out over the garden, which appeared and disappeared through the mist. The distant mountains were shrouded, invisible, but he could feel their heft leaning toward him, the paper-thin layers of compressed mica and settling shale. How different was this silence from the quiet years of his retirement, he thought, when he and Rose had worked in the garden together, tying and cutting, pruning and weeding, planting and mulching. They had sat together, resting, watching the monarchs drift over the borders. They had wiped the sweat from each other's brow. He had felt sometimes, on those long, uninterrupted days, that they were the last people on earth, the last of their kind. He had wondered how different it might have been if they'd had children. And he thought now that one could feel triumphant as the last of two, a matched pair of animals entering the ark, or the mirror images of a butterfly's wings, things that belonged together, that were not whole unless joined; but it was another thing entirely to be simply the last—to be the one left behind.

He felt cold now; he stood and whistled for Pearl. She flew suddenly at him out of the mist, veered around his head. He put up his hand for her, welcomed the damp and chilled weight of her. And then he remembered Evita, the mother bird. He put Pearl on his shoulder, stepped into the fog, and headed down toward the loft to let Evita back in. As he reached the lower terrace, the mist parted for a moment and he saw Evita circle the roof of the loft and then alight there, her head turned, listening.

And then it seemed as if he could not move fast enough, had not ever been quick enough, for he felt the disturbance in the air above his head, felt the mammoth webbed shadow of the owl as it flew over him, saw the blanket of its wings shaken out like a cloak, heard the impact as the great bird's talons clasped the pigeon and bore the body away over the river toward the dark wood. It was, after the short scream as the owl's talons bit into Evita's breast, quiet. Conrad was dazed. He lifted his hand a moment toward the

sky, then turned slowly to regard the black spaces in the woods on
the far side of the river, their baffling silence, the mist closing in.
He opened his mouth, but there was nothing to say. On his shoulder, Pearl hunched into his neck. What had that scream sounded
like to her, a creature tuned to the aperture of sound itself, the pinprick on the scale, the passage from one world to the next?

Pasquale was still sitting on the nest. Conrad stooped to peer in
at him but turned away after a moment, frowning at the floor. He
heard the bird rustle his feathers, shifting position. Conrad was
not sentimental; he had seen pigeons killed before, though usually
it was hawks who took them, a battle of feathers and spurs in air.
But he did not want to look at Pasquale now. He passed on down
the aisle, sifting grain into each pan.

And then, because he could not think what else to do, he took
down the broom and began to sweep, raising clouds of dirt and
feathers, the empty hulls of seed, everything that was left. Pearl, offended by the rising dust, left his shoulder and flew to the landing
board. But Conrad leaned hard on the broom, felt the fragile stick
bend beneath his weight, felt how close he was, just at that moment, to falling.

Six

EARLY THE NEXT morning, an hour before dawn, Conrad began boxing his pigeons, shuffling in the dark, taking one after another gently between his hands and feeling the heartbeat beneath the warm feathers in his palm. He loaded twenty of his highest fliers, birds who required a good stretch to stay healthy, into crates, and made several trips carrying them up the hill to his truck.

Standing on the gravel driveway, he looked up at the sky. Despite the dense clouds, which had lingered since the day before, since the storm that had ushered in Lemuel, there was an empty feeling to the morning. As he stood there looking up, he had the odd sensation that all the constellations and near planets had vanished, that the earth itself had been blown off course into some vacant orbit. The sky was velvety and dark. Conrad shivered a little. It would rain again before the day's end, he guessed.

He planned to drive his pigeons up toward Lake Champlain, a distance of some one hundred miles, where his friend Harry LeMoyne, also a fancier, would hold them for an hour or two and then release them to fly home, giving Conrad time to beat them back. Conrad was not much interested any longer in flying competitively, but he liked to give his homers some distance flights from time to time. He had often taken them to Harry's over the years. The two men, chatting companionably, would release the birds together, watching them circle upward and acquire their bearings in the breeze. Sometimes Conrad would linger through the morning to drink a cognac or two at the twig table outside

Harry's front door. At home, Rose would have clocked the pigeons, eager to report their times to Conrad when he returned.

It became his habit over the years to send a message to her via one of the pigeons, usually the archangel, a small, compact bird with lustrous, dark bronze plumage. Rose particularly admired this pigeon, with its shining blue wings and copper breast. It had been an expensive gift, from Lemuel, of course. And Conrad liked the idea of sending her love letters through his pigeons, liked the idea that his words, though he always felt they fell short of what he meant to say, spent some time in the high altitudes, acquiring a particular dash and romance.

As a boy he had dreamed of racing his birds in a war, over the rippling white sea of the Sahara, or swift and silent through the spray of rocket fire raining from enemy guns poised above a rocky escarpment. Gentle with his hands and tending to clumsiness, disinclined by nature to hunt or play sports, the young Conrad appreciated his pigeons' stealth, their disguise of innocence, the intellectual victory they made possible.

He understood that his pigeons gave him a certain edge over other boys and, later, over men who might best him in a different sort of contest. That he could stand on Lemuel's rooftop and collect his birds on his outstretched arms made him feel that he had entered into a pact with nature's most mysterious forces. He liked that his pigeons traveled by mystical relation to the world's most powerful and invisible forces—the shifting arc of the sun, rainbows of polarized and ultraviolet light, the heaving ballast of atmospheric pressure, and the body of sound itself, its whine or bellow up through air as its source approached or receded. Welcoming home his returning flock, he imagined that he, too, possessed through some grant of nature a precious modicum of the world's powers. Each time he witnessed his birds returning—as he stood on Lemuel's rooftop or, later, on the grassy swale before his own loft—he wanted to drop to his knees as they fell fluttering from the sky, their wings holding air. And he felt both grateful and afraid at once, as though it were not his birds that had been released in unfamiliar territory but he himself, now discovered again, now found, now saved.

He had called Harry to make their assignation the night before, after a sad supper of tinned lima beans heated up over the blue gas flame and doused with ketchup.

Returning to the house from the loft when the true darkness of night had begun to fall, he had hoped that a basket might have been left for him, and he'd stepped outside to the front porch. The street was empty, though a flock of crows blew out violently from the black green yew by the gate when he opened the door. Conrad had gazed down the street, had seen the lights wink on at May Brown's, one after another, the widow looking for someone, moving quickly from room to room in a game of hide-and-seek. A pair of io moths, the black eyespots on their reddish hind wings opening and closing as the moths hovered near the porch light, rose and fluttered away in tandem into the twilight. Conrad was surprised to catch sight of that unfamiliar little white terrier again, the same dog he'd seen the first time he'd found a basket on his steps. The dog jumped up from the far side of the gate and streaked away down the road when Conrad stepped onto the porch.

This had been a day of nothing but disappointments, he thought —first Nolan Peak dismissing him and his letter; then that owl taking Evita; and now, no dinner. He sat down on the top step. Reaching into his pocket for his handkerchief, his fingers found the necklace of beads. Pulling it from his pocket, he lifted it to his nose. And then, after a minute, he laid it on the step beside him. What he wanted, at that moment, was to be done with the encumbrances of his life. He wanted to lay all his belongings down in a circle around himself—all his worldly goods. He wanted to see the material evidence of his life scavenged by the crows and the woodpeckers, the foxes and the narrow, bald-faced possum—his watch jerked across the ground by a phalanx of field mice, its gold face disappearing, winking, into the shadowy ferns; his money clip grasped by a darting mockingbird, who would fly away with it to a distant tree, screaming in pleasure. He wanted to see the buttons plucked from his shirts, the threads unwound from his jacket. He wanted to be unraveled, to do away with what felt like the poisoned substance of himself, the burden of his own oppression since Rose's death. He put his hand over the beads a moment, then lifted it away, leaving the necklace curved over the stair, abandoned.

Sitting in the dark later that evening, listening to Schumann's Opus 73, the composer's *Fantasiestücke,* Conrad had called Harry, who had seemed genuinely glad to hear from him. And then he had stepped outside, into the garden. He sat down on the grass by the reflecting pool, a dark aperture in the earth. All around him, by infinitesimal degrees, the moonflowers opened their white faces and turned toward the sour scent of his misery, fanning their perfume into the breeze. The cry and answer of the tiny tree frogs hidden in the branches of the low shrubs resounded in a throbbing volley over Conrad's head, the heartbeat of the garden itself, rhythmic and consoling. He had lain down, his head cradled on his elbow, and shut his eyes. The sweeping wands of the spirea, Rose's beloved bridal wreath with its down of white flowers, fell gently over him.

An elephant stag beetle, its forked, antlered jaws studded with a serrated ridge of teeth, crept forward from the undergrowth. Conrad had opened one eye to see the insect's shiny prothorax and formidable weaponry; it settled itself with its back to Conrad, its jaws trembling at the night air, a distant dripping. Conrad inched out a finger—these beetles, despite their elaborate defenses, could never right themselves if flipped to their backs. He touched the hard shell, hinged like armor, and the beetle stayed still, alert and vigilant, praying under his hand.

When he woke it was almost dawn. He was damp and chilled, and his hands were stiff, but he had slept the quietest, most dreamless sleep of his life. Gathering his pigeons that morning for the drive, he understood that he had been given a gift, but he did not know whom to thank.

CONRAD DROVE THROUGH town on the way to Harry's, stopping for the light at the corner of Main and Green Streets on the square. By habit he glanced up to the granite wall of the bank beside him on his left. A plaque had been installed there just below the second-story windows, following a flood that had submerged the town in water for two terrible days in 1942. A brass hand, one finger extended, pointed to a line marked by the numeral 12 in ornate letters. Below the hand was an inscription: SEPTEMBER 18, 1942: THE DAY THE WATERS ROSE.

Conrad had seen photographs of the flood in the *Aegis*'s office. He and Toronto had found them a few years before while planning for Laurel's bicentennial celebration; Harrison Supplee had thought that selected old photographs (framed by Toronto, who was handy with tools, and gilded by Conrad) might be sold to raise money for the town. One Sunday afternoon, Conrad and Toronto had let themselves into the office, made coffee in the pot, and sat down under the browning arms of Betty Barteleme's philodendron in the front room to look through boxes.

Toronto had read to Conrad from brittle clippings as they sat on the floor, sorting through stacks of old prints. According to the first stories, printed a week after the flood, a week of steady rains, the legacy of a dying hurricane, had burst the series of stone-and-earth dams along the Mad River at Lake Arthur. Millions of gallons of water had sped down Mt. Abraham at speeds of twenty-five miles per hour, forcing the river over its banks and into the streets, businesses, and homes of Laurel. Property losses had been estimated at $11 million. "But a week later," Toronto said, reading aloud, "Laurel's residents are mourning most acutely the lives of two youngsters taken by this dreadful natural disaster."

Toronto frowned at the paper in his hand. "It must have been terrible," he said, putting the newsprint aside and passing a photograph to Conrad. "Look."

The photos showed a landscape almost unreal in its alteration. The river had flooded streets and fields, surging through businesses and homes, carrying off livestock and automobiles, furniture and pianos, whole trees and front porches. Dead animals trapped in aggrieved postures in the forked branches of felled trees; an isolated chair caught spinning lazily in a whirlpool; walls of debris fifteen feet high buttressing storefronts—the pictures were shocking, sad, frightening. Conrad could look at them only briefly. And that the waters had receded in less than two days, a breathtaking reversal, leaving the town choked with rust and mud, seemed to him a perfect demonstration of the brutality of destruction—it can all happen in a second, he had thought; they might not even have known it was coming.

He was so preoccupied with these thoughts while waiting at the intersection that he did not notice the light changing. When the car behind him honked, Conrad startled, jolting the truck forward against the crosswalk. But as he did so, he saw in horror the terrified face of the pedestrian in front of him—her arms flung out against the advancing hood of his truck, a blue vein like a ribbon at her neck, the black windows of the bank reflected in her eyes.

A flash of light hit the street before him—a trick, the sun emerging for one blinding instant from behind the clouds; sparks flew as if from an anvil. It was too late to stop: Conrad felt the truck move forward beneath him like a ship proceeding into the lock of a canal, into some temporary hold in space and time, a false level. And yet, the collision he expected did not occur; instead he felt himself pass through the girl's body; he felt a coolness, like walking through damp sheets hung on the line to dry.

When he pulled over to the curb, he was shaking. After a long moment, in which his head filled with a maddening prickling sensation, he finally raised his eyes, looked into the silver rectangle of the rearview mirror.

The girl was on the far side of the street, walking away from him down the sidewalk. She wore a white dress, long and unevenly hemmed. She carried in her arms a large bouquet of cream-colored flowers. Conrad stared at her a moment, then rolled down his window. He could not hear the sound of her footsteps, but the scent of the flowers was strong and unmistakable, the musky spice of hothouse roses. When she reached the far corner of the street, she turned slightly, and Conrad saw the smooth profile, shallow as the head on a coin, and serious as a queen. It was Hero.

WHEN CONRAD AND Rose had decided to marry, after over a decade of friendship through their late childhood and adolescence, Lemuel had wanted to make all the arrangements, of course. Such a spectacle was what he lived for. Like Rose, he thought life ought to be lived with a theatrical flourish, that certain events called for drama, for costume and music, for a careful adjustment of the lights, a pregnant pause.

Leaning against Conrad's arm in the Sparkses' kitchen one night, Rose had made the announcement with uncharacteristic simplicity, and Lemuel had leapt up from the table to embrace them, catching them both in a great hug, squeezing hard to rouse some more lively display from them. Conrad, holding Rose's waist, had felt anxious for a moment. It was one thing for him and Rose to have made the decision—lying quietly face-to-face and smiling foolishly at each other in Rose's wide bed in her childhood bedroom—and another to hand the news of it over to Lemuel, for whatever production he would make of it. By nature a private man, even in his youth, Conrad felt both thrilled and uneasy when involved in the sort of high jinks Lemuel liked to mix up.

Lemuel liked to surprise people with gifts and pronouncements. On the morning of Conrad's eighteenth birthday, Lemuel had flung open the door to Rose's bedroom just before dawn, handed Conrad his clothes, and, hurrying him along, taken him to the river. From the deck of a friend's sailboat, they had watched the sun rise over the city, a bottle of vodka and a loaf of black bread between them.

"The world is yours, Conrad," Lemuel had said, throwing his arms wide, vodka splashing from the bottle, as the light of the sun crept up over the buildings, gilding them with gold. "It's a wondrous thing to be eighteen."

And Conrad had tried to feel that sense of power. He had, for a moment, enjoyed the thrill of the morning, he and Lemuel hoisting the sun themselves.

Lemuel liked all matters celestial. He kept an almanac in the kitchen and made sure his family was apprised of the momentous matters of the heavens—eclipses of the sun and moon, the Leonid meteor shower, rings around Saturn glowing for a moment, visible through an amateur's telescope for the first time in a millennium. More than once Conrad had found himself conscripted to tote a hamper to the park or the rooftop, young James and John half-asleep at his shoulder, to watch the terrifying and marvelous movement of the planets, Lemuel narrating sonorously from some book—Byron, or Wordsworth, usually one of the Romantics.

"Swiftly walk over the western wave, Spirit of Night!" Lemuel would raise his voice, nearly shouting Shelley's lines, invoking some answer from the heavens. "Out of the misty eastern cave, Where, all the long and lone daylight, Thou wovest dreams of joy and fear, Which make thee terrible and dear,—Swift be thy flight!"

And each time, watching Lemuel stand in the fading starlight among the chimney pots, a book in his hand, glasses on his nose, a finger raised, Conrad had felt awed not just by what he witnessed —the moon turning black before his eyes, a giddy shower of shooting stars—but by Lemuel's knowledge of what was going to happen. His father-in-law, Conrad knew, held his ear to some language only he—and sometimes Rose, too—could hear.

THE SPARKSES, WITH a liberality that at first made Conrad uncomfortable, had never seemed to mind that Conrad slept in Rose's room on his visits back to New York from college in Ithaca.

"Good night, you two," Adele Sparks had said casually, smiling and glancing up from her embroidery the first night Rose took Conrad's hand and announced they were going to sleep.

"They don't mind?" he had said to her as they ascended the waterfall of the Oriental rug that flowed down the stairs.

"Of course not," Rose had said. "It's only natural."

And so the details of the wedding had become Lemuel's province, and he had taken to it with pleasure, a man who finally finds material worthy of his talents.

"This calls for a celebration," he had cried that night in the kitchen, gripping their arms, his eyes bright. "Champagne! The "Wedding March"! Firecrackers! Come on, you two! Show a little life!"

And he had led them all up to the roof, Adele Sparks drawing a shawl around her shoulders, Rose wrapped in a corner of that shawl as if for that last time she could be safely contained within her mother's arms. Lemuel fired one champagne cork after another into the sky over the lights of Brooklyn, the pigeons setting up a rustling and warbling alarm in their loft.

Afterward, in the kitchen again, Rose had leaned toward Conrad and kissed his cheek. "I'm going to take a bath," she'd said, and slipped from the room. Lemuel refilled his own glass and Conrad's and then canted back in his chair. His wife came to stand behind him, her hands upon her husband's shoulders, smiling at Conrad.

"We're very happy," she said to him. She bent quickly and kissed the top of Lemuel's head, his thick hair, already growing white. "Lemuel and I met as children as well, you know," she said. "There's something perfect about it, isn't there?"

Conrad had felt at a loss for words, though by then he knew the Sparkses well—they had watched him graduate from high school and, on the strength of his excellent average, win an engineering scholarship to Cornell. They had included him in their own family, almost as if he were a son, since that first winter he had looked after Lemuel's birds. But he knew that there was something they had never talked about, despite their easy acceptance of his and Rose's relations. Tonight he felt he wanted to ask about it, about the spells that Rose sometimes drifted into. Months would go by, sometimes a year or more, and she would show no sign of ever returning to that state that Conrad came to associate with the saddest music—the fugues Lemuel played sometimes on the organ in the Sparkses' front parlor, shaking his head—or, more often, with silence, in which Conrad would sit miserably in the kitchen, Adele offering finally to make him comfortable on the settee in the parlor for the night. But then it would happen again, and by now he had learned to recognize the look of it, how her appetite would wane and her face acquire a dull, secretive look. Within a few days, she would have vanished entirely, locking herself in her room, sometimes for days at a stretch, her door closed to everybody except, sometimes, her mother, and less often, Lemuel.

After Lemuel's visits to Rose's room, after he had stormed down the stairs and out of the house, there would be the sound of crashing furniture and glass coming from Rose's room. Conrad, sitting in the kitchen, would wince at each report. John and James would roll their eyes at the ceiling, and Adele would move quietly about the kitchen, white around the lips. Because they never told him what happened then, because Rose herself would not speak of it afterward, pressing a finger to his lips, or kissing his mouth to quiet his careful questions when she finally emerged, looking thin but with bright spots of color in her cheeks, he had never been able to ask. He would be so happy it was over that he would not press her, though he sensed that there had been more spells than he'd had opportunity to witness. But now, having taken the formal step to make Rose his wife, he felt he deserved to know. What happens to her? he wanted to ask. She won't tell me. I'm afraid of what it is.

Now he looked at Lemuel and Adele, their beaming faces, and felt speechless. Lemuel cleared his throat, set his glass down on the table, and leaned forward to take Conrad's hand between his own. "Still mad at me?" he said.

Conrad looked back at him, surprised. "For what?"

"Poaching your pigeons!" Lemuel said, laughing, and he reached into his breast pocket and retrieved an envelope. "You know what I have in here?"

Conrad shook his head.

"Look." Lemuel put the envelope on the table between them, patted it, and pushed it toward Conrad. Conrad reached for it slowly and opened the envelope, tearing the paper. He unfolded the sheet inside, a certificate for one hundred shares of stock in a railroad company, the paper edged in gold.

"What's this?" he said, looking from Lemuel to Adele and back to Lemuel.

"Your gambling debt," Lemuel said. And when Conrad looked confused, he continued, "From your pigeons! The ones I caught."

Conrad looked mystified. "But that was only a quarter a pop," he said slowly.

"Ah, yes," said Lemuel. "But if you plant an apple seed, what happens to it?" He slapped the table with his fist. "I planted your losses, and look! A miracle! They grew into winnings! Not a fortune, I admit. But over a decade, with some intelligent and, here and there, adventurous investing, they have made a respectable journey into the land of profit."

Conrad stared at him.

"Go on," said Lemuel. "Take it, it's yours. It's a nest egg." He smiled, satisfied. "It'll get you and Rose started."

Conrad knew how happy it made Lemuel to make a gift of something, particularly if he could surprise someone, particularly if the gift was valuable but had been acquired without the usual costs. He was forever winning things in poker games—fur coats, which he would heap into Adele's protesting arms, shares in a boat owned by the father of one of James's classmates. Though his own parents had been poor, Lemuel believed in both his own cleverness and his luck, and his faith seemed to reward him continually with success. Lemuel found twenty-dollar bills where other people found nickels. But some things, he knew, take time. He'd never minded, for instance, staying up all night with an ailing pigeon in his arms.

"How did you know?" Conrad asked him now. "How did you know I would still be here?"

Lemuel looked up at his wife.

"We just knew," she said to Conrad, smiling. "We knew from the beginning. We've seen how you are together, how you feel about each other."

Conrad saw her eyes glistening. He looked down at the stock certificate in his hand. "I will be good to her," he said. "As good as I can."

"Of course," Adele said, nodding.

"But—" Conrad stopped. "Can I ask you something? About Rose?" He looked at Lemuel, saw the older man's eyes shift away from him. He turned instead to Adele, her sympathetic gaze. "When Rose gets—you know. When she locks herself in her room. What should I do?"

It wasn't what he meant to say, he thought. What he meant was, Why does she do that? What's wrong with her?

Adele sighed, pressing her hands to Lemuel's shoulders as if to stay him. "Ever since Rose was a little girl," she said carefully, "she has been troubled by—things her father and I do not understand. She has always been—sensitive."

Conrad glanced at Lemuel, could see his eyes riveting a hole in the tabletop, as if something that disgusted him had formed a stain there.

"There's no medical reason for it," Adele continued. "We did investigate that once, many years ago. I thought there might be something that could—"

"It does not give me pleasure to say this," Lemuel said then, interrupting his wife savagely, "especially not tonight, but there is something in Rose that is cowardly. She's beautiful, a beautiful girl. She's talented. She's had all the advantages in the world. And yet she wants to attach to herself all manner of miserable thoughts, wants to indulge in a morbid bloodletting. You can't do anything about it. It's high drama, all right. I thought it would go away as she grew up. But it didn't." He spat out the last words.

"Lemuel and I don't see it exactly the same way," Adele said then softly, rubbing her hands on Lemuel's shoulders. "He thinks she does it on purpose. He thinks she does it to—challenge him." She shrugged lightly, looking at Conrad and tapping her heart. "Be careful," she said. "It's fragile."

Years later, at Adele Sparks's funeral, Conrad would see Lemuel —so tall and strong, so assured—falter for the first time, his long stride down the aisle of the church staggering and then breaking as he came to his knees at the casket, his arms thrown wide over the polished wood. Lemuel had wept as if there were no one else present, though every pew was full.

After Adele's death, a death they had all felt acutely, Conrad knew Lemuel had never again approached Rose in her room when she retreated there, never again berated her, as if his own taste of sorrow—could it have been his first?—had made him fearful. Instead, he had, alongside Conrad, simply waited anxiously for Rose to reappear, counting the hours or the days. And each time she did, he would cry the way he had cried at his wife's funeral, understanding at last that grief is not accountable, that it lives wherever it chooses, and that the worst thing is this: after the first time, one always has the memory of it.

That night, the night of his formal engagement to Rose, Conrad kissed Adele and Lemuel, the embrace with Lemuel one that cracked his spine, and climbed the stairs in the Sparkses' house. He quietly opened the door to Rose's room. It was completely dark—

the interior of a heart, he thought. The heavy drapes at the windows closed out even the low gleam from the streetlights and the pale moon. His steps fell muffled on the carpet as he crossed to the bed, undressed quietly, and slipped under the sheets and quilts. Rose was naked, asleep, warm, her thin body and damp hair smelling of bath salts, lavender and chamomile. When he took her in his arms, she did not wake, and he lay there until he fell asleep, his hand over her rib cage, amazed each time it rose and fell under his hand. Lying awake next to someone sleeping, next to Rose sleeping, he thought, was the most frightening thing of all. Each time you close your eyes on that precious form, it might be the last. And each time, you do it anyway. You take that risk. You have no choice.

ROSE AND LEMUEL had fought about the wedding, of course. Lemuel, a fallen Catholic and pronounced atheist—despite his career as a church architect—wanted it held in a cathedral. Not for sacramental reasons, he explained, but for the pomp: the choir, the swinging incense, the stained glass. "We pagans like a good party," he said.

Adele, who managed to be devout without tangling herself up in arguments with Lemuel, agreed with his choice. Through Lemuel's work, he had many friends in New York's religious hierarchy—friends who seemed completely prepared to overlook his beliefs, or lack of them, for the recompense of Lemuel's intellect and high spirits and Adele's generous supply of coffee and wine and good food.

"Lemuel is the original prodigal son," the parish priest told Conrad on one of his visits to the house to help plan the wedding. "He has spent his whole life in service to God's house, all the while arguing that there is nobody home. Now would you trust a man like that when he says he doesn't believe? Lemuel believes. He just doesn't like to admit it."

But Rose wanted the wedding on the rooftop, and because she would not be swayed, that was where it took place, the priest sighing and crossing himself, knowing he owed Lemuel more than one favor. His stipulation was that there were to be no guests.

"You want me to perform the holy sacrament on the roof of your house—all right," he said to Lemuel. "But you can't make me do it in front of my congregation. You want guests, they'll have to come to the reception. Downstairs."

So Rose and Conrad were married on the roof, with the entire Sparks family, Conrad's baffled parents, and the idiot monkey, a white lace ruff around his neck, looking on. And when Conrad leaned down to kiss Rose, who wore a white dress of her own making that reminded Conrad, when he saw her step out onto the rooftop at last, of the toga she had been swathed in the evening they met, Lemuel marched briskly to his loft and released his pigeons en masse, shooing them up into the sky with whirling arms. They rose into the blue, a cloud of virginal white, with Rose and Adele clapping, and James and John, conscripted by Lemuel, crashing their cymbals together. Surrounded by a storm of white feathers, Conrad had grabbed Rose, lifted her off the ground, and pulled her to him as if she, too, in her dress of shifting white, threatened to rise from the roof, float away like Chagall's airborne bride. And she had held his face in her hands, rubbing her nose across his, and said, over and over, "My friend, my bird boy, my friend."

DRIVING TO HARRY's in the early dawn, his pigeons behind him in their carrying crates in the bed of the truck, Conrad passed through the low, rock-strewn fields, ticking off the miles to Harry's.

He did not really see the landscape around him, though, for he was traveling in a different way back through his own memories: his afternoons with Rose on the rooftop with Lemuel's pigeons, Rose kissing their beaks and passing them grain from between her own lips; their long walks hand in hand through Brooklyn and over the bridge to the city; their Sundays in the salty-smelling movie house, watching Gene Kelly dance, Rose's head on his shoulder; their evenings at the Museum of Natural History, where they passed silently down the shadowy aisles between scenes from the beginning of time, frozen tundras and shade-soaked forests, a blue light surrounding the whale suspended from the black and invisible ceiling.

He remembered Rose's graduation from high school, when she had walked to the podium again and again for one academic prize after another, proud yet embarrassed, wearing another of her homemade dresses, dresses that always made her look faintly out of place.

Conrad had seen then, though he had sensed it already, how she was set apart from her peers, how her strange intellect and unpredictable nature had distanced her from other people her age. Her closest friend was, like Rose herself, an oddity—a musical prodigy with thick glasses and a severe limp brought on by a childhood attack of polio.

And yet Rose had guided him through so much, Conrad knew, from their hours in bed, where she arched to his tentative touch, to the abstract subjects of his college studies, which often felt impossible to him. She had shown him—her hands darting with a compass or slide rule—the dancing figures of geometry, their ballet, shapes twisting in air; made him see the beauty of it.

As they grew older together, her spells, as he began to call them, came less often, though still he winced at the memory of them.

Once, just two years after they were married, when the early heat and unrelenting blackflies of June had oppressed them both, he had seen one of Rose's spells coming, had dogged her anxiously, hoping, perhaps, to ward it off by his own vigilance. "I am no good, no good," Rose had said, furiously tearing up weeds in the garden; she had seemed somebody he did not know speaking then. "Look at me, Conrad," she'd said, raking her fingers over her face, drawing down the skin below her eyes. "I'm a failure. I'm afraid of everything. My father knows it. And he hates me for it. Why don't you?" And she had shut him out of their bedroom.

From behind the closed door he had heard the sound of drawers being yanked open, of Rose muttering to herself, angry. And Conrad had himself been angry then. Sitting on the floor outside the door, he had called in to her. "What are you *doing*, Rose?" His tone, he knew, had been that of a parent—threatening, warning a child about to misstep. But she had not answered him, and when a silence finally fell in the room, he had assumed she was asleep.

He had gone then to his workshop on the lowest level of the loft, where he had been working for some months on developing the anode-and-liquid-gold technique that would eventually make him his career as a gilder. Working quietly, his pigeons rustling above, trying to rid his head of Rose and what she might do, he had touched the anode to a pebble, flooding it with gold, and then, catching a feather from the floor, to one feather after another, webbing the barbules and barbicels of each exquisite construction until he held a nosegay in his hands, a fan of gold. It wasn't perfect, not yet—the mixture was too slippery and failed to adhere properly—but he was pleased nonetheless. He had held it to the window, watched how it caught the light. Marveling, he wanted to make a gift of it. And so he returned to the house and climbed the stairs. But the door to their bedroom was open, and Rose was gone.

Lemuel had called him that night. "She's here," he said, when Conrad answered the phone. "She's all right. She's been talking with Adele."

And Conrad had exploded then, cursing Rose. "God *damn* it," he'd shouted. "What is the *matter* with her?"

Lemuel had put down the phone; Conrad heard the sound of voices in the background, held the receiver with fingers clenched white.

"Conrad?" Her voice on the phone was so small and faint that Conrad was transported for a moment back to his childhood, Rose's childhood. He had seen Adele take Rose in her arms once, though she had been eleven or twelve at the time, and smooth her hair from her forehead, folding the child's legs over her lap. Rose had wept about a schoolgirl cruelty, a ball thrown with a vengeance at her defending hands, knocking her to the floor of the gymnasium. In her voice now, so remote and tiny, he heard her tears; yet he also heard her laughter when, blindfolded, he had been led to the rooftop and presented, on his departure for college, with a quilt Rose had sewn. Suspended from Lemuel's loft, its rich tapestry of velvet and silk had glowed in the sunlight, each square stitched with his name in gold thread.

"What?" he whispered now into the phone.

"I'm sorry," she said, whispering, too. And then, after a pause, "I have a present for you."

I don't want a present, he thought, recoiling. I want you to come home. I want you not to have left me.

"Conrad," she said. "I'm going to have a baby." And Conrad had reeled as though struck.

"You are?" he managed at last. "You are?" Joy had flooded him;

though following close behind it, so close that later he wondered whether he had experienced one of Rose's spells of prescience, was something else. Fear. What was she doing in New York then? Why had she left?

Rose had come home the next morning, disembarking from the train with a smile so blinding Conrad had felt his heart swell to unimaginable proportions within him. He reached for her small hand to help her alight from the train, felt her impossible fragility, her bravado, her intelligence, her soft heart. But twenty-four hours later, in a spill of blood, the child, not six weeks in Rose's womb, had left her. And no others were ever to follow.

WHEN CONRAD ARRIVED at Harry's shortly after nine, the old man was waiting at his doorstep, scanning the sky. "Looks like a storm," he called as Conrad parked the truck. "Forecast is nasty."

Conrad looked up. The sky was indeed darker, but a low light still lay beneath it. He didn't think it would rain. Not yet.

"They'll be all right," he said, shaking his friend's hand and returning his rough embrace. "You forget my birds. They're aces. Never lost one yet."

Harry smiled, rolled his eyes. "My friend," he said then, holding on briefly to Conrad's arm. "I'm so very sorry. I wanted—I wish I could have come to the service." He indicated his eyes with his fingers split, jabbing at them in annoyance. Both eyes were clouded with cataracts. "They've taken away my wheels. I couldn't find anyone to bring me."

Conrad pressed his friend's hand in return. "It's all right," he said. "It doesn't matter."

Harry nodded, miserable, putting the backs of his hands briefly to his eyes. "Come on," he said at last. "I'll help you unload them."

Conrad nodded. But as he turned to head toward the back of

the truck, he paused. "Harry," he said tentatively, turning around. "Would you believe me if—" He stopped again, looked at the ground. "I think I'm seeing things, Harry. First, the other night, I saw—an angel. It was Lemuel. You remember him? Rose's father?"

Harry nodded, raised his eyebrows.

"I know it sounds crazy," Conrad said, and he moved then to lift down the first crate of pigeons. "I would have said *you* were crazy, if you'd told me this. But I saw it—this thing. Big wings and all. In the garden, Rose's vegetable garden." He stole another glance at Harry, whose face was serious. He sighed. "And then today, on the way here, I had an accident—or almost an accident." He put his hand up to his forehead, felt the dry contour of his own skull. "I drove—I drove right through—a girl. Crossing the street in front of me. She was fine, but I swear it was like I drove literally right through her. I—" He lifted up his hands helplessly. "I don't know. The angel, Lemuel, he told me Rose loved me. And now—" He bent down to peer in at his birds, touch a finger to the cage. "Now it's like I'm being—watched."

He stood up again to face Harry, shrugged, lifted his palms. "I'd thought it was all over. My life, I mean. Without her. But now I think it's not. I think there's something left to happen."

Harry leaned over and knocked Conrad's head with his knuckles. "You're going to lose the rest of your marbles. That's what." But he put his hands up, defensive as a boxer. "It's all right," he said. "I don't quarrel with anyone anymore. You've seen an angel, that's fine with me. You've been running over people who don't exist. So—all right. Of course, Rose," he went on, winking, "she had it in her anyway. Probably was an angel all along herself."

Conrad smiled at the thought. Rose would have liked it. He took a deep breath. Harry was right. There wasn't anything else to say. "Okay," he agreed, taking Harry's arm. "I still need food and drink, though, and I'm not getting enough of it. What do you have for an old man? Then I'll go on home while the getting's good. I'm not as sure a bet as my birds."

In his tiny, galleylike kitchen Harry poured them each a beer, then brought a round of salami, a wheel of cheese, and some crackers to the table outside. His own wife had died nearly a decade before of breast cancer. Conrad and Rose had been to the funeral, Rose clutching Conrad's arm in desperation the whole time.

Finally, looking up and considering the darkening sky, Conrad had risen to his feet. "I'll check on them before I leave," he said to Harry. "You'll send them off this afternoon?"

Harry raised his hand as Conrad walked toward his truck. "Watch out for falling rock," Harry called, a joke between them, from the time Conrad's car had been struck by a boulder as he was leaving Harry's, skirting the edge of the mountains on his way home. People laughed about those road signs. Conrad was the only person he'd ever heard of who'd actually been struck. Now Conrad smiled as he walked away, raised his hand to Harry in a salute.

On the grass beside his truck he crouched and looked in at his shuffling pigeons. And then, suddenly inspired, he opened the truck door, found a pen and a piece of paper—an old bank receipt —in the glove compartment. He collected the fiberglass tube and leg harness for the pigeon. Leaning on the hood of the truck, under the rushing clouds, he stopped, thought, then wrote: "Dear Rose. I love you, too. Thank you. Conrad."

Not enough, he thought. But *still*. He rolled the paper tight, fitted it into the tube, and attached the tube to the archangel's leg.

"For old time's sake," he whispered, stroking the bird. And though the tears ran down his face then, he placed the bird back in the cage, checked his watch, and headed for home.

Seven

THOUGH IT WAS still early in the afternoon, the sky was almost black with threatening clouds by the time Conrad pulled up in front of his house and backed the truck onto the pebbled driveway.

Next door, May Brown had hung her wash on the line stretched between two old champion oaks, the splayed hands of their leaves turning wildly in the wind. The luminous sheets and white shirts wrenched against their clothespins.

Staring through the windshield at the dark windows of his house, Conrad remembered why he hadn't wanted to leave home for so many weeks after Rose's death: it was shocking to come back without her there, like opening the door and discovering you'd been robbed. His eyes traveled over the path and up to the porch steps. No basket, either, so there would be no dinner, unless he wanted to cook it himself.

He felt ashamed at the anger that overtook him then; he had no business being angry about the inconsistency of these deliveries. After all, that anybody should be looking out for him in this way was remarkable enough; he should just be grateful. But he felt disappointed all the same. She ought to have a schedule, something I can depend on, he thought. And almost in the same moment he realized once again that he didn't know who *she* was. For that matter, why *she*? It might be anybody. If it were the Pleiades running this round-robin of meals for him, for instance, a notion that had occurred to him before, they'd be better organized than this.

He rolled down the truck window, caught the mineral scent of the river. From far away, carried along the river's gray, choppy waters and up the hill to his ears on a current of rising air, he caught the distant, bright ring of the chain knocked against the metal gatepost in Horace Fenton's pastures downriver, heard his faint call to the cows as he rode the swinging gate to let them pass. "Come on home," Horace called, low and mournful, an echo. "Come on home."

Next door, May's kettle on the boil released a sudden, high-pitched scream; Conrad jumped in his seat at the sound, jumped again as one of the open casement windows to her kitchen knocked back against the house with a sharp report. Conrad felt his heart throb wildly in his chest. A branch snapped nearby. And then the air was drenched with a sudden, wet electricity, a swarm of insects rising on silver wings from the low marshlands bordering the river, over the airy, empty heads of the pale pampas grass flattened in the wind.

He was worried about his pigeons now. They didn't mind the rain, but an electrical storm could throw them off course, as if they depended on the topography of the earth's electromagnetic fields to steer them home, a language of sensation, an invisible matrix as known to them as the chains of rock outcroppings and looping streams and rivers running in map lines through the green forest.

He opened the door to the truck and swung his legs out. But as he did so, he heard a nearby whistling through air and a soft thud, the sound of a projectile landing in the dense earth nearby. Conrad looked down at the ground but didn't see anything. Still, he wasn't imagining it—he'd heard the sound. Something had fallen from the sky.

Dropping to his hands and knees, he began combing warily through the tall grass that bordered the driveway, its rough margin blooming with the loose, creamy spikes of mugwort.

He jerked back when the flowers were disturbed by an alarmed rustle, the frantic noises of a mute creature. As he leaned forward, a violent fluttering parted the leaves, and he saw the bird, light tan with iridescent feathers, a yellow band around one leg. One wing was bent. Folded, it scraped the ground. Conrad could tell the injury was several weeks old, for the feathers were shorn away but cleaned of blood. As Conrad hovered there on his knees, the pigeon keeled over to one side, finally exhausted, and Conrad saw also that one eye had been plucked out, leaving a hole the size of a cherry stone, chalk white and vacant. Conrad slowly extended one hand, hesitated a moment, and then touched the pigeon's back. A slight shudder ran through its body, then nothing.

Slipping his hand under the pigeon's breast, Conrad held his breath. It was there, a slow pulse separated by long intervals. And Conrad wished then, as he had wished once before at Rose's bedside, that simply by wanting it, simply by some heroic act of concentration, he could change his whole life, everything that had come before—every moment of foolishness and stupidity, every instance of timidity and fear, every act of temerity and cruelty. Would that be enough, he thought, to earn a miracle? He pressed his fingers to the pigeon's breast, squeezed.

And then something struck the back of his head as he knelt there, a pinprick of pain that loosened in him a ganglion of fury. He lifted his eyes, felt the first random drops of rain like hail strike across his head and shoulders in a yoke, surprisingly heavy. Struggling angrily out of his jacket, he folded it awkwardly, lifted the bird, and placed it carefully on the cloth. He rose to his feet with the pigeon cradled near his chest and stood then to face down the accumulated threat of the afternoon, the gathering storm, the dark windows of his house. He turned toward the porch, the fierce heat of anger on his face running with the scattered rain. And then he stopped, for there on the top step of the porch, laid there in the timeless instant when he had knelt—was it in prayer?—over this lost bird, was a basket. A wreath of steam rose from the willow lid.

He turned to catch the deliverer, to be a witness, to say what he saw, but there was nothing. Just his garden gate slowly closing and a pattering sound, light as snowfall, which might have been the rain.

HE ATE EVERYTHING in the basket, sitting on the floor by the French doors, the repast spread out on newspaper, the wounded pigeon resting in a blanket by his knee. A beef stew, clover rolls dusted with flour, a tin of gingersnaps, a carafe of dark beer—it tasted as good as anything he'd ever eaten. It occurred to him fleetingly that he didn't need to eat it all, that he might do well to save some, but he couldn't seem to stop. Through some combination of the cook's skill and his own bottomless hunger, he was given an endless appetite, a craving that felt, even as he enjoyed the meal, vaguely unconnected to food. It was odd how the contents of the basket, while always comforting him, also aroused in him a desire for more.

Between mouthfuls, he forced a dropper into the bird's beak, dripped herbal tea into its craw. And gradually the pigeon revived, rustling within the warm folds of the blanket, opening its one eye and fixing Conrad with a look that he took to be one of gratitude.

At last, finished with his meal, Conrad licked his fingers for the last of the gingersnap crumbs, leaned back against the legs of the chair, gathered the bird onto his lap, and gently inspected its wing.

"Now, what happened here?" he asked, gently extending the pigeon's wing. He probed near the missing eye with a finger, but the pigeon retracted its head sharply into its breast. "I think you're a homer who's never going home again, my friend," he told it. "At least not without a chauffeur." He inspected the band on its leg.

He didn't recognize the code—no numbers, just a series of letters that spelled out HI ROLLER.

Conrad stood up, the pigeon in his arms, and walked to the open French doors leading out to the garden. The rain of an hour or so before had been a false start—just a fistful of cold drops and then no more.

"Well, let's get you a proper meal," he said. "Introduce you around."

As he stepped outside, he felt how the temperature had dropped; the warm atmosphere of the sunstruck earth had turned dank, and the coolness palmed his cheek. He crossed the terrace, past the black circle of the reflecting pool, that bottomless well. Stepping up to the retaining wall, he looked down over the sloping terraces below.

And then he froze at the shape he saw moving there, small and dark, a bowed head, something, someone standing there inside the vegetable garden. The stroking motion of his hand over the pigeon's back ceased. Rose?

No, no, too short, too squat, he saw; too thick at the waist. An angel? They come like this? In broad daylight? Short and square? He glanced behind him at the house. Had he missed someone there, an intruder who had shadowed him, evaded him, standing in a dark corner, behind the door, in the recess beneath the stairs? The basket, he thought. Was this who'd been feeding him?

When he began to descend the steps, slow and tense as if he might have a fight on his hands, he saw the figure more clearly, though it did not move as he approached the garden. The face was obscured by a scarf tied over the head, the plane of the jaw averted. Conrad shifted the pigeon to one arm, walked to the gate, lifted the latch. At its warning click the figure turned, startled.

"You said you'd welcome visitors in the afternoons," Betty

Barteleme said, her eyes wide. "But I didn't think I should bother you."

Conrad took her in—her cheap black coat with the wide, twisted belt cinched around her middle, her good shoes filthy now and ribbed with mud, her face white beneath a faded paisley scarf. A brooch at her chin, a cameo, pinned the scarf there.

"Miss Barteleme?" he said, amazed.

"I came to see for myself," she said. "But I'm not a snoop, I'll have you know that."

"No, I—" Conrad began, confused, but she interrupted him.

"I saw your letter," she said. "When I was tidying up yesterday. It fell on the floor by Kenny's desk. I picked it up to put it back and then I—I read it." She stopped. "I haven't been able to stop thinking about it ever since." She glanced at him quickly, then turned away again. "But I'm not a snoop," she repeated, sniffing. She extracted a pale blue tissue from her sleeve, touched it to her nose.

"No, I'm—"

But she interrupted him again. "This is where?" she said. She looked around, nodded slowly. "I can see it. I can." She put her hands out. "A big angel, with wings like—an angel's." She closed her eyes. "He puts his hand on your brow"—she reached and touched her own forehead, lightly, with one black-gloved finger—"and you're—comforted, aren't you?"

She opened her eyes. "My mother saw an angel when I was born, you know," she said quickly, though Conrad could barely hear her, did not know. How could he know?

"It was in her sewing room. I was not a week old," Betty went on quietly. "She said she turned around, feeling something there behind her, and saw him, saw him bending down and smiling at me, his hands on my cradle. She wasn't afraid at all, she said. She knew he meant me no harm. 'Oh, you're special, Betty,' she would say to me. 'You've an angel's breath on your face.'"

Betty stopped, turned to Conrad. "But you don't see it there, do you?"

Conrad took in her face, the puffy eyes, the jowls, the violently black hair escaping from under her scarf. He did not know what to say.

"I don't either, though I've looked and looked," she said, reaching into her sleeve again for the tissue. "It's a plain face, I know. More than plain, even. I don't know how that could be, how an angel's breath could have done that." She looked up at Conrad. "You don't think it was—a joke?"

"Oh, no, I—" But his voice failed him. Rose had been so beautiful.

"And now—" Betty drew in a long breath. "Now I have to think, you see. Decide what to do. You don't know him—Nolan—Mr. Peak," she corrected herself. "He's a man of honor, true *honor.*" She said this last fiercely; Conrad was surprised at her vehemence. "He would never do *anything* he thought wasn't strictly — by the book. And I have never, in all our years, never gone against him."

She had drawn herself up now, stood facing Conrad fully. "Of course, he's never asked me, but I know he sees what I think about things. I catch him watching me sometimes. He wouldn't let on about this, you see, because he has a man's sort of pride, he's—" She took a deep breath, held Conrad's face in her eyes. "But this time—this time, he's mistaken. He thinks there's no such thing as angels." She put her hands up to her face, covered it with her gloved fingers.

Conrad took an anxious step toward her, but she waved him away, collected herself. "Your wife," she said, taking a deep breath, looking out over the terraces beneath them, the waves of green interrupted here and there by patches of soft color, the roses and the lilies, the chrysanthemums, the fringed heads of the butter-colored dahlias. "She had a real green thumb on her, didn't she?"

Betty folded her gloved hands, knit her fingers together, sniffed. "Of course, she was lucky, she had the time for it. I just do my African violets. You can do those on a windowsill, you know. Perfect for a working girl like myself. But your wife—" She shook her head at the waste of death, as if it were a lack of judgment or a sin of excess. "She had a heart of gold, too, didn't she? Green thumb and heart of gold." She laughed a little. "I used to see her at the cemetery sometimes when I'd go to sit by Mother. She always had a big basket of flowers, arranged them for people's stones. And that child—you know, the funny one who works out there now, Kate and Eddie's girl—oh, she followed your wife all over the place. They had flowers in common, I suppose. But it was something else, too, wasn't it? Sometimes I'd see them, walking around out there together, pointing at things, kneeling down on the ground together, looking and touching. Like a mother and daughter, I thought, or two sisters. I don't know how your wife got her to talk. Won't say anything to me when I try to wave hello. She's done wonders with the gardens out there though, you know. Keeps them up very pretty." Betty nodded slowly, as if Conrad had agreed with her.

"Your wife always had a bunch of those pink roses for Mother, who loved them so. She used to come and read sometimes to her, too, after Mother lost her eyes. Poetry. That's what Mother liked."

Betty clasped her hands before her stomach, as if it hurt her. "But you already know that," she said. "You know all about that."

But Conrad hadn't known. Betty Barteleme's mother? He didn't think he'd ever seen her, ever even known her mother was here in Laurel. Or had Rose mentioned it to him, choosing something from the bookshelf to read to her before she went off, and he'd just forgotten? He shook his head. And the notion of Rose and Hero, wandering the cemetery together, *like a mother and daughter.*

He'd known Rose worked there sometimes. The Friends of Mt. Olive maintained an heirloom rose collection on the grounds; he remembered Rose corresponding with various growers about it from time to time. People used to send her canes through the mails, wrapped up in plastic bags. There was a whole group devoted to it, preserving the old varieties. He'd once said to her that he thought it sort of a waste, having it out there at the cemetery.

"Why not have it someplace where people can enjoy it?" he'd said.

And Rose, putting on her straw hat, ready to go, had stopped for a moment in the hall and thought.

"Who says no one enjoys it?" she'd said after a minute.

Like a mother and daughter. After that one miscarriage of Rose's, early on, they hadn't ever really talked about having children. That it might have been his fault, their lack of progeny—he'd hated the disappointment of that, imagining that he might have failed her in that essential way. And he never wanted her to feel that it was her fault, either. He had assumed that, like himself, she didn't talk about it out of respect for his feelings. But perhaps it had always been there for her, he thought now. He had mostly forgotten about it, except for moments now and then when he found himself imagining what Rose's child would have looked like, a replica of her, her childhood all over again, replayed for him like a favorite piece of music.

But that wasn't quite right, was it? Hadn't he thought, too, that they didn't need a child? Hadn't he thought there might be less of Rose for him if there were a baby, someone who could possess Rose in ways Conrad himself would never know? The sheer ugliness of that thought made him feel shrunken now, cut down.

In Hero, in that lost girl, what had Rose found?

Had he not known half of it? What had he missed?

He returned his eyes to Betty's face and saw instead back into his life, to a bridge there that collapsed into rushing waters, no passage across.

"Well," Betty said quietly after a minute, seeing his expression. "We always find out too late, don't we?"

CONRAD BACKED AWAY, let her stand there, her head bowed. He closed the gate quietly behind him, walked carefully to his loft. A handful of his pigeons were there, waiting on the landing board in the chalky light of early dusk, looking at him. "I forgot all about you," he said aloud, startled. How could he have done that?

He put the lost pigeon in one of the open roost compartments, where it could leave if it had a mind to, though he didn't think it could fly very far—if at all now—with that wing. He moved to fetch grain, fed his own pigeons as they came in now, perhaps seeing him there below. They dropped one by one to the landing board after circling the roof. He began to shut them in, counting them in his head. "I'm sorry," he said to them. "I've never done that before. Forgotten you."

And then he realized finally, as he counted, who was missing— one missing. The archangel. He stopped, breathing hard. Where was the archangel? He stepped backward over the grass before the loft, scanned the sky, the dark clouds. Nothing.

Conrad waited a long time, standing in the growing cool of the early evening. Betty Barteleme vanished from his garden as though she, too, like Lemuel, like the angel, had been only a spirit. He waited awhile and then, fearful of climbing back up to the house as it grew dark, began to hurry up the hill.

The bird never appeared, never came home. Not that afternoon, nor that night, nor the next day, nor any day after that.

There was a one-eyed jack now in Conrad's roost, a pigeon that had become lost en route, had felt itself caught up and run off course by the sloping currents that crossed the country in a parabola of aching wind, and had fallen at last at Conrad's feet, a survivor whose passage had cost him an eye and a wing, part of the precious instruments that steered him home. This survivor found himself in new country now but was already assimilating the telltale signs of this new place, the angle of the terra-cotta roof, the arm of the silver river curled around something precious, the precise geology of this changed world.

But the archangel was gone, and with him, Conrad's last letter to his wife.

THERE WAS ONE lamp left on in the living room, a faint beacon that led Conrad up through the growing twilight, through the garden terraces to the house. He closed the French doors behind him, sighed at the mess, stooped wearily to pick up the litter of his picnic, still on the floor.

As he rose, the dishes in his hands, he caught sight of himself across the room in the gilt-framed oval mirror that hung there. The sight halted him; he did not know this apparition in the glass. And he realized at that moment that since Rose's death he had created in himself a second presence, a corresponding figure that replaced him, accompanied him now like a shadow. Seeing himself for so many years in Rose's eyes or at least in relation to her, he had never felt himself divided in this way. Now, though, he imagined that the self that had been married to Rose had been sealed off, silenced, with her death, though it lay harbored within him still like a mute or an amnesiac.

It was seeing himself like that, looming in the mirror, that stopped him, his eyes with that sunken, gaunt look, his white hair standing on end in wild tufts. This was who had replaced him. This—abnormality.

He put the dishes down on the desk, moved closer to the mirror, raised his hand to the glass. I don't know you, he wanted to say to the stranger there. Who are you?

He put his hand over his bad eye, and realized that his depth perception was being affected more than he had thought by the condition, for the figure in the mirror failed to jump to the left, the usual result of his good eye's adjustment to the deficit of the weak one. The image remained there, staring back at him; he wasn't sure whether he would strike it if he swung at it, or merely strike thin air, the impossible boundary between them either inches deep, or miles.

Why did he call her name then? Why did he say it aloud— "Rose!"—with such urgency, as if he'd stepped to the edge of a cliff and, turning around to ask her to come forward and share the view, found her gone, missing, a tuft of grass where she had been, a sparrow hopping away.

"Rose!"

He called to her into the mirror, as if the silent self there would, hearing her name, awaken, restore him to himself, produce Rose as if leading someone forward onstage: See? Here she is. And it occurred to him then that this state, in which the parts of himself— past and present—could no longer be reconciled, was perhaps something like what Rose herself had experienced from time to time, this feeling that she was lost to herself.

It was grief that did it, he thought. It was grief that stole the soul, taped over its mouth, wound it in cotton batting, and locked it in a trunk. You had to be Houdini to escape it, running through the mazelike prison of your own injured mind like a trapped rat, aiming at the pinprick of light at the end of the tunnel.

But he did not think it could be done. Whoever this stranger was, looking back at him, he seemed here to stay.

THE VIEWS FROM the road to the cemetery were lovely, especially at sunset, even on an evening when the sky was filled with clouds; a lingering glow lay across the humped shoulders of the mountains like the thin slice of light showing beneath a door. Conrad had not been to Mt. Olive since Rose's funeral. Now, a mile or so from the gates, he pulled the truck over to the side of the road, got out, and stood on the sandy shoulder by the stone wall.

After a minute he returned to the truck and took his binoculars from under the seat. When he raised them to his eyes and aimed down at the scene beneath him, he was immediately struck by the sensation of weightlessness that overcame him, as though his bearings, his place in the world, had become suddenly uncertain. Within the lenses a small view of Laurel emerged, partially eclipsed by trees and the sloping shoulders of the mountain beneath him. He thought, as he often did when considering the mountains, how once, despite its formidable heft, this whole region had boiled with geology's terrifying capacity for conversion, perfect matter transformed into something airy and rippling, the schist melting into a flow like water itself, the entire face of the earth shaping itself into a new place. Sometimes, lying on the ground, watching the clouds' slow and elephantine progress in the sky, he had tried to feel his way down to the core of the planet itself, its fierce and bitter center. The sensation had almost frightened him, as if some cord connected him to the center of the earth, a tug deep within his spine.

Now, moving the binoculars slowly over the view beneath him, he took in Laurel's town square, the golden, Oriental roof of the bandstand glowing in the falling dusk. To the west he saw the black curls of roads climbing up toward the high point of town; a few roofs, small and square, lay like scraps of paper among the trees. The natatorium at the hill's crest, built by Havelock Eddison, who had in his younger days swum competitively at college and believed still in the healthful regime of daily laps for all his neighbors, shone strangely, its glass roof flowing with pale green light.

He lowered the binoculars for a moment and stared. The view, contained within the overlapping arms of the mountain, reminded him at that moment of the snow globe that Rose had kept on her dresser. It was an inexpensive one, the kind sold all over New England to tourists who came for the fall foliage and the skiing. The glass bell jar contained a tiny scene, a village nestled in a bowl of miniature snowcapped mountains, the tiny windows of the houses iced with yellow, the roofs brown and black, unevenly painted. Minute fir trees, green and dusted with white, grew close by the houses. When you raised the toy and shook it, the scene was suddenly clouded in a swirl of false snowflakes, which would settle gently on the tiny town, burying it in white.

Rose, whose tastes were usually informed by Lemuel and Adele's exquisite appreciation for the finer things in life, had had an inexplicable fondness for this snow globe.

"Look," she had said, finding it in a store one afternoon while they were shopping. And she had shaken it, causing a mighty storm within the glass, the snow shifting like sand. Conrad had glanced over, unimpressed. But Rose had remained standing there, watching the mighty storm whirl within her cupped hands. She had bought it that afternoon, brought it home, and placed it on her dresser.

Once, Conrad had come into their empty bedroom and had been startled to find the snow falling gently, silently, from the globe's glass ceiling. He had stopped, transfixed; and then Rose had opened the door from the bathroom, a towel wrapped around her. She had smiled at him.

"What did you think?" she had said, laughing, reaching for the globe and shaking it again, raising the strange wind within it. "An immaculate snowstorm?"

But there was indeed something immaculate about this view, Conrad thought. In the sky above him the clouds formed their massive figures, hourglass shapes bending and twisting at the waist. He thought of his angel, of Lemuel's wings fanning a wind that bowed the trees, flickered the lights, a door in the sky swinging open.

Nothing moved in the view beneath him. It was still and silent as the world within that snow globe, a paradise in which nothing had yet happened, no error had been committed.

He passed through the gates to the cemetery. The grass there was a vibrant green, the trees taller and more noble. In the sky the clouds had parted slightly in a crease, and the long rays of the setting sun fell across the hillside, through the leaves of the trees. Flowering vines curled over the mausoleums, buried them in blossoms, the white star shapes of the clematis, the orange horns of the trumpet vine. Blankets of dense green ivy lay draped at the feet of statuary, angels with their calm, upturned faces. Little lambs, their stone legs folded beneath them, lay shadowed among the late lilies.

Conrad drove along the main road between flower borders wild and exuberant with color—yellow and pink and smoky blue, pale orange like the translucent bodies of the carp in his reflecting pool. Purple martins crossed in the evening air on their bladelike wings.

Rose's stone was set off by itself, just beyond the broad circle of shade thrown down by an old copper beech. He parked the truck by the side of the road, got out, and then could go no farther. He did not look directly at her stone, though he was aware of it, as if someone he knew had entered the room behind his back and was standing there, waiting for him to turn around. He looked out across the bowl of the hill, the varying markers set like prehistoric relics on the grass, some, substantial shelves of granite, others small and lime white, tilting and crumbling. In the urns and bowls set before the stones rested bunches of cut roses, masses of yellow lilies and black-eyed Susans, fistfuls of loose purple phlox.

He closed the door to the truck, stepped away from it. The grass was soft beneath his feet. A distance away, through the trees, he saw the yellow lights of the caretaker's stone cottage. He began walking in that direction, passed into the darkness of a nearby grove of oaks.

He startled at the shrill baying of a dog, the sound veering toward him. From over the hill a small white terrier came, speeding across the grass, which was now almost black in the departing light. The screen door to the cottage swung open; Conrad heard it bang shut again and saw the girl step out into the last of the day's light, her hair falling over her face. Conrad put out his hand, touched the rough bark of a tree, moved close to its wide trunk.

The dog drew near her, circled her legs twice at a mad run. Conrad saw her put out her hand, graze the air above the dog's compact, leaping body. She walked out across the clipped lawn, which merged gradually with the unmown meadow. She stepped forward, parting the high grasses fringed with light. And then she stopped, her silhouette dark against the emptiness before her, the chasm that separated the cultivated acres of the cemetery's lawns behind her from the steady rise of the mountains beyond, a torrent of blue.

And when she put her hands to her mouth, called out into the air, Conrad heard first her voice and then its echo, a volley of end-less questions disappearing into the distance.

What had she said? Whom had she called?

Conrad stepped forward, away from the tree, strained to hear. She lifted her hands, called again, her voice resounding in the emptiness, the same note repeating like a skipping stone over the still air, no one there to answer. "Hello," she called. *Hello . . . hello . . .* And then she dropped her head, as the last echo of her voice faded away.

BEFORE HE DROVE away, Conrad approached Rose's stone, stood at a slight distance from it, attending to the absolute silence there. He looked around him at the soft folds of the darkened hills, the wavering lines of markers running down and away over the grass, disappearing. And then he stepped forward, meaning to touch his hand to the stone itself, a gesture he thought he could manage but found he could not. He stood there, staring at the inscription, just Rose's name and her dates, ROSE SPARKS MORRISEY, 1915–1985. And then he noticed what he had not seen before: looped over a corner of the stone, dropped casually as if by a bird that had flown over the green grass, its tiny shadow skating rapidly over the graves, was a string of rose beads, its faint scent sweet and light and everlasting.

Eight

CONRAD RETURNED HOME from Mt. Olive and pulled Sleepy Hollow close to the French doors. He leaned forward, staring out into the darkness. He wondered if Lemuel would ever appear again. He rubbed his eyes, tried to fashion from the melting darkness the semblance of Rose herself moving toward him. Maybe the whole garden, the house clinging to it by a trailing root, would be lifted from its place on the ground, swung skyward like a floating island. He remembered Rose, her hands brimming with pebbles, clearing the ground for the first small plot they had tilled. "Lightening the soil," she had said. She never visited the garden without filling the pockets of her apron with stones.

Despite his desire to be vigilant, he fell asleep at last. Hero's voice lingered in his ears, a sound from a dream that one struggles to answer, fighting the paralysis of the body and the clamped jaw.

He woke sometime in the middle of the night, chilled and mournful. He sat upright and looked out the window. Next door, May Brown's lights were ablaze, though it must have been two or three in the morning. Ever since her husband had died, peacefully in his sleep at her side a few years before, May had been afraid of the dark.

Conrad had come across Rose and May sitting in the garden one morning shortly after Paul's death.

"I'm so afraid, Rose," May had been saying, her hands gripped around a teacup, her back bent, her head dropped toward her lap. "I'm so afraid."

Rose had leaned toward her friend, touched her gently on the shoulder. "Why not leave the lights on?" she suggested. "There's no law says you have to turn the lights out, is there?"

And May had glanced up at her. "No," she'd said. "No, I suppose there's not."

Conrad looked out at May's bright windows a moment, then climbed the stairs and lay down on the bed. He wasn't afraid of the dark. That wasn't it. He remembered Rose's body beside him, his arm draped over her hip, his hand under the pillow holding her wrist. They had always slept like that, even at the end, when her body had become so light, so insubstantial, that Conrad had been terrified to lie down beside her. She was disappearing, molecule by molecule, under his hands. One day, he imagined, he would wake and simply find her gone, the bed empty, a death so thorough that not a trace of her would be left.

It still seemed impossible to him that just two days before she died he had helped her to the bath, folded her limbs into the warmth. She had looked up at him with grateful eyes, her white shape underwater shattered like something seen through wet glass, through ice.

"You want to come in?" she had asked, smiling at him, breathing hard, and reached out to touch his knee as he sat beside her. "Remember?"

And he had remembered, of course, the baths they had taken together at her parents' house, the two of them locked together in the big, claw-footed tub, the ferns that hung at the window shaking dry bits of brown leaf to the floor, the stained glass transom over the door throwing colored light across the tiles. Rose had loved the bath, had filled the water with salts and powders, had soaped away at his back as he sat hunched awkwardly in front of her, scratching the stubble of his hairline at the back of his neck.

And sometimes, afterward, they had lain together on the thick rug, Rose so hot, furiously hot, Conrad's shaking hands clamping her hips to his own. They would climb back in the water afterward, limp and giggling. Rose would lift one leg, hook it over the rim of the tub, inspect her foot. "Don't you think a foot is a strange thing?" she'd say. And Conrad didn't know how to tell her that he found her foot, all of her, impossibly beautiful, the high arch and knob of her heel, the neat toes, the pink flesh.

He had always felt that way about her—that something in her left him speechless, without the words for what he felt. He could see her even with his eyes closed. Even now he could still touch his tongue to the cleft of her collarbone, the shape of something designed to fly, could still feel the soft pillow of her thighs beneath him. That her body, that warm, lively body, had been veering infinitesimally toward this, toward this disappearance, troubled him. He worried that he had not been careful enough, not certain enough of what he had possessed.

He remembered seeing a play with her in Manhattan once, when the old male actor who played the lead had collapsed upon the stage. The audience had been confused for a moment, not knowing whether this was a true catastrophe or part of the performance. And so they had all sat there, sat for too long, waiting, their collective breath held, until the stage had exploded, the other actors shedding the skins of their roles, surrounding and then raising the fallen man in their arms, calling out to the audience, "Is there a doctor in the house? A doctor?" The curtains to the stage had jerked closed partway and then opened again, closing, opening, as if no one could decide whether this was the beginning or the end. And yet they had all been unsure, hadn't they? Had wavered uncomfortably in their seats? What was this? Truth or fiction? Rose had gripped his arm, her hand over her mouth. And afterward he, too, had felt sickened. This failure to tell the difference between death and a pantomime of it—it cheapened them, made them all small and unworthy.

What is this place I am in? he wondered now, lying on the bed, looking into the dark. He reached out his hand; the sheet beside him was cold.

Rose had moved through the world as if riding a wave, watching her garden flower and die back, tearing up the ribbons of spent leaves and digging them back into the earth again, dust to dust. But he had been fighting simply to stand up in the current. He had been layering the world, each moment, with gold leaf, willing it to stay just as it was. The whole idea of the future, with its promise of eventual loss, had scared him too much. He turned his face to the pillow, curled his knees to his chest.

At last he slept again, the house creaking beneath him in the wind. It was the wind before a storm, a storm that would prove to be, in the end, as mighty as any since the great hurricane of nearly a half century before. His garden tore at its roots, the great trees groaning, the arbor keeling. In their loft his pigeons stepped restlessly side to side. And next door, May Brown moved from room to room like a somnambulist, empty eyed, polishing the surfaces of her tables with a white cloth that carried no trace of dust, her house ablaze against the night and the approaching rain.

CONRAD WAS WOKEN by a sound like a bird colliding with the windowpane—the newspaper's dull thud against the porch floor. He sat up in bed, reached to the floor, and rummaged there for a pair of trousers. The wind outside seethed and moaned. Distant doors and shutters banged as if a family of strangers had moved in below, were busy taking occupation of his house.

He retrieved the paper from outside, carried it to the kitchen, set it on the table, and sat down. He turned the pages slowly, looked up once, and reached to the sugar bowl, extracting a lump of stale sugar, which he tucked into a corner of his mouth.

He began reading through the letters to the editor, blinking against the diminished vision in his left eye.

At first what he felt was a certain mild surprise, as the familiarity of the words began to wash over him. And then, realizing what was before him, he gave a snort of astonishment, pushed his chair back from the table a measure, and picked up the paper before him.

He couldn't even for an instant imagine what had come over Nolan Peak to print his letter. But before he had time to consider what could have happened, the bell at his front door rang.

The Pleiades were gathered on his front porch, Henri in front with a copy of the paper folded under her arm, her hand clamped to her head to hold her hat, a brilliant yellow fedora, in place against the tug of the wind.

"We realize you said the afternoons," she announced, "but we have a commitment at four, and besides, we wanted to talk to you right away."

Conrad backed into his hall to let them in, felt them blow past him on a cool tide of air. He pushed the door closed.

"The dining room," Henri said, ushering the other Pleiades past her.

Conrad followed them hurriedly, tried to sweep away the piles of papers and dishes on the table.

Henri looked at the disarray with a sigh. "Oh, Conrad," she said. "We've failed you, I'm afraid."

She took off her hat and, after brushing vaguely at the table's surface with the back of her hand, set down the paper. "Never mind," she said. "Rose wasn't much of a housekeeper herself." She adjusted her glasses and shook out the pages.

"Now," she began, but before she could continue, Mignon French leaned impulsively over the table toward Conrad, her soft, creased hands clasped before her, and said in a breathless voice, "Was it just the most amazing thing you ever saw?"

Conrad opened his mouth, but Grace Cobbs jumped in. "Rose would have been so *happy*. I'm sure she *is* so happy, even right now. We're just absolutely *thrilled* for you. We just *know* she's—"

"Was it *really* Lemuel?"

"The old *goat!* I always knew he—"

"Why, it gives me chills, just—"

They were all talking at once. Conrad looked from side to side at them, the six women chattering away, laying their hands lightly on one another's forearms. How did they manage to settle anything between themselves? He'd noticed, watching Rose and her friends over the years, that they all seemed to talk at the same time. But at last Henri's clear voice reached him through all the others.

"You realize, don't you," she said, "that some people will think you're crazy?"

Conrad turned to her.

"I saw Harrison Supplee this morning," she went on, nodding, "and he said today marked a new low point in the history of the *Aegis,* a day when Nolan Peak would print such foolishness as this."

"Oh, Harrison's such an old *stick*," said Mignon, pursing her lips in a tart fashion. "He could do with an angel himself. Shake up his stuffing a little."

"In any case," Henri said, "we just wanted you to know that we're all for it."

Conrad looked at her blankly. "All for what?" he said.

"Your proposal. The garden." Henri looked at him over her glasses. "Rose's garden."

Conrad stared at her. He shook his head. "I don't know what you're—I'm—"

"Well, Conrad! It's all right *here*," Henri said, and she gave him a disapproving look, as though he were a schoolboy, baiting her. "Heavens," she said. "You ought to know what you yourself have written." And she pushed the paper over the table toward him.

Conrad patted his pockets for his glasses. They weren't there, of course. Nora Johnson stood to survey the room and, after a second, spying them on the sideboard, handed them to him. "Here you are, dear," she said.

"Thank you," Conrad said distractedly. And then he started to read. His letter was just as he remembered it.

Except at the end there was a PS.

Whoever heard of a PS in a letter to the editor?

But there it was. "In light of this angel's appearance in my garden, those wishing to honor his arrival and the memory of my wife, Rose Morrisey, may do so by donating plants, bulbs, and trees or the funds to purchase them to Mt. Olive Cemetery, care of Hero Vaughan."

Conrad sat back in his chair.

"Conrad! What is it?" Mignon cried. "Get him a glass of water, girls. He looks faint."

But Conrad waved his hand. "No," he said. "No, I'm all right, it's just—"

"What?" said the Pleiades all at once.

There was a momentary hush. "I didn't write that," he said at last, and looked up, his eyes traveling over their faces.

There was an appalled silence. "Not *any* of it?" Nora said at last. She looked shocked, near tears.

"No, no," Conrad hurried to correct her. "The first part, about the angel—I wrote that. That's all mine. That's all true. But the— PS part. I'm afraid I didn't have anything to do with that."

There was a silence round the table. Helen Osborne put her hands flat on the shining wood, as if conducting a séance, and closed her eyes. "A mystery," she said.

"How very—strange," Henri said slowly. "Very strange."

"You know, though," Mignon said after a moment. "It's still a good idea. We all felt that, didn't we?" She looked at her friends. "It's exactly what Rose would have wanted. She loved her gardens, and that poor, strange young woman adored her. We all know Rose would have loved the idea. That's what we said." She turned to Conrad. "I think, my dear," she said seriously, "that you might just want to consider it an act of divine intervention."

"Exactly," Henri said. "Who cares where it came from? We don't. Am I right?"

There was a chorus of agreement from the Pleiades.

"And in *any* case," Henri said with a certain amount of evident relief, "that is what brought us here. We'd like to be the first to contribute." She looked around. "We'd like to set in a rose garden," she said, nodding. "All the ones Rose liked best. Some hybrid teas—we don't mind having to fuss with them—and some floribundas. 'Wendy Cussons', and 'Sutter's Gold', and 'Silver Lining', and—what was the other she liked?"

"'Arthur Bell'," Conrad said softly. He remembered that one because he'd given it to Rose for her fiftieth birthday, the year it was developed. A yellow rose with a powerful, sweet scent. He looked around at the Pleiades.

They rose together then, on cue but off center somehow, a familiar constellation missing a single star, lurching crookedly in the night sky.

He did not know what to say. He lifted his hands in a gesture of speechlessness and saw that they were shaking.

"Don't," Mignon said softly, reaching toward him. "Don't say a thing. We know just how you feel."

And for the first time since Rose's death, Conrad believed it was true.

HE HARDLY HAD time to recover from the Pleiades' visit, though, before the bell rang again.

It would ring all day as a procession of people—folded copies of the *Aegis* under their arms, which they would present like tickets—came to his door and asked to see the garden, see the place where the angel had stood. They paused on the paths between the beds, shifting back and forth on their feet, glancing at the sky, the wind snatching at their hats and hems, setting up a din in the trees.

Lenore Wyatt, with her daughter and infant granddaughter, came and held her hand a moment to Conrad's cheek, the baby staring up at him with serious gray eyes. When Lenore's hat, a cherry-colored beret, was blown from her head and sailed down the terraces toward the river, Lenore looked after it in surprise and then laughed.

Kenny Toronto's wife, Stella, came, her hair in one gorgeously thick, long plait down her back, a white tennis hat on her head. She kissed Conrad on both cheeks. "I can't stay," she said. "The kids are in the car. But Kenny wanted me to tell you—we're happy for you." She smiled at him.

"Did Kenny—?" Conrad didn't know exactly how to phrase the question.

"Oh, it wasn't Kenny's doing," she said, laughing. "Only the devil and Betty Barteleme have any influence with Nolan." She winked at him, kissing her fingertips as she turned to leave. "Come by and see us. We've got a bald eagle. Looks exactly like a mutual friend of ours."

Mignon returned by herself in the early afternoon and held Conrad's arm as he walked her down the steps to the garden. Of all the Pleiades, Conrad thought Rose and Mignon had been closest. They had an eagerness behind their good manners, an impetuousness easily aroused by pity or humor.

"I just wanted to come once by myself," she confided. "Can't hear myself think with the others sometimes, though you know I love them."

Leaning against the gate, pulling her light coat around her, she shut her eyes briefly. "I miss her," she whispered. And then, opening her eyes again, eyes so blue they always made Conrad think of babies, she looked at him and said, "I wish I could have been of more help to her—as much help as she was to me."

She turned her head, looked down over the gardens. "You know, I told her once that they have pills for people who suffer the way she did. I tried to be lighthearted about it. You know, encouraging her. Perhaps that was wrong. But she just shook her head. She said she'd learned that it had a cycle, that she could tell it was coming and just had to wait it out. But it frightened her, didn't it?"

Mignon looked seriously at Conrad. After a moment, when he said nothing, she went on. "I think she was afraid that one time she wouldn't be able to last it out. That it would get the better of her. And do you know what she told me? 'I'm not as bad as many, Mignon,' she said. 'I've learned that.' We used to joke that maybe she could take up drinking in secret, like Henri. That might make it more bearable."

Conrad opened his eyes wide. "Henri?" A drunk?

Mignon looked at him a moment, surprised, and then laughed.

"Oh, we all pretend not to know," she said. "She'd be mortified."
She reached to adjust the scarf over her hair. "You know, Rose always said you were wonderful about it."

Conrad felt the hair at the back of his neck prickle.

But Mignon went on. "She said you just mostly pretended it didn't exist. 'That's just about right,' she told me. 'I've got my community of fellow sufferers. I don't want Conrad belonging to that club. He has to be the one I come home to.'"

Mignon smiled up at him. "So that's all right then, isn't it?" she said. "If you can't go there with them, the best you can do is to be there when they get back."

She reached over and touched his cheek. "We all suffer something, don't we?" she said. "Some of us just go down harder than others."

MIGNON'S HUSBAND, LOUIS, who came by with the car to fetch his wife after half an hour, had been decidedly unpleasant.

Conrad had escorted Mignon back up the hill and to the front door in time to see a car race past the house, a beer bottle flung to the lawn, a teenager's trail of mocking laughter hovering over the plumed stink of exhaust. Louis, who had come around the car to open the door for Mignon, stared at the bottle, fallen harmlessly to the soft earth, and then frowned at Conrad. Conrad lifted his arm in a tentative wave, but Louis turned his head aside, taking his wife's limp arm as she came slowly down the path.

"Come on now," he said to her, low and impatient. "Just get in the car."

He glanced up at Conrad. "You're working them up all over again, Morrisey. You're getting the girls all worked up." And then, after a heartbeat, he added, "Isn't one funeral enough?"

Mignon stopped then, as she was getting into the car. "Louis," she said reproachfully. "There's no need of that."

"Horseshit," Louis said, hurrying around to the driver's seat. "It's just a lot of horseshit."

But Conrad could see that he was embarrassed. Louis didn't look up at Conrad as the car pulled away from the curb, though Mignon ducked her head toward him and gave him a little wave with her fingers.

CONRAD WAS AMAZED at the number of people who came through his garden that afternoon, the number who confessed their own angel sightings or, more often, the sightings of their parents or grandparents, as if it were a phenomenon that was dying out in the modern age, the times too crowded with earthly miracles, with events more transparent but equally strange.

One girl, a young woman he did not recognize, had stopped him. She drew an old photograph, wrapped carefully in tissue, from her purse. It was a portrait of a mature woman, in her forties perhaps, her black gown severe, her hair brushed into a high, tight knot atop her head, her lips barely parted in a smile.

"This was my great-grandmother Marianna. She was Russian," the girl said to him, showing him the picture. Conrad nodded, smiled politely, but the girl went on. "She saw angels every day of her life. They kept her company wherever she went." The girl took a deep breath. "The men angels wore bearskin coats, and their faces were so bright you could hardly look at them. And the lady angels, they wore dresses of braided golden rope."

She shivered slightly as the wind picked up around them, blowing her hair across her face. "Isn't that something?" she asked Conrad, who suddenly had to suppress the urge to reach out and brush the girl's hair from her cheeks, away from her eyes.

She stared up at him. "Once, my great-grandmother was supposed to cross this bridge; it was near her village, in Russia," she said. "It was snowing. And she was stopped at the edge of the river by one of her angels, a man angel, who told her not to cross, that the bridge was unsafe. You see? And so she didn't cross but stayed there instead, the lady angels blowing on her hands and feet to keep them warm. And all night my great-grandmother stopped anyone who might be thinking of crossing that bridge. All except for one man, who wouldn't listen to her, who didn't believe her. And when he was in the middle of the river, the bridge broke away beneath him and he was drowned.

"They tell me I look just like she did when she was my age," she said, and she held the picture up to Conrad again, turned her shallow chin to him in profile. "Don't you think so?"

And Conrad had nodded, amazed.

AROUND MIDAFTERNOON CONRAD went up to the house to make himself some tea. The cold wind fighting at his back all day had made him ache, and he felt tired and hungry. Standing in the kitchen, waiting for the water to boil, he looked out the window and saw Nolan Peak moving furtively through the overgrown garden, the tops of the trees lashing in the wind, the flower borders flattened.

Nolan arrived as though he did not wish to be seen, sidling down the garden steps, looking intently at the ground as if following a set of tiny tracks. Conrad watched him for a minute and then turned off the gas under the kettle and stepped outside.

Nolan was standing in the center of the vegetable garden, frowning, his hands deep in the pockets of his coat. Conrad walked quietly over the grass and stopped at the gate. He glanced up at the sky; it rushed overhead like a river, the clouds churning. After a minute he cleared his throat slightly and called out, "I should thank you."

Nolan jumped, spun around, and glared at Conrad. "Oh no. Not *me*," he said.

Conrad looked at him in confusion. Why did all his conversations seem so baffling today? "For my letter," he said, thinking to explain. "For printing my letter." He paused. "I didn't think you would."

"I wouldn't have. I *didn't*," Nolan said. "I mean, obviously it *has been*, but not because I had anything to do with it. What I have is a—snake in the grass." He kicked at the earth under his shoe. "And all I see here, *as* I predicted, is a garden. A *vegetable* garden."

Conrad ran his hand over his head. He opened the gate. "Well, I guess I'm confused," he said. "Miss Barteleme said—"

Nolan froze, held up a hand. "What?"

He was facing Conrad now, his palm opened toward him, the gesture of a traffic cop.

Conrad stopped, feeling uncomfortable. He cleared his throat again. "Well, she came by here. She said she'd read my letter. I don't think she quite agreed with your—position on it. And then, when I saw it in the paper, I assumed—"

"Assumed *what?*" Nolan looked as though his collar had suddenly become too tight. Conrad saw the bow tie, green with yellow spots, bob up and down several times.

"Assumed you'd changed your mind. That she'd gotten you to change your mind."

Nolan stared at Conrad. "She read it," he repeated.

"Well, yes, she—"

"She read it and she thought I was wrong. About printing it."

"Yes, she—"

"Oh," Nolan said slowly. "Oh, I'm starting to see. No, no—" He held up his head again, as though to stop Conrad. "I'm starting to see how it is." He turned aside, looked hard at the ground.

Conrad regarded him, his coat with the too short sleeves, his silly-looking Tyrolean hat.

"Miss Barteleme," Nolan said slowly, "has an infinite knowledge of—" But he didn't finish his sentence. The bow tie worked up and down, up and down. "She never said anything to me," he said.

Conrad felt himself relax at Nolan's tone, which had dropped from anger to bewilderment.

"I depend upon her, you see, to—" Nolan put his hand up to the back of his neck, rubbed at some old discomfort there. "Her good judgment," he finished at last, rather quietly. Looking around vaguely, he spotted the garden bench, walked over, and sat down on it. "Miss Barteleme," he said, "believes in angels."

Conrad sat down beside him.

"She's the only one who could have done it," Nolan said, staring at the ground. "I'm there late at night, you know, writing my editorial. She usually waits for me, to lock up. She always waits for me. When I left last night, though, she was still there. Busy with the files. 'You run along, Mr. Peak. *I'll* wait for the printer.' That's what she said." He pushed his hands along his thighs, a gesture of helplessness. "She must have done it after I'd gone home." He put his head in his hands. "And she never said anything to me."

Conrad glanced over at him. Suddenly it was quite clear to him that of all possible betrayals, this was the one Nolan had least expected. Nolan believed that a kind of brute anarchy was at work in the world, one dilemma after another, life as a Sisyphean nightmare. In a way Betty Barteleme was the one reliable force in his life; Betty with her mix-and-match pantsuits, Betty with her eyebrows plucked into an attitude of serious purpose, Betty with her hair the uniform black of ebony, no matter how old she became.

Betty was known throughout town as Peak's lieutenant. She stood at the back of the room at city council meetings, a squat, humorless presence, and when Nolan rose heavily from his chair to approach her, she would open her purse silently and place two aspirins in his outstretched palm, this transaction completed without a single word having passed between them, without so much as a glance. If you called the *Aegis* having just seen Nolan walk in the door, you knew that Betty's invariable reply to you would be, "I'll see if Mr. Peak is available now." She was famous for once physically blocking the door to Nolan's office with her heroic, pastel-suited body when a hostile vagrant, odoriferous and degenerate and armed with a treatise on the approaching millennium, had demanded to see the man in charge. Toronto had called the police, but it was clear to everyone that Betty had saved the day.

Louis French joked for months afterward about putting a collar around her neck and using her as a night watchdog at Harrison Supplee's hardware store. But Conrad knew that it was Toronto who had finally put a stop to the jokes. Some boys on the high school baseball team had growled and barked menacingly at Betty one afternoon when she'd stopped by the field to deliver a phone message to Toronto. She had burst into tears and fled to her car. Toronto, watching her go, had stood regretfully for a minute, hanging his head. And then he'd called the boys over to him, made them sit in a circle around him at first base, and told them how brave she'd been, how fearless. "One day," he said, "one of you might have to defend someone you love. Let's hope even some of you can be as brave as Betty Barteleme." And because they loved and admired him, the boys felt ashamed. The next day there was a vase of lilacs on Betty Barteleme's desk when she came to work. Toronto understood that she thought Nolan had sent them, and he never corrected her.

Now Conrad looked sympathetically at Nolan's bowed head.

"I don't think that's quite fair, do you?" Nolan said to the ground after a moment, though Conrad didn't think he expected or even wanted an answer. "I'm not an unreasonable man. Am I viewed as unreasonable?"

Conrad didn't know exactly how to answer this question, but he felt sorry enough for Nolan to try to say something comforting.

"Well, I wouldn't have said so. Not unreasonable." Conrad put his hands together, rubbed them against the cold. "Maybe she just thought there wasn't any point. That it was one of those things you'd never—see eye to eye on."

"She didn't come in today," Nolan continued as if he hadn't heard him. "Called in and talked to Kenny. He said she wasn't feeling well. And I thought, at the time, that that wasn't like her. I don't believe Miss Barteleme has ever taken a sick day as long as I've known her. I thought she was—not that sort of person."

Conrad laughed in spite of himself. "What sort of person?" he said. "The kind that gets sick?"

Nolan glanced over at him, glared again.

Conrad leaned back against the bench. "Everyone gets sick sometimes," he said quietly.

"Not Miss Barteleme," Nolan replied glumly.

"Well, there's nothing to be done about it now. My letter's in there." Conrad thought a moment. "There were a lot of people here earlier, you know," he said. "To be honest with you, I was sort of surprised."

Nolan snorted. "I should think so," he said.

"Oh, not in the way you think," Conrad said mildly. "You know, I wouldn't have said I was that sort of person. A person who—sees things. But I'm discovering that it's more common than you might imagine. Seeing things, I mean. People do it all the time." He realized as he spoke that he sounded exactly like Rose. It was something Rose might have said, in that same tolerant tone. Or Lemuel himself.

He glanced over at Nolan, who was sitting hunched over beside him, his head in his hands.

"You're a bird man," he said. "Did you ever keep pigeons?"

Nolan didn't lift his head. "I just look at them. The birds," he said. "I just watch them."

"Well, come on," Conrad said, standing. "Come have a look."

Nolan rose reluctantly to his feet, and the two men descended the steps to Conrad's loft. Nolan inspected the building with interest while Conrad showed him around, describing his flock, its history and lineage, the flight capability of various birds. At last they stopped before the roost compartments. Conrad knew the high winds were exciting the pigeons. They shifted restlessly in their cages.

"They always fly home?" Nolan asked. "Every time?"

Conrad smiled. "It's a mystery," he agreed. "But it's true." He thought for a minute. "You want to see? Wait a minute." He went into his workroom on the lower level and hunted around until he found a leg harness and a pencil and paper. Returning to Nolan, who was still standing in front of the roost boxes, staring in at the birds, he handed the paper to him and said, "Here. Write something. We'll send him out, and you can see for yourself."

But Nolan demurred. "I don't know what to write," he said. "What do I write? I'm writing to myself?"

"Well, it's only for proof," Conrad said. "Just so you can see. Write your name or something." He waved his hand. "Just put your mark there."

And then he stopped, thought of the archangel, his lost bird, his last, lost letter to Rose. He turned, looked Nolan full in the face.

"I used to write to my wife," he said. "If I'd taken the birds for a long flight, I'd send her a message. She'd always be here when they got back, you see, clocking them for me." He paused. "It was something I could count on," he said.

Nolan stared in at the birds. "I don't have anybody to write to," he said at last.

And Conrad saw that he was embarrassed, that he was going over in his head all the people he knew, anyone to whom he might say something, something that mattered.

"Well, I'll tell you something," Conrad said, sitting down slowly on the top step. He thought of everything he knew about pigeons, all the evidence of faith lodged there, the stories he realized he'd always depended on for a confirmation of the value of hope. How was someone swayed toward belief, toward happiness?

"During the First World War," he said at last, "frontline troops used to carry pigeons with them. It was how they communicated with headquarters if it was too dangerous to spare a runner to send back. They'd send word by pigeon instead, giving their position, describing what was going on, that sort of thing." He stopped, thought a minute. "Ships took them to sea, too. And in World War II, the Royal Air Force outfitted the birds with tiny cameras rigged so that the shutter would snap a picture at timed intervals. The birds would be dropped from planes, and they'd fly home having shot aerial photos the whole way back. Men parachuted from planes, too, with pigeons strapped to their chests. Sometimes they even sent pigeons ahead, hoping a friendly patriot would recover them and send back word about enemy positions and so on."

He waited a minute, glanced up at Nolan, who was staring impassively at the birds.

"Eventually, of course," Conrad went on, "the Germans figured out what was going on and started shooting at them." He picked a feather from the cuff of his trousers, fluttered it away with his fingers. "Nobody understood exactly how the pigeons always knew how to get home again. But they trusted that whatever they had to say would find the person it was intended for."

He craned around again to find Nolan with his eyes. He offered the pencil to him. "You just have to trust it," he said. "It's a mystery, and you just have to trust it."

Nolan stared back at him and then after a moment took the pencil. He leaned over with the paper on his knee and, after a few seconds of apparently deep thought, wrote for a minute or two. "Here," he said finally, handing over the paper. He cleared his throat. "I have written to Miss Barteleme. I have told her—to come back. To get well soon."

Conrad smiled up at him. "That's fine," he said. "I believe Miss Barteleme will be looking for this bird."

TOGETHER THEY LOADED one of Conrad's pigeons into a crate. Conrad selected a roller, capable of impressing Nolan with its high-diving antics, its acrobatics, how it could fall fearlessly from a great height. Conrad picked up the crate, and they headed up the hill through the garden.

"Where do you want to go?" he asked Nolan finally. But the wind had picked up even more, and his words were carried away.

"What?" Nolan leaned over the bed of Conrad's truck, cupped his hand to his ear.

Well, we're a fine pair, Conrad thought. He can't hear and I'm losing an eye. He motioned to Nolan to get in the truck.

Once they were inside with the doors shut, he asked him again, "Where do you want to go? To let the bird out?"

Nolan thought. "What about the reservoir? Lake Arthur?" He leaned forward and looked out the windshield. "You know," he said suddenly, "I've got a bad feeling about that sky. I think we're going to get hit hard."

Conrad leaned forward as well and looked up. The sky had been threatening for days, but a terrible struggle was taking place overhead now, the mountains a bulwark against the clouds, trying to contain an ocean behind them.

"I was up there yesterday," Nolan went on, still staring through the windshield. "At the reservoir. Walked along the dam for a ways, doing some bird-watching. Fall migration's started. I like to go up and see what's around this time of year. But I'll tell you—" He stopped a minute. "That dam doesn't look good. They made a big show of shoring it up after the hurricane in '42, you know. Havelock Eddison, that old lunatic, donated a Cadillac, drove it right into the lake in front of the dam. And the Army Corps were up there, fooling with it. But it's been a wet summer. The water's high. And I wouldn't bet anything on that dam." He set his mouth grimly. "Wouldn't bet a damn thing."

Conrad backed the truck out of his driveway.

"I haven't been up there in years," he said to Nolan. "My wife used to like to picnic up there, near the falls. She was always finding things to dig up and bring back." He steered them down the hill, toward town and the road that led in snakelike curves up the far mountain. "She used to call it the Lost Lake."

Nolan didn't say anything, just craned his head and looked up at the sky again. "I don't take any bets," he said. "Not with a sky like that."

ROSE HAD BEEN right about the lake, Conrad thought, when they walked in through the silent woods to the water's edge, black ripples lapping lightly with a small sound at the top of the old stone-and-earth dam. It did seem like a lost place, a place where something had happened once, though so long ago that no one could remember exactly what.

You might lose your memory here, Conrad thought. You might kneel down to find your face reflected in the watery mirror and forget who you were, the eyes looking back into your own a stranger's. He stopped, stared across the water ribbed with silky silver ripples. He shivered slightly and hurried to catch up to Nolan.

The trees here were pruned high, an upper-story canopy of oaks and hickory. Their leaves muffled the sound of the wind. Conrad carried the crate with his pigeon through the unnatural darkness, following Nolan, who nosed along like a scout, stopping briefly every now and then to cock his head and listen. Finally Nolan stopped near the water's edge, turned to face the trees, and stared up into them for a moment. He pulled a pair of binoculars from his coat pocket. Lifting them to his eyes, he panned slowly through the treetops. After a minute, he removed the glasses, wiped at the lenses with his handkerchief, and then raised them again.

Conrad shifted the cage to his other arm.

"Well, look at that," Nolan said quietly, not moving the binoculars from his eyes.

"What?"

"Here." Nolan handed him the glasses. "Up there. In the trees. Just look. Wait."

Conrad set down the crate and took the glasses from Nolan. He realized again how bad his eye had become, for he couldn't see anything at all for a minute as his good eye struggled for focus. But at last the branches became clear, though something darker, like spreading paint, moved within the brace of leaves and twigs.

And then he saw that it was birds, the bodies of hundreds or even thousands of birds come to rest in the tops of the branches, a thick darkness that shifted like ink, huddled sections rolling gently in the branches as one group of birds parted to make way for another, the flock settling and resettling, a watery sluice opening and closing. He swung the glasses slightly to the right and then the left, then backed up a step and moved the binoculars in a wider arc. He realized that all the trees as far as he could see were dense with closely feathered wings pumping smoothly, a communal heartbeat high overhead. And yet they made no sound at all. No complaint, no warning.

He dropped the glasses to his chest, turned to look at Nolan, who was squinting, staring up into the leaves.

He opened his mouth, but before he could say anything Nolan stepped forward and clapped his hands.

At the sudden noise a piece of the sky above them lifted and swerved away. The air was full of the sound of beating wings, a buffeting sensation, confused and alarming. Conrad drew back instinctively as if to protect himself. A chorus of screeching cries filled the wood.

But in an instant it was over. The sky above them sealed again; like a rock rolled before a cave's mouth, the birds resettled in the branches, blocking the light. They made an unfamiliar ticking sound.

Conrad stood there, his breath held, and thought he had turned to stone, here in this lost place where the wild creatures of the air had come to roost on the mountain, gathering in the treetops, a rain of stinking hickory nuts and acorns jarred from the branches, falling soundlessly to the soft earth. These were the last uneasy motions of the world, its pointless final adjustments. And he saw Rose's body on the bed, the shape of her discomfort. He had tried to adjust her head on the pillow, tilting her chin away from where it wanted to fall on her breast. But she had resisted him, had opened her eyes, opened her mouth, and he had thought that she would come back then, that she would hear him, that he could say everything that then rose to his lips, the miraculous sentences ready at last, the thoughts so clear and bright—it would all come to him. He wanted to tell her. And there was something she, too, wanted to say, as if after a lifetime together there was one word that had evaded them, which was now rising like the sun appearing at the window, light flooding into the darkness, breaking over the sill and coming across the floor, rising up the bedclothes and the folded sheet, touching her hands and wrists and arms, the small curve of her listening ear, one word that would be made manifest. He had hovered over her. She had spoken, but he had missed it in the roar of white light that overcame them, his back rounded over her, his hands denting the mattress by her shoulders. It had passed right through him, an interval of illumination, and taken her with it, leaving him behind.

NOLAN HAD WALKED off, a small figure twenty yards away, advancing slowly, balancing along the thin line of the dam.

Conrad watched him bend down, retrieve a long branch, and drive it in toward the water. Conrad hoisted the pigeon crate again, picked his way over the tangled tree roots along the edge of the lake, and stood at the shoreline.

Nolan turned around carefully and came back along the dam toward Conrad.

"Never seen anything like that before, have you," he said, though it wasn't a question.

"What's happening?"

Nolan shrugged, looked up. "They're waiting," he said. "Migration's started, but I guess they know bad weather's coming, and they're just staying put until it blows past. Sort of a voluntary detention." He grimaced and shoved the stick he was still holding into the water again. "I'll tell you something else." He fished around with the stick, turned up a dripping tangle, a rib cage of black, sodden leaves and broken branches. "These spillways are all choked up. Four or five inches of rain and it'll be over the top. This dam's never going to hold all that water. It's going to blow."

Conrad was queasy. He looked up into the trees, the birds waiting there, shoulder to shoulder. He felt impatient and annoyed. Nolan's grim manner was alarming him.

"Well, surely someone's been up here before this," Conrad said. "Looked it over."

"Oh, I don't know," Nolan said airily. "There's dams like this all over the state, all over the country, in just about every little town you can think of on the East Coast. Wherever there's water. They were built a century ago, or more. It's like bridges. There's bridges ready to fall down all over the place, too. They don't get fixed until they break. And then it's too late." He turned around and looked out over the water, its restless cargo.

"It'll be just like before," he said. "Helen, that was the hurricane in '42. They put in some discharge pipes after that, but nobody comes around to check on them. And they're all blocked up now. Even the spillway's full." He turned around to face Conrad.

"See, this is where Laurel lies," he said, spreading his hands flat, palm down, in the air. "This is the lay of the land," he continued, and he tilted his hands, swooped them downward, imitating the driving flight of a seabird. "Water will go this way, down the channel in the mountain." He swayed slightly as if floating above the land itself, feeling its contours, shafts of warm air, cool air, the view beneath him. "Just like last time. It will come down the mountain, come through town, and go right out the other side, following the river."

Conrad stared at his drifting hands, the tilting table of the landscape.

Nolan wagged his right hand. "Most of Laurel is up on the high shoulder, here, to the east. That was smart of them. I guess it was obvious that you don't build too much right next to a river that's mostly fed by the wash running down the mountains. Water can go up and down too fast, because when it rains you don't get just the two or three inches falling on your own head. You get it from over the whole area. Every little stream picks it up and channels it right into the river."

Conrad frowned. He knew enough from his days as an engineer to know that Nolan was right. Heavy rains near mountains were the worst, for exactly the reasons Nolan cited. And all that igneous rock—there was no place for the water to go but right along the surface of the land. He looked down at the lake, the tree roots looping like coarse stitches along the shore.

Nolan stepped off the dam, passed around Conrad. "Coming?" he asked, turning around.

Conrad stared at the water for a moment. He sniffed, taking in the sour scent.

"Coming?" Nolan repeated.

Conrad turned around to face him.

"There's nothing you can do about it," Nolan said, and he sounded almost angry. "You don't have any control over it at all."

THEY STOPPED UP at the road, walked to the edge of the escarp-ment. Conrad set the crate on top of the wall. He gestured to Nolan. "You can get him out."

Nolan stooped, peered in at the pigeon. After a minute he reached in and took him out. He held him in his hands, and a smile came over his face. Conrad was briefly touched. He, too, was always moved at the feel of a pigeon resting in his arms, how weightless it was.

And then Nolan stepped up close to the wall, and together he and Conrad looked out at the view, the massive, sliding contours of the mountain's foothills, deceptively soft. Torn runners of purple cloud trailed down the ridges. The wind pulled and pushed at the men's jackets.

Nolan lifted the pigeon, and then, with a quick motion, it wrenched from his hands and flew away in a rising arc.

They watched until it disappeared.

Conrad took up the crate. "You can come on back to the house and wait," he said. "Though he'll probably get there before us."

Nolan followed him back to the truck. He didn't say anything while Conrad started the engine, backed up, and turned around to head downhill. "You can just leave me in town," he said finally. "I walked up to your place anyhow."

Conrad glanced over at him, surprised. "I thought you wanted proof," he said.

For a minute Nolan was quiet. "Guess what?" he replied at last. "I trust you."

Nine

PULLING IN TO his driveway twenty minutes later, Conrad almost hit the little terrier that shot across the gravel in front of his wheels. He braked hard, even though he'd been moving slowly, and lurched forward sharply against the steering wheel, the breath forced from his chest as if a massive hand had struck his sternum. He closed his eyes against the brief shock of airlessness. After a moment, recovering his breath, he sat upright in time to see the dog, *Hero's* dog—white, with tiny black ears—trot safely around the side of the house toward the garden.

When the dog was out of sight, Conrad took a deep breath and got out of the truck. And then he saw the basket on the top step of the porch.

He looked at it for a moment, half expecting the lid to rise of its own accord, and then he crossed the grass and sat down heavily on the step beside the basket. He put his palm to his chest, the place where he hurt after colliding with the steering wheel a moment before. He glanced down at the basket. When he reached over and idly fingered the lid, he felt the heat of whatever was inside rise up against his hand.

He raised his head and looked out over the grass of his front lawn, its stiff points. Without the sun, the world had emptied itself of shadows, sinking into a colorless gray. But the ground glittered oddly, full of the dancing sparks that ignite before the eyes when one is about to faint, light compressed to shrinking particles. Conrad felt his fingers tingle.

"Hero!"

He called out her name in the silence. The air was empty; the wind had fallen in a sudden lull, a hush that spread across the mountains, down along the valley, over the serpentine black body of the river, flowing over the dark green earth. He could hear the loud ticking of the grandfather clock in the hallway by the front door, a German relic inherited from Lemuel and Adele. A strange portcullis hung over the entrance to a small cavity in the clock's face. Every hour, the portcullis would rise, and two wooden cuckoos would leap forward on accordion extension arms to chirp the time. One of the cuckoos, though, had been silent now for more years than Conrad could remember, the silver gears inside its breast slipped and cracked. You had to mentally double the number of chirps if you wanted to know the time. Unless it was an odd hour. Then you could never know for certain.

He heard two notes. But it must be closer to five, not four, he thought.

"Hero?"

She didn't say anything, but he knew she was there, standing thin as a reed behind a tree, or crouched inside the hollow heart of the boxwoods, or leaning up close against the downspout by the side of the house. Listening.

Conrad stretched out his arms, wiggled his fingers. The feeling was returning to his hands, an unpleasant sensation, short, electrical bursts.

"You're a wonderful cook, Hero," he said then, speaking to the air. "Just as good as she was. And she was a great cook." He thought. "Among other things."

He looked down at his feet, his big shoes splayed on the porch step.

"I know she thought I couldn't take care of myself," he continued, still looking down. "She was right. What you've given me has—tided me over. It's been like—magic." And it had been magic, he thought, the return of his appetite each time the basket appeared, the meal inside a restorative, a tonic, evidence of the world's willingness to provide.

"Thank you," he said, realizing how late he was, how remiss.

He looked up, sensing she might appear then. But nothing moved across the square of lawn. He heard a door bang shut across the hedge at May's.

"May hears me, she'll think I've gone crazy, talking to myself," he called, trying to laugh at himself. "She'll think I've lost my marbles. First angels, now ghosts."

And he stood up then in the ringing air, prepared to receive Hero, prepared to have her step forward from among the trees, show herself. He hoped she would come.

But nothing moved. The trees held still, their branches spread wide like the attitude of a man in flight, falling. He looked up at the sky, the heavy roof of clouds overhead, here and there embroidered with fine, crinkled lines of light, an intricate finish.

"Some people are afraid of the dark," he said then vaguely, but he didn't know what he meant anymore, whether she was there or not.

"Some people are afraid of—" He stopped. He didn't know what he wanted to say.

He slid his gaze to the side of the house, a prescience coming over him. Something moved there. A long arm of dark-leaved ivy trailed loose from the house wall, lifted in the light wind that had begun again in terse exhalations among the leaves. He thought of all the infinitesimal motions of the world, the obstinate, heartbreaking progress of an earthworm, eating its own route forward.

"I'd be happy—" he began, turning back, but had to stop. He

wiped his sleeve across his face, across the plain devastation there. "I'd be happy to have you come and—visit. See the gardens. Anytime," he went on. "You could come anytime.

"Please," he called, more loudly now. "I'm always here."

May's white face appeared behind the glass of her kitchen window, staring at him.

Conrad turned away from May's curiosity, crouched down by the basket, out of view.

"Hero," he said. "I don't know what kind of world you live in, what you've been through. I'm afraid I can't even imagine it. I should be able to, I know. But I always tried to tell her, afterward—it's good to have you back. That's what I said. It's good to have you back."

He picked up the basket, held the warmth of it close to his chest, and turned to open his front door. But before he closed it behind him he looked out once more.

She was standing across the road, framed like a statue in an ivy-covered alcove of the high stone wall. An old bicycle, which he hadn't noticed before, leaned against the wall beside her. Her face was averted, and her eyes were cast down. She didn't move.

Conrad raised his hand slowly. He waited, thought he saw her fingers twitch at her side.

And then, just before he stepped back to close the door, he saw her arm rise, a gesture from the other side, from far across the road, the white stripe of the median dividing them—a distance that suddenly, as he closed the door at last, blocking her from view, became nothing at all.

HE ATE, THEN fell asleep sitting up in his chair, his mouth hanging open. And when he woke a few hours later, it was to the sound of rain, not a drumming but a continuous roar. Stepping to the

French doors, he passed outside and stood under the awning. The air was melting, the earth already soaked. Conrad thought he could feel the mountain's layers of metamorphic rock tugging heavily against one another like massive ships, leaning into gravity's hold. From inside he heard the grandfather clock, six calls from the cuckoo. Midnight.

Around him the house held its breath. The runner in the hall was disarranged as though a child had run its length, scuffing his feet. The cloth lay unevenly, lumped in the center. Mail had spilled from the table by the front door, a sharp-edged pool of white on the floor. The chairs stood empty around the dining room table, pushed back at odd angles as if the occupants of a dinner party had risen suddenly in alarm, had been called away. He stood in the hall by the stairs, hanging his head. He remembered the young men from the ambulance crew hoisting the gurney to bear Rose away down the stairs, aiming her toward the door.

Upstairs he pushed open the door to their bedroom against the soft blackness. In the absence of her living, breathing self, he wanted to touch something of hers. He wanted to feel the fabric of her dresses against his arms, her nightgown under his fingers. He wanted to put his hands into the small soles of her shoes. The watery light from the street lamp fell against the double doors of Rose's wardrobe, wavering against the rippled veneer, parting at its dry seams like the bark from a tree. He opened the doors. Rose's scent hit him so powerfully that he stood transfixed for an instant.

He pulled wide the doors of the wardrobe, saw the light fall over the slips of dresses hanging inside, everything just as she had left it, the sprigged florals and the gleaming skirts, the gathered blouses and worn cardigans folded over their hangers. He reached for one thing after another, took each out and held it up, ran his hand along the folds and drew the fabric hungrily across his mouth. He knelt on the floor, drew out her shoes and fit his hands inside, remembering the feel of Rose's foot in his palm. He saw her standing in the garden, feet rounded slightly outward, rocking back and forth, **thinking**, piles of weeds at her feet. He lifted the shoe and felt her weight within it, the bended knee, the lifted skirt.

He emptied the wardrobe methodically, laying her clothes on the bed. And when at last he had finished, he stood still a moment before approaching the wasted mound, throwing himself across the smell of her. He crawled over all that was left, the silk shifting beneath him, his shoes catching the thin fabric, crumpling it. He gathered the clothes in his arms, buried his face in them, his back shaking with the emptiness of what lay beneath him.

But as he lay there, his cries quieting, he imagined he heard footsteps, Rose passing lightly through the rooms downstairs, her quickening tread, coming and going. From far away, in the kitchen, he heard the radio suddenly come on, bursting into a waltz, and he rose from the bed, moved to the top of the stairs.

"Rose?" he whispered.

The clock at the foot of the stairs beat and whirred.

He came downstairs, stood frowning beside the clock. Then, with a sudden movement, he reached forward and held fast to the chain that suspended the weights, the dangling lead pinecones. The clock made a spinning, protesting sound and then ceased.

"Rose?" he called into the dark hall.

He was confused then, couldn't remember whether he had just come inside or was preparing to leave. Was he going on a trip? Where was his bag? Was he waiting for Rose? Had she just called to him from another room?

And then, on the hat stand by the door, each arm topped with a gold bead, he saw the long yellow slicker he'd been issued when he started volunteering as a school crossing guard. It had been Rose's idea, a way to get him out of the house each morning after he'd sold the gilding business and his patented anode, a month after his seventieth birthday. He'd been tired of the traveling by then, even tired of the work itself, though from time to time he'd do a small job as a favor for someone, something he could manage in his workshop—repairs of one sort or another, frames or clocks or bits of jewelry.

He'd been embarrassed by the crossing guard job at first but had gradually grown to like it. It had a kind of authority to it that he appreciated, striding out into the center of the street, holding his hand up against approaching traffic, the little children streaming past him. In the morning, Rose would fix him a cup of coffee, usher him out the door for his walk to the bottom of the hill. One of the bus drivers, a heavyset woman with a pile of orange hair atop her head, sang like a Valkyrie as she drove. She would wave gaily to Conrad as she turned the corner, and he could hear her rich soprano melting out of the bus's windows, the children bouncing gaily on their seats behind her.

He'd given up the job in the spring, when Rose was so ill that he didn't like leaving her alone in the house.

Now he shrugged into the coat, stepped outside to the porch. He put the yellow hat on his head, moved out into the water. It was raining so hard that Conrad could hardly see where his feet landed, his legs dropping away into nothing, into a quicksand of black. His stride faltered.

He passed May Brown's, lights ablaze as usual, and imagined her retiring to bed in a profusion of electric bloom, her skin blue under the hectic glow, her eyes closed. How could she stand it, he thought—the memory of waking to Paul dead beside her, his eyes staring into nothing.

He understood that he veered away from the treacherous content of his own mind, wishing instead for an impossible emptiness, a place to rest that was still and blank as a sheet, sheared of anything that might cause him pain. He wanted to retrieve from his life only the moments of happiness, wanted to string them faithfully, to create a chain of linked associations he could run his fingers through, a set of charms against his own fear. But images of Rose's last weeks seemed to overlay everything. His entire life— and hers—had coalesced into the span of those last, terrible days. That was all there had ever been.

When he turned the corner at the bottom of Paradise Hill, he could hear the river. It made a hairpin turn there after its straightened course through town, fanning out into shallower water and running down behind his house and out into the rough fields beyond, where Horace Fenton's cows stood stock-still, ankle-deep in the bracing cold water.

Conrad and Rose had liked having the river so close, had picnicked on the rocks in the summer, chilling beer bottles in the crannies between boulders, dangling their feet in the pools, sometimes swimming in the basins boiling with ampoules of green air. Rose had planted primroses in the sandy soil by the willows. He remembered standing on the highest terrace, looking down at her as she knelt on the ground, a tiny figure, the broad brim of her hat bobbing as she bent to her work. She had seemed so small beside the river, he had thought, the scope of her ambition too large, impossibly large. And he had been anxious, watching her work. She imagined too much, risked too much.

But over the years, rising each time from the despair that overcame her with the reflexive habit of a parasite buried deep in the body, she had covered every square inch of their property on her hands and knees. Patient, penitential, she had fitted into the shallow topsoil thousands of bulbs and corms and roots. She had never sought a cure, he realized, beyond the habit of her own life. She had been prepared to give her pound of flesh for every acre on which she staked a claim, the price for living in this world just as much, exactly, as she could stand to spare.

And what had he done? He had come along behind her, flooding the world with gold, stopping everything in its tracks before it could change, wither off, die. Rose had just kept planting, replacing one thing with another, seeding the earth under her feet with a thousand tiny, voluntary worlds.

He passed into town and walked slowly along the deserted town square, rain drumming his head. The pavement ran with water. The gas lamps at the double doors to the hotel burned through the sheeting rain, two yellow cat's-eyes. Here and there a ghostly blue glow emanated from the rear rooms of stores where security lights were turned on.

A single car, a battered green one, was parked at a haphazard angle in front of the Congregational church.

The walk had calmed him now. The sight of so much that was familiar felt reassuring and friendly—the notched brick of the bank's walls, the downspouts training water with a joyful music into the storm drains, the stilled spokes of the silver wheels in the bicycle shop window. Neat loops of shiny black fencing ran around the green, and the bandstand with its gilded trim, fragile as a spiderweb, was illuminated under the bursts of blue lightning. Conrad was warm now, his stride sure and long, his body breaking through the rain.

He looked at the buildings around him, shining with the rain's reflective light, and realized what a marvelous job it would have been to gild the whole square, not the walls themselves but their outlines, like Christmas lights tracing each door and window, filaments of gold laced together, hung in the air.

And he remembered the moment when he had showed Rose

how the anode worked, when he had finally perfected it, his thrill at watching the gold spin from the tip of the instrument, like a vein fountaining gold blood. She had been in the bath that morning, and he had come up the hill from his workshop, a rose in his hand.

"Watch," he had said, bursting into the bathroom, for it was perfect now. And holding the flower out to her, he had touched the anode to the petals, saw them flood with gold as the liquid spilled over their waxy surface.

Rose's face, pink from the warmth of the bath, had lit up. She had held the flower in her hand, turning it and turning it.

"It works!" she had said wonderingly, smiling up at him, delighted. And he had remembered his boyhood fantasies then, his first poor flock of pigeons flying obediently from his outstretched fingertips as he let them go, flying from the chimney of his top hat, from inside his sleeves, from inside his heart, his audience astonished, their hands before their mouths at his magic.

"Well, yes," he had said, excited, watching her. "It doesn't hold much, and the flow's still too uneven. But the mix is about right. I just have to figure out a continuous-feed device or something. Then I could do a whole mountain with it."

And then Rose had stood up in the bath, water sliding over her tiny breasts and down the cleft of her buttocks. She turned her shoulder to him.

"Here," she said, looking back at him, wagging her shoulder.

"What?" He had recoiled, laughing. "I'm no Midas, Rose. It'll burn you!"

"Oh, just try it. Just a little," she'd pleaded.

And so Conrad, at first hesitating, had leaned forward finally, touched the anode to the soft impression of her shoulder, a magician with his wand. She had winced as the drop of gold fell to her skin, crystallizing there, burning into her flesh. But it had stayed, a golden beauty spot, the only mark he'd ever put on her. And she had been so pleased.

Now he scanned the buildings, imagined them fringed with gold, the prettiest sight in the world. He reached out to the walls as he passed down the street, Harrison Supplee's hardware store, the heavy walls of the courthouse, the dense stone of the bank. He skirted the bandstand, once, twice, splashing up water, his yellow coat flapping open, grazing the ground. And then he passed the Congregational church, bent his head back to admire once again the steeple rising white against the black sky. And as he did so he saw something wavering in the crow's nest of the open belfry. He hesitated, perplexed. Pigeon? Owl? Bats in the belfry?

But it didn't move again, and so he walked on, his slicker shining in the rain, until he passed from the square and vanished into the scrims of rain, leaving no footprint, no mark behind. And it was not until he neared his own door that he heard the bells, solemnly pealing into the storm and up to Paradise Hill.

HE'D BEEN SO happy, walking in the rain, remembering Rose's pretty shoulder, the transforming power of gold, that the sound of the church bells confused him, their sequence recalling to him the dark granite church near the Sparkses' house in Brooklyn, its bells ringing for a wedding or the close of services. He and Rose had stopped sometimes to watch the wedding parties flow from the opened doors, the bride gliding forward, the onlookers pelting her with fistfuls of rice, the groom ducking, shielding his new wife's unveiled and tender face from the scattering grain. He and Rose had stood across the street, arms linked, watching the milling crowds on the church steps, the bride handed carefully into a waiting limousine, the dark car pulling away slowly, the falling notes of the bells raining down.

What is this? he thought now, listening.

The music of the chimes filled his head as he passed through his doors, and though the rooms were dark he could see clearly, each object floating up toward him, asking to be remembered. It was a perfect day, ribbons of pale blue light undulating over the gleaming floors, flowers from the garden standing in vases around the rooms, grasses trailing from bouquets, the kitchen table heaped with tomatoes and squash, pink potatoes and the intricate, unfurling heads of lettuce, a copper beetle trembling on a leaf.

And what was this? Rose, bare to the waist, washing her hair in the sink, humming lightly, the golden beauty spot on her shoulder shining, winking at him. He stood and watched appreciatively the way her shoulder blades worked like tiny wings, the soft crescents of her breasts, her long hair raining water, the comb spinning droplets in the air. As the water sailed from the comb, blue and silver, Conrad saw how each drop contained a tiny world—the sunny kitchen, the flared skirt of the garden, the swell of Paradise Hill, the White Mountains beyond, the high delirium of the blue sky—all of it on the head of a pin, tiny and immaculate and bright. And Conrad was filled with wonder and love at what a good life it had been. That he had been born, that winged creatures had alighted on his hand, that this woman had eased into his life in childhood and stayed by his side, working her magic, seeding Paradise Hill with flowers, encouraging in his heart a thousand generosities and acts of love—all this was to him, at that moment, the most miraculous of miracles, the ordinary world rich and mysterious and fragile as a dream.

And he put out his hands to turn her toward him, to show her the look on his face, the rapture there. But as he stepped forward into the shower that fell from her swinging hair, as she turned toward him, the comb lifted in surprise, he saw how each droplet had begun to darken. Like film exposed to light, the edges curled with shadows and smoke. The universe suddenly clouded. Each drop of water, with its perfect replica of the world he knew, blackened and flew apart, and Conrad stumbled against the table edge, collided with a chair, and threw up his arms.

IT WAS THE storm, he realized. He was breathing heavily, staring into the dark, his hands gripping the back of a chair. The lights were out. It was a simple thing, easily understood. A transformer burnt by lightning, a tree crashing down over the sagging hem of utility wires. But he'd had her there, for a moment. That had been real, too.

His breathing quieted, but against his clouded eye the furniture grew immense, without depth, its familiar contours bulging and swaying. Carefully he felt his way along the counter toward the sink. He kept a box of kitchen matches on the windowsill there, candles in the drawer. He rummaged until he found a stub of candle, then struck a match and set the candle in a saucer on the table.

How cold he was now, and how wet. He realized he was still wearing the slicker and shrugged out of it, taking it to the pantry and hanging it on the hook on the back of the door, where it dripped a dark pool onto the stone floor. On the shelves, Rose's glass jars of preserves shone in the faint light from the candle. He remembered kneeling painfully with the dustpan and whisk broom to sweep up the shards from a broken jar, Rose standing behind him, holding on to the counter. It was when it had first begun, her illness. She had been putting up blueberries, but her grip on the slippery glass was unsure, and she had dropped three jars that morning.

"I don't know what's the matter with me," she had said, looking away from him, holding on to the counter's edge.

"It doesn't matter," he'd said. But when he'd stood, the dustpan filled with broken glass, he had looked at her and she had been miles away, and so thin. He'd noticed that, and the trembling in her hands, too. She had met his eyes then, a long look, and in that moment everything that was to come, though they couldn't really have known it, shouldered up between them, a mountain suddenly rising from the plain, their first sight of what would separate them.

He made his way now into the dark dining room, found more candles in the center drawer of the sideboard. He lit another and was walking back into the hall when a frantic pounding came at his front door, startling him. Hot wax spilled onto his wrist.

He stood by the silent clock for a second, rubbing his burned skin.

Who was at his door at this hour? In the middle of the night?

But when he opened the door and May Brown burst into the hall, her raincoat buttoned up over a nightdress, he realized that of course it would be May. Who else would wake up because it had grown suddenly dark? She must have sensed it, even lying there asleep.

"I've been knocking," she said, wild and accusatory. "I was afraid you weren't home. Though I couldn't think where you *would* be if not here." She swung a flashlight, trained it up into his face. He winced. "Actually, I took a walk," he said, and leaned around her to close the door against the wind and rain. He took a step back and regarded her white, terrified face under the pleated folds of a clear rain hat, the cellophane sort that folds up into an impossibly tiny square. "Here," he said, gesturing toward her. "I'll take your hat."

She gave a trembling sigh and then reached up to untie the bow beneath her chin. She handed the hat to him. He took it from her and hung it on the hat stand. "Take off your wet coat, May," he said. "I'll get you something of Rose's to put on over your nightgown."

He found Rose's blue gardening smock in the hall closet, averted his eyes politely while May hung up her raincoat and put on Rose's smock, overlapping it across her chest as if she were cold.

"I'm sorry," she said then. "Rose was right. I should have had a generator. It's black as *pitch*." She said this last word as though the night were something dirty, something that had crept in uninvited under her door. "I couldn't see anything. I had to talk to somebody. I thought you might be up. Do you mind?"

"I'll make us some tea," he said. "Come on. I've got a candle in the kitchen."

She followed him down the hall, chattering away. "Quite a storm out there, isn't it? I can't believe you were out walking in it. How long do you think it will last? I didn't hear a weather report."

"Lord, May, I couldn't say," Conrad said, pulling out a chair for her and collecting two more candles. He lit them, trying to make the room as bright as possible, and set them on the table, then turned to fill the kettle and light the burner on the stove.

May leaned forward, raised her palms toward the candles as though they might warm her.

He reached into the cupboard, found the teapot and two mugs, set them on the table. The arrangement looked insufficient. "Are you hungry?" he said. "There's some—" But then he realized that there wasn't anything to offer her, and he saw, looking up guiltily, that she understood this.

"No, no," she said quickly. "Just tea. Tea would be lovely. I'm sorry, Conrad. I'm just so terrified of the dark. And I thought, Well, Conrad, he's alone, too. Maybe he won't mind the company."

"I don't mind," Conrad said. "I can't seem to sleep anymore anyway."

May nodded. She understood this, too. She looked around the room, turning her hands before the candles, toasting them. "Isn't it funny," she said slowly after a minute, "how she still seems to be here."

Conrad turned around from the stove. "Do you think so?" he said, staring at her.

May looked vaguely around her again.

"Yes," she said. "Yes, very much so." Her eyes flew toward his face and then away. "Do you talk to her?"

Conrad thought about this question. "No," he said at last, honestly. "I don't think so."

"Paul talks to me," May said then quietly. "Just the other day, I'd lost my keys. And while I was looking for them, all over the house I looked, I heard him say, right in my ear, 'They're in the blue bowl, May.' And there they were. And that's not the first time," she said, glancing up once, quickly, and then away again. "It's happened a lot. Oh, I can't say how many times. I thought he might say something to me tonight when the lights went out. But he didn't. I guess they don't know everything," she finished.

Conrad laughed at that thought, that even the dead, with their heavenly perspective, couldn't see what lay around the next corner.

Steam twirled from the kettle spout. He brought the kettle to the table and filled the teapot. Then he pulled out a chair and sat down.

"So, here we are. Two widows. I mean, a widow and a widower," May said, wrapping her hands around her cup.

Conrad said nothing, staring into his mug. Voices in your ear, apparitions at the sink. Angels in the garden. Maybe it was all part of it, he thought. Part of what came afterward. The mind protests so mightily against the absence, that it creates these momentary restorations. But he hadn't created Lemuel, he thought. That was beyond him.

"I saw that girl Hero on your porch the other day," May said then, and Conrad's head jerked up. He had forgotten she was there.

"I guess she misses her, too," May went on. She took a sip from her cup. "I thought maybe she'd gotten friendly with you."

"No," Conrad said. "Actually, I've never been able to talk with her exactly." He looked over at May. "What do you know about her?"

May shrugged a little. "Not very much. Not any more than you do, I suppose. I know she was out at that hospital for a while, poor thing. And I remember that she was a sickly child. Paul and Eddie were friendly, but Eddie never talked much about her. And I didn't know Kate well. I think it was difficult for all of them. She's never been—healthy." She thought a moment. "But Rose said she'd been doing so well, out at the cemetery. Being out there, working in the gardens, had helped her. I imagine Rose did some intervening to see that Hero got the job out there. I thought it would be lonely and grim with all those—you know—" She looked back at Conrad shyly, apologetically, and then lifted her eyebrows in a sigh. "But Rose said Hero told her it was peaceful. She can't take people too much, I don't think. Too much hubbub for her. She has breakdowns, Rose said."

Conrad looked down into his mug and frowned slightly. "But she could take Rose," he said. "She talked to Rose."

"Anybody could talk to Rose," May said.

Conrad nodded. He knew that was true. Complete strangers used to take up with her, sharing confidences, bringing her gifts. It was just something about her. And Rose knew she'd helped Hero, that her kindness had been appreciated. He could imagine their first meeting, he thought, how Rose would have walked right up to Hero with some wildflower in her hands and asked Hero about it. And that would have led them to walking over the gardens together, talking about flowers, puzzling over some odd specimen, an unusual trillium or an unknown narcissus. Hero could have talked about flowers, he sensed, more easily than about anything else. At least at first.

And later, after they'd become friends, when Rose knew she was dying—had she asked Hero to do this, to take care of him after she was gone? Had she written out the recipes? Or had it been Hero's idea? Were these anonymous baskets of food her way of thanking Rose, of continuing to love her?

Rose had always known how to approach people, how to make them comfortable. Conrad realized he wanted—though he understood that there was desperation in the wish—to help Hero now.

"Well, what was she doing on your porch then, I wonder?" May said suddenly, as if just remembering the thread of the conversation.

"She brings me food," Conrad said after a pause. "She's been doing it all along. Ever since Rose died. I only just figured out who it was."

May looked up at him, openmouthed. "Is that right?" she said. "She's been cooking for you?"

Conrad nodded.

May smiled at him. "Well, that's something. Isn't that something. The kindness of strangers. Although, I guess Hero isn't a stranger, is she?"

"Oh, I don't know," Conrad said then, thinking. "I think she's the original stranger."

May nodded wisely. And then, with a little gasp, she said,

"Wait. I almost forgot. I found something for you, speaking of strangers."

She reached into her nightgown. "I've been clearing out things, the cupboards and so forth. I don't want to leave anybody a mess when I go."

"Oh, May! You're still a young woman, for God's sake," Conrad said then quickly, but as he spoke he saw how ridiculous that was. Of course, she was old. She was probably older than he, though maybe not by more than a few years. He and Rose used to make fun of Paul and May, quarreling and complaining at each other as they worked in their garden, May gesticulating here and there, Paul waving her off, moving stolidly from one task to the next. And yet they had been there every evening once Paul got home from work, moving together in a perpetual, companionable argument, building their garden. Paul raised gladioli, which May cut as fast as they bloomed, bearing armloads of them to Conrad and Rose. "Aren't they something?" she agreed proudly, as Rose exclaimed over them. "He has such a way with them. I don't know how he does it."

But now May was an old woman, her gray hair cut short and curled tight to her head like a cap, not like Rose's, which she had always worn long, even when it turned gray, braiding it behind her head and winding it in two coils pinned at the nape of her neck. He saw that May's fingers, as she held her hand toward him, were knotted and bent, splattered with liver spots. Her wedding ring had bitten into her flesh; the skin bulged around it.

"Paul took this," she said, handing him a photograph. "You know how he was with the cameras, always taking pictures. Such a mess in that darkroom. And of course I haven't any idea how to dispose of all those chemicals and things. I've just been putting it off. I expect they're pure poison." She sniffed. "But I found this.

And considering who was in your garden the other night, I thought you'd like it."

It was a picture of Lemuel and Rose, taken, Conrad judged, a few years before Lemuel's death. Rose must have been fifty or so, Lemuel nearing eighty. In the photograph, marked at the edges with Paul's blue pencil crop marks, Lemuel and Rose stood side by side in the tunnel of trees near Conrad's loft, the river a suggestion of black behind them, the trees in full leaf. Lined on Lemuel's and Rose's outspread arms were the pigeons, their wings raised, and on Lemuel's head perched one of the pouters. It was a trick Lemuel had perfected with his own flock, taught to Conrad and then to Rose, touching them lightly to adjust the position of their arms and then stepping back, putting his finger to his lips in a kiss. In the picture Rose's eyes were closed, her mouth smiling, but Lemuel's eyes were wide open, as if he knew that something was about to happen. The impression, if you just glanced quickly at the picture, was that Lemuel and Rose had sprouted feathers, were ready to lift from the ground. Conrad remembered the feeling, though he hadn't done it in years, the tickling of the pigeons' feet on his arms, the sensation of weightlessness, the sudden certainty that he could, on an act of faith, fly.

"Don't move," Lemuel would always say, backing away from them in a crouch, his eyes holding the birds captive. "Don't even breathe."

The first time Conrad had stood there in a kind of ecstasy, the grid of the city spread out beneath him, the wind in his ears, until Lemuel had clapped his hands and the birds had startled, released him, flown up into the sky.

"You don't want it to last too long," Lemuel had said, striding back to him that first time, pumping his hand as if in congratulations. "Lasts too long, it starts to seem like everything else." He'd pinched his fingers together. "Just for a moment. That's the trick."

But in the picture, Paul's picture, how long had they stood like that, waiting for Paul, fussing with his camera, to take the shot? Lemuel was a man of infinite patience, Conrad knew, of mystical certainty. In a brief experiment with beekeeping, Lemuel had installed several hives on his rooftop one year, had enjoyed the elaborate garb required to tend to them, the veiled hat and white suit. But within a few weeks he had persuaded himself that the protections were unnecessary, and he liked to move quietly among his bees in just his shirtsleeves, claiming that the occasional sting was advantageous to his health. And after a while, grown bold, he had learned how to gather the bees around his head and face in a swarm—a bee beard, he had called it, delighted—without once being stung. Conrad, terrified, had marveled at Lemuel anew then, had imagined that not everyone could take such risks with the world. You had to believe, Conrad knew, but he thought he would never have so much faith.

And now, in the photograph May had passed to him, Conrad again saw Lemuel's insistence, his firm insistence on the world's own patience, its willingness to tolerate, even tenderly, a man so devoted to mystery that he dove into it again and again, foolishly and with pride, with a challenge in his eyes, with love. For Lemuel had stood there longer than a second for that picture, Conrad thought, as if, as you grow older, you can't get enough of the magic of being alive, the knack for it leaving you a little bit every day. So you start hunting it down, bearing down on the body you love as if each time will be the last, as if now you need to take risks to court it, lure it back to you, show you are still able, still willing. So Lemuel, too, had hung on, holding his breath while the pigeons gripped his arms. He had been unable, unwilling, to let go of that moment of transport, that moment when he might fly.

"Thank you," Conrad said now to May. "It's a good picture."

May bobbed her head, pleased. "I thought he must have looked just like that," she said, leaning over and looking at the photograph. "In your garden."

And then Conrad realized she meant the angel. He looked at the picture again and saw the difference. Because in the picture, you could see how it was still Lemuel, still just a man there, performing a trick, a sleight of hand, how he knew it was no mystery, not really. And in the garden that night his face had shown something else—had shown, in fact, the mystery itself, now a part of the man, now the substance of the man himself. And Rose, standing there beside her father, the man who had always dared her to fly, her eyes closed—well, she had flown now, hadn't she?

Conrad set the photograph down on the table and rubbed his eyes. And then he looked up and fixed May with his gaze, her cropped head, her old hands, her familiar face.

"May," he said. "Can you dance?"

"Well, I—whatever do you mean?"

"You know," he said, standing, taking her hands, raising her from her chair. "Dance. To music."

And then he led her, rushed with her, to the living room, stopping in the center of the carpet, Rose's wildflower meadow. "Wait a minute. Don't move." He bent before the cabinet, heaved out his old shortwave radio. He clicked it on, bent over the blue tube, and fumbled with the dial in the dark. A babble of voices, someone speaking German, foreign languages, surged into the room. At last he found music, Strauss, a waltz.

And then he returned to her, a tiny old woman standing alone in the center of the room, and he held out his arms to her, courtly and gallant, and swept her up. They passed the French doors, and he kicked them open with his foot. The sound of the rain barreled into the room, almost drowning the swinging chords. Conrad reached up and pressed May's hand into his shoulder, caught her hard again around the waist, and stepped into the pattern of the waltz, his own cold hand holding hers, moving her in time—step, spin, step; step, spin, step—winding and winding around the room in the dark, making circles on the floor, trying to remember the steps, his own heart clenched in his chest against everything that was gone.

Ten

WHEN THE FIRST crease of gray light appeared at the horizon, Conrad stood up from his chair at the window. Rain fell outside with the steady noise of a waterfall. May sat slumped on the blue sofa, her eyes closed, her thick ankles protruding from under her nightdress and Rose's gardening smock.

She opened her eyes in confusion when he touched her lightly on the shoulder. "I'll take you home," he said gently. "It's almost light out now."

He led her down the hall, opened the door. They stepped out onto the front porch. Conrad handed her down the steps, opening an umbrella over her head. They walked across the spongy grass, Conrad's hand under her elbow. At her door he waited while she fumbled with the latch and let herself in. She turned back to him.

He smiled up at her. "You'll be all right now?"

"Oh, yes. It's nearly day."

Conrad tilted his umbrella, squinted up into the rain.

"Thank you," she said.

He nodded. "You never forget how to dance."

She smiled. Her hand rose briefly to her mouth.

"Sure you'll be all right?" he asked again.

"I'll be fine now," she said, and smiled again, like a girl. "Thank you."

Conrad turned around and walked back down May's front path. Crossing into his own yard, he passed around the side of the house, out to his terrace. He looked down Paradise Hill, out into the rain streaming through the early morning light. What he saw shocked him, for the river below was not just high, not just swelled up to its rocky banks, but branching over it in tiny rivulets, threading through the grass. The thin trunks of scrub trees floated up from a froth of water where there had once been dry land. Conrad walked to the edge of the steps, stared down the hill. His pigeon loft was now only a hundred yards or so from the river's edge, across a meadow that Rose had sown with wildflowers, the shifting heads of poppies, the wild, twirling faces of daisies and black-eyed Susans.

He descended to the loft, slipping now and then on the slick stones of the path. The gray morning sky was full overhead, pouring water. Inside the loft he shucked off his raincoat, moved among his agitated birds, talking quietly, pouring fistfuls of grain into the pans. "That was a nasty night," he said. "Thunder worry you?"

His helmet pigeon, the one he used as a decoy to draw down the others, bobbed its bare black head at him. The Gazzi Modenas —offspring of the flock Lemuel had passed on to him—and the nuns—soft-feathered pigeons Conrad appreciated for their affectionate quality (though Lemuel scorned their ability as fliers)— stepped lightly in their cages, back and forth, the embroidery of their bronze and white feathers shifting. Pasquale rustled on his nest, and Conrad suffered a pang for the beautiful Evita, borne off in the owl's talons. At the cage where he'd installed the lost pigeon, Hi Roller, he stopped and cocked his head at the stranger. "Settling in?" he inquired after a moment. But the bird averted its one eye, stared away from him.

In his workshop he stood at the open door and stared out into the rain. He looked out over the river, saw its furious pace down through the meadow. The mountains were invisible, drenched in low clouds. They acquired, for being unseen, a disproportionate height, a vague menace.

Conrad tried to gauge how much rain had fallen to have made the river rise so fast, and swiftly calculated the slight incline across the meadow to his loft. Were his pigeons in any danger? He'd feared for them only once before, during a week of intermittent rain when the river had risen like this, just enough to lick over its banks. Then, he and Rose had boxed the pigeons and driven them up to Harry's, though the rain had stopped the next morning, the water receding by afternoon to its usual height.

And then he remembered the reservoir, the choked dam, what Nolan had said. Was it really possible? He tried to imagine it, the stalled flocks waiting in the trees there, suddenly blown skyward as the dam exploded, a tangle of torn roots and broken branches, the sky full of beating wings, a massive alarm. And the bells, the church bells. Had he only imagined that sound last night, the doleful sound of warning?

He put his hand to the joist by the door, pushed slightly at it, testing its strength. Drops of hardened resin clung to the pine boards, little amber-colored beads, as if the wood were still alive and might, under some enchantment, sprout new buds, new branches, the whole building bursting into leaf, a forgotten bower.

And then, without waiting another minute, he hurried back up the hill, climbed into his truck, and headed into town.

The only place open this time of day would be Eddie's, he knew. Though the Vaughans owned a house in town, Conrad didn't think Eddie ever stayed there anymore. After Kate's death, Eddie had seemed to prefer closing down the restaurant at night and sleeping a few winks on the cot in the back room by the giant, round dishwasher, with its comforting tumult of suds and clinking plates. The state of the Vaughans' house, which had gradually fallen into disrepair, had been a subject of some annoyance on the part of the garden club, which liked to hold an annual tour through that part of town, where the houses were oldest and considered most charming. Conrad remembered Rose shaking her head over it one day, coming home from a meeting about the tour.

He had been sprawled out on the sunny terrace on a settee, having come home the day before from a long trip to Philadelphia, where he'd been gilding the gates to a new park on the Schuylkill River.

Rose had sat down at his feet and taken off her hat. "It's not so much of an eyesore," she'd told him, grumbling. "They're all so exacting." She heaved a little sigh of annoyance. "And I think Eddie's girl is living there. I wish they wouldn't disturb her about it."

"Well, why doesn't *she* fix it up?" Conrad had asked lazily, shoving Rose over a little to make room for his feet.

She adjusted her position, turned to look at him thoughtfully. "Connie," she said at last, "you're just a fountain of good ideas."

And Conrad, who hadn't cared about the garden club in the least, had reached up and pulled Rose down on top of him. "What have you been doing while I've been gone, anyway?" he'd said, nuzzling her neck.

Driving into town now, he thought about Eddie, thought about a hot breakfast. Pancakes, a couple of eggs, toast, hot coffee —the notion filled him with longing, and he headed down Paradise Hill toward town. But as he neared the bottom of the hill, he saw that the road in front of him was awash with water. Conrad braked, held hard against the steering wheel as the truck hit deep water and shifted sixty degrees across the road. After a moment, though, the tires caught, and he righted the wheel, plying slowly through the current, plumes of spray spinning from his wheels.

Conrad glanced to the side, took in the dark houses, black pools of water lying in uneven patches over the lawns. Here and there, cars were sunk up to their hubcaps. At one house the yellow front door was open, and a man in a bathrobe and galoshes stood frowning out at the street, surveying the water lapping his picket fence. This was where the river turned, just behind these houses, Conrad realized. No wonder the water was so high here.

He steered slowly through the water, fearful of stalling the engine. Where the road began to rise slightly, he was able to pull out of the confining stream and turn into town. In the square, water ran high along the curbs, lapping the sidewalks. A thicket of broken branches crowded the storm drains. The awning of the hotel was torn, flapping in the wind and rain, and the canvas tenting for the bandstand had pulled away in parts, as though a giant hand had ripped it and flung the strips over the drenched grass. There wasn't a soul to be seen. It was Saturday morning, Conrad remembered, and still early, a little before six. Maybe everyone was still asleep.

When he turned down the hill toward Eddie's, he saw lights for the first time and realized that Eddie must have a generator. He could hear its low hum. He pulled the truck off the road, glancing out into the channel of the river, now racing high and thick between its mortared banks. Eddie, a black umbrella over his head, was standing across the street from the restaurant, balancing on the edge of the river bulwark like a small, dark insect, looking down into the churning water.

Conrad raced the engine once before turning off the ignition.

Eddie turned at the sound. "Mighty high," he called over the roar of the water.

Conrad got out of the truck and walked across the street to stand beside him.

"Water's up all over town," Eddie said.

"I saw," Conrad said. "I came through the square."

"No power, either. And they're having a problem with the generator at the hotel. Lucky they only got a couple of people staying there. Probably come down here for breakfast if they want anything hot." Eddie continued to stare into the water, its boiling surface. "They got a backup at the *Aegis,* of course, but the captain's gone down with his ship."

Conrad turned to look at him. "What?"

Eddie turned, hopped down awkwardly from the bulwark, his leg prosthesis following him stiffly. "Let's get out of this," he said. "I'm getting soaked."

Conrad followed Eddie inside, where they deposited their wet coats on a chair sticky with dampness. He pulled up a stool at the counter, and Eddie pushed a cup of coffee at him and then turned to crack three eggs onto the splattering surface of the griddle. He broke the yolks with the back of a spatula, shoved at the runny mess.

Conrad took a sip of coffee. "What happened? At the *Aegis?*"

Eddie put two pieces of white bread into the toaster, shoved down hard on the handle. "Peak went to pieces," he said.

Conrad looked up from his cup. An image of Nolan standing morosely on the dam at Lake Arthur flew up in his head, sent a flutter of alarm through him. What had Nolan said then? *You don't have any control over it at all.*

"Didn't you hear it?" Eddie went on. "Last night? That was him up there, ringing the bells. Told them it was a warning, when they got up there and brought him down. He'd had some kind of stroke. Been drinking, too."

Conrad stared at Eddie. The notion of Nolan drunk filled him with sadness. And then he remembered an evening from a long time before, the summer he'd been gilding the bandstand, in fact.

One night, having just finished work, he'd been sitting on the steps of the bandstand, cleaning his equipment before going home. The square had been deserted, but Conrad could see through the windows into the hotel's dining room, where a few guests still lingered at the small tables over coffee or tea, their heads close together. He'd leaned back on his elbows, enjoying the soft breeze, and looked up at the sky. Stars were out. The tipped urn of Aquarius balanced coolly along the celestial equator. Orion rose in the bluing east with his golden glove.

Conrad had startled when the sharp report of a hammer against wood rang out on the opposite side of the bandstand. It had felt as though someone were battering a two-by-four between his shoulder blades. Jumping to his feet, he had turned around to see Nolan, his white shirtsleeves rolled to the elbows, nails clenched between his teeth, furiously banging away, tacking a fluttering piece of paper onto one of the posts.

"Christ!" Conrad wiped his hand over his mouth. But Nolan didn't even look up at him.

Conrad stood for a minute on the steps. A fine sweat had broken out over his forehead. The noise had scared him half to death.

"You just about gave me a heart attack," he said finally, exasperated. "Didn't you see me sitting here?"

"Sorry." Nolan shifted the nails to the other side of his mouth. He moved a quarter turn around the bandstand, began hammering in another nail.

Conrad walked across the floor, leaned over the railing, and looked down at the sign: LOST CAT. ORANGE. NO TAIL. REWARD. CALL THE AEGIS.

Conrad stood up. Across from him Nolan drove in the nail with a few more strokes, punctuated by dull thuds when he missed and struck wood instead. At last, apparently satisfied, he bent down unsteadily to pick up the pile of papers spilled on the grass at his feet.

"Lost your cat," Conrad said, putting his hands in his pockets. "Too bad."

"Not my cat," Nolan said, and when he looked up into the glare of the utility light, which Conrad had hung when the sun had gone down, Conrad saw that his face was red, his hair disheveled. "My mother's. *Bennett's* cat."

"Oh." Conrad waited a moment. "Well, they often come back, I understand," he said at last. "Don't they just go off sometimes, on their own, and then come back again?"

"Not if they know what's good for them," Nolan said. He stared up at the fluttering sign and then suddenly lifted his arm and gave the nail a savage whack with the hammer. "There must be a million places in the world," he began, and looked vaguely away across the shadowy green. "A million places where—" But he never finished his sentence.

"Good night," Conrad called as Nolan walked off, weaving, into the dusk.

Nolan had raised one arm behind him, the one with the hammer, but he hadn't turned around. At the curb he'd stumbled. Conrad heard his distant voice, a short curse. A few minutes later, as he was loading his equipment into his truck, he heard the sound of the hammer meeting tree bark, an artillery of rage.

Now Eddie leaned back, glanced down at the toaster. "He told them the dam was going to break. He wanted people to know, he said, so they could get out in time." Eddie turned back to the griddle, mashed fiercely at the eggs. "Sad thing is, he's probably right."

Conrad shook his head. "Well—" He couldn't exactly think what more there was to ask. He imagined Nolan in his too short coat hanging from the bell ropes, his face twisted and crumpled, the bells pitching their giant weight into the rain, Nolan hanging beneath them, trying to swing clear to someplace else. He shuddered slightly.

"Wouldn't see the doctor," Eddie went on, folding his arms and leaning against the counter. "He was mad as hell, in fact, when they brought him down. Babbling on about angels and—hey—" He stopped suddenly, stood upright, the spatula raised in his hand. "That was some letter you wrote."

Conrad dropped his head in embarrassment. It all seemed so long ago, with so many strange things having happened since, that he was having trouble sorting out the truth of it. "Mmmm," he said indistinctly, hoping Eddie would just drop it.

Eddie put his hands on the counter in front of Conrad. "My daughter saw that letter. Hero did," he said. "Cut it out of the paper and brought it down here to show me. She hadn't been down here in a long time. I was pleased she came on."

Conrad still said nothing, hanging his head lower over his coffee cup.

"Well," Eddie said discreetly, turning back to the griddle. "I would have thought it would have been your wife, anyway. She was the real angel."

Conrad glanced up as Eddie put the plate before him and set a fork down beside it.

"Just like my Kate," Eddie said. "A real angel."

Conrad picked up his fork, realized he was starving. "Where's Nolan now?"

Eddie snorted, wiped his hands on a dishcloth. "They called Betty Barteleme, right from the church. She came down and got him. Still in her bathrobe! Now there's devotion for you."

Conrad looked up at Eddie again in surprise, his mouth full.

"Wasn't anyone else to call," Eddie went on. "His mother wouldn't have anything to do with him once she heard he'd been drinking. Harrison Supplee came down here afterward. I was just closing up. He said Peak fell to his knees when Miss Barteleme came in the door. Fell to his knees and put his arms around her legs." Eddie lifted the coffeepot, refilled Conrad's cup. "Supplee was disgusted, of course, but if you ask me, it was meant to be all along. I've seen that woman come down here a million times, running down the hill with some message for Peak while he ate his lunch. She thought he was some kind of god."

Conrad smiled, thinking of Nolan's letter, and took another mouthful. "Is he all right?"

"I don't know. I imagine so, though Supplee said his face looked funny and he was bent over like his shoulder hurt. Might have been from pulling on the ropes, though." Eddie came around the counter and sat down beside Conrad, wiped aimlessly at the Formica. "She'll get him checked out. She's responsible about that kind of thing. You can count on her for that."

A silence fell between them. Conrad chewed steadily through his breakfast. "One thing, though," Eddie added after a moment. "He did make everybody nervous about that dam. The National Guard is up there now with a whole lot of sand, checking it out. Supplee called the governor's office last night. And I'll bet Peak was right, even if he did have a funny way of getting the word out. I wouldn't bet a cup of coffee on that dam. That's the thing about Peak. He's not what you would call an appealing sort of person, but you know he wouldn't bullshit you."

Conrad pushed his plate away. "I was up there with him yesterday," he said. "At the dam. He showed me." He wiped his mouth. "Thank you," he said. "That was good."

"No problem," Eddie said. "On the house."

He held up his hand when Conrad started to protest. "It's the least I can do," he said. "I would have done anything for your wife, Conrad. Brought her breakfast in bed every morning if that's what she wanted." He took a breath. "My Hero's been up at the cemetery holding down a job for six years now. I never would have thought I'd see that day. And your wife's responsible. Ever since that first time, when she came by the house and showed Hero how to fix up the garden there. Your wife did what no doctors and no drugs have ever been able to do. She gave Hero something to be good at. Gave her some peace of mind.

"I'm not saying she's normal now," he went on, standing up and straightening the napkin holders along the counter. "She's never going to be what you or I would call—normal. But she's got that nice little cottage up there, and her little dog, and all those pretty flowers and things, and I think she's almost—happy. You don't know—" His voice caught, and he took a breath. "You don't know what it would have done for Kate to know that. To know that she's happy."

Conrad watched Eddie. "She's a good girl, Eddie," he said then. He was surprised that Rose had taken his advice—if it could be called that—about Hero and the Vaughans' garden. He thought for a minute. "You know, she's kind of been taking care of me, since Rose—"

Eddie turned to him, surprise on his face.

Conrad raised his hands in a shrug. "She's been cooking for me, Eddie. Bringing me food. Leaving it on my porch. And I've never been able to thank her. Not really. I can't ever seem to find her exactly."

Eddie sat down heavily on a stool. "I'll be," he said slowly, staring at Conrad. "Is that right? Cooking, huh?" He gave a big smile. "Well, that would *really* make Kate happy." He sat still, nodding vigorously, smiling at Conrad.

Both men turned then as the door opened and Harrison Supplee and Louis French, Mignon's husband, came in to the restaurant. The wild, static sound of the storm outside rolled briefly into the warm room. Harrison stopped at the table nearest to the door, bent over, and shook his long legs within his waders. Conrad watched him rear up in the high boots like a praying mantis, stretch his shoulders against some discomfort. He looked pale and waterlogged. He had high, finely shaped eyebrows, which gave him a delicate, faintly sorrowful appearance. Conrad saw Louis take him in with a sneer of disapproval, a look suggesting that Conrad had been caught sitting out on all the work. The men advanced to the counter.

"How's things?" Eddie asked.

"Black as night," Harrison said shortly. "Power company won't touch a wire while the river's rising." He took off his cap, set it on the counter, and folded himself awkwardly onto a stool. "National Guard's bagging the dam, but they've started evacuating folks already. They're sending everybody up to the natatorium."

Louis French took the stool beside Harrison. "Know how many inches of rain we've had? Twelve. Twelve inches."

"And it's all just sitting there, waiting to blow," Harrison said gloomily. "It's going to be just like last time if they can't find a way to hold that dam. I've said many times that Laurel deserves better than that old piece of crap. I've said it so often I think I burst a blood vessel." He smacked his pale, creased forehead with the palm of his hand.

Louis reached for the cup of coffee Eddie pushed across the counter to him, took a sip, bulged his cheeks. "Know how much a bathtub full of water weighs?" he asked no one in particular. "One cubic yard equals one ton."

"Three-quarters of a ton," Conrad said quietly. He knew such things from his days as an engineer. "One inch of rainfall over one square mile has the potential energy of six thousand pounds of dynamite. That's about three times the force of the *Enola Gay*'s load."

Louis didn't look at him, shifting his eyes sideways as if Conrad hadn't even spoken, but Harrison gave a snort of surprise.

"Well, I guess we have Peak to thank for getting the ball rolling," he said. He shook his head. "Crazy old fool."

"Anybody heard from him?" Eddie asked, refilling Conrad's cup. Conrad looked up and nodded his thanks.

Harrison gave a short laugh. "He was up at the natatorium already this morning, dressed to kill in some old army flak jacket, cameras draped every which way around his neck, Betty Barteleme right behind him with a notepad. 'You can't keep a good man down, Harrison.' That's what she told me."

Eddie raised his eyebrows.

"He looks like shit," Harrison said, and took a noisy slurp of coffee. "Looks like he's about to keel over. Toronto's trying to get him to go home." He wiped his mouth with a napkin. "He did us all a favor, though. The least we could do is save him from himself now, lock him up someplace until it's all over. I'm afraid he'll drag Betty Barteleme off on some idiotic mission with him. I told Toronto just to clonk him over the head with one of those cameras of his."

Conrad looked up at Eddie for a second. Then he turned to Harrison. "If they're evacuating," he asked, "isn't this place included? I mean, it's right on the river."

Harrison leaned over and glanced briefly and significantly at Conrad. Then he looked at Eddie, who had turned his back to them suddenly and was scraping the griddle. "That's why we came by," he said quietly. "Eddie, you need to close up shop." He waited a minute. "The whole of River Road and up to Pine Street. Everybody out."

Eddie kept his back to them, withdrew a rag from his belt, and wiped it over the surface of the griddle. There was a silence while each man, Conrad thought, considered his coffee cup, the cooling dregs, what was left, and the prospect of what might come, the unimaginable future. He thought that each of them was seeing the river in his mind's eye, imagining the current's labored flow through town, the path of its destruction.

"Like you said"—Eddie spoke without turning around, and the men watched his back—"it'll be just like last time.

"Remember?" he said then, turning at last and facing Harrison. "Remember, after it stopped raining, how we all stood on the hill, where the natatorium is now, and looked down into town?"

No one answered him.

"It was beautiful, in a terrible sort of way," he went on quietly. "I was home by then. It was after my leg. Kate and me stood up there, on the hill, along with everybody else. Hero wasn't even born yet, but we thought Kate might be carrying. We just stood there, looking down, and nobody said anything. And it seemed like it was all over, that we'd never come back here, that it would stay that way forever, just the roofs sticking up here and there out of the water. It was like we were cut loose, in a way. I couldn't believe I'd come home to that." He shook his head. "It was hard to believe a few days of rain could change everything so much, so that you looked down at your life and it seemed like something that had happened a long time ago, to someone else."

No one said anything for a minute.

"Lot of people got ruined," Louis said then.

Harrison shot him a look. "Eddie," he said. "I promise you. River comes through here, we'll just build you a new place. More up-to-date. Just like before. You did it before, Eddie."

But Eddie didn't answer him, just stared out over Harrison's head toward the window. He could see the water coming, Conrad thought. He was considering whether he could stand his ground against it.

"We were wrong," Eddie said, as if Harrison had never spoken. "Kate wasn't carrying then. It wasn't until later, until after we'd rebuilt this place, a few years later—Hero was born then." Eddie was still looking off over the men's heads. "Not a flood child after all," he said. "A restoration."

Harrison glanced at Louis and Conrad, appealing for their help. "Old warhorse like yourself," he said then, making his voice light. "This ought to be getting your blood running." He reached over and laid a narrow hand on Eddie's arm. "This place could use a bath anyway."

A sudden urgency filled Conrad, the first real stirrings of fear. He didn't want to be sitting there anymore. He wanted to get out, and he wanted Eddie out, too. He stood up, nodded at Harrison and Louis. "Come on, Eddie," he said. "I've got the truck. I'll help you get a few things out."

Harrison and Louis stood then as well, moved toward the door.

Harrison stopped at the table and collected his coat. "Don't waste time now, Eddie," he said. "Dead man can't fry an egg." He glanced at Conrad once more, jerked his head in the direction of the road. "We'll be seeing you," he said. And then they were gone.

Conrad waited. He did not look directly at Eddie, did not want, he realized, to look upon this old man's world, cramped and lonely within the four stained walls of the restaurant. He did not want to imagine it in the pitch dark, engulfed in black water, the room's contents swallowed by the river, bottomless and terrifying. He thought of Hero safely on her hill as though a hand had lifted her there, set her carefully on high ground, out of harm's way. Whose hand? Rose's, he realized.

He tried to make his voice sound persuasive. "What'll it be?" he asked Eddie. "The register? Toaster? Couple of chairs?"

Eddie looked around him vaguely, as if Conrad had interrupted some train of thought. Then he stepped over to the cash register, lifted down from the wall behind it a picture frame. Behind the glass, pressed against a sheet of yellowing paper, was a four-leaf clover, brown and dry. Eddie wiped his arm across the dusty frame. Then he handed it to Conrad.

"Kate found this," he said. "On the hill. That day we stood up there after the flood. She looked down, and then she just bent over and plucked it from the grass, like it had called out her name or something. 'Look, Eddie,' she said to me. 'See? For the Four Leaf Clover Cafe.'" He laughed. "And that's what we put on the new sign. The Four Leaf Clover Cafe. It used to make her mad that everybody still called it Eddie's. She never did though. Always called it the Four Leaf Clover Cafe, like it was something lucky that had happened to her."

Conrad looked up at Eddie, at his tired eyes, pink rimmed. How old was Eddie? Seventy-five, at least, Conrad judged. What's happened to all of us? he thought in sudden alarm. How have we all become so old?

"Go on," Eddie said. "Take that with you. A little extra good luck for the man who lives on Paradise Hill, the man who sees angels. Spread the wealth, Conrad."

He turned away, began stacking plates. "Don't wait on me," he said. "I've got the car out back. I'll just gather up a few things. Empty the register."

Conrad stood there uncertainly. He should wait for Eddie, he thought, but didn't know how to insist.

Eddie didn't look at him again. He disappeared into the back room, spoke over his shoulder. "They could probably use some help up at the natatorium," he called. "I'll see you up there."

"Okay," Conrad said, but Eddie had disappeared. "Okay, Eddie."

He waited a minute. "You—take care," he called. But there was no answer.

EVEN BEFORE HE closed the flimsy weight of the door behind him, though, Conrad thought that he would never see this again. Eddie's, all the other buildings scattered along the dirty shoulder of the river, Eddie himself, would be wiped away completely from the face of the earth, no record remaining, no trace. He remembered the pictures of the aftermath of the 1942 flood. There had been something unreal about those images; they were strangely silent, as if everybody in town had died, their bloated bodies bobbing against the ceilings of their houses, bedclothes wrapped around them in shrouds, their expressions surprised, injured, hurt, as if to say, We had no warning.

Stepping across the street, he looked down over the edge of the wall into the river. The heavy rain jostled and pitted its surface now nearly to the top of the wall; just a few more feet and it would roll over the edge and onto the cracked and buckled pavement of River Road, running like a fault line into the distance.

A warning. Is that all it takes? he thought. It's what Nolan believed, what had sent him up into the bell tower, made him ring the bells to wake even the dead. Was it enough just to be warned? But wasn't everybody warned, from the moment they breathed their first cold breath of true air? From that first moment, a circumference was drawn around them, a line that described and contained their lives, their beginning and end. He'd known Rose would die, that he himself would die. He'd spent his whole life anticipating it, he thought, so afraid of this place he'd come to now, so afraid of this desolate aftermath, that any sign of infirmity along the way had struck him with fierce and unreasonable terror. You could be warned, he thought, and still not escape.

But then he thought about his own house, high on Paradise Hill, safe from the rising waters. He felt across his coat, to the framed four-leaf clover resting there against his heart. All around him were people answering the knocks at their door, people who could stand and run, who even now were making for safety. But there were others, too, he knew: People still asleep in their beds, or just rising slowly in the unnatural silence, unaware. People who would never be able to run from what was headed toward them, a wall of black water. How would they survive? Hand to hand, he thought, mouth to mouth, someone else's hot, reviving breath in their lungs for an instant, someone else breathing for them when they could not, the most essential form of charity.

He thought of Lemuel and his insistence on the world's beneficence. He thought of Rose, of how often her faith had been shaken by her own grief, of how often she had recovered it in an act of generosity. And he thought of Hero, her anonymous deliveries to his door, patiently gardening for the living and the dead. What is heroism, he thought, if not a moment of faith at exactly the right time?

He turned away from the water then, hurried across the street to his truck, climbed in, and turned up the hill toward the natatorium. Spread the wealth, Eddie had said.

Go home, Conrad, Lemuel had said.

Home was Paradise Hill, but Conrad knew where he needed to go first.

Eleven

IN THE PARKING lot of the natatorium, Conrad steered slowly through the queues of dark figures leaving their cars and moving toward the open doors. Though it was well past dawn now, the morning was stubbornly dark, and headlights blazed through the rain. Cars clogged the graveled lot. People moved in maddeningly slow procession, their faces averted from the slanting wind, their belongings heaped in their arms, their children gathered close.

He stopped the truck at one point to allow a group of people to pass. When the group crossed before his headlights, Conrad recognized the Pleiades, huddled together under two large black umbrellas. He stared through the streaming windshield at them. Henri turned her white face toward him for a moment, blind against the glare of the headlights, her eyes squinting. Her face was creased, as if she had just been woken. Under a rain hat her hair was awry, slipping oddly to one side—a wig, Conrad realized, shocked. Mignon had her by the arm, was tugging her along, but Henri's step was uncertain. None of them seemed to recognize his truck, and Conrad let them pass, watching after them until he saw them shoulder safely through the doors of the natatorium.

Where were their families? he thought, feeling dazed. The line of figures, bowed like refugees, continued to pass before him. But then he realized that most of them were, like himself, alone. Except for Mignon, whose husband was out with Harrison, and Nora Johnson, whose husband was still a volunteer with the fire department and was presumably out knocking on doors, all the rest were widows.

When he caught sight of Toronto hurrying in front of the truck, he rolled down the window. The rain soaked his shoulder and neck in an instant, bitterly cold. "Kenny!" he yelled above the sound of the storm. "Toronto!"

Toronto stopped a moment, looking around in confusion; then, recognizing Conrad, he raised his hand, hurried around to the passenger side of the truck, climbed in, and slammed the door behind him. He smelled like rain, Conrad noticed—like water itself.

He reached up and unclasped his coat at the neck, stretched against the stiff rubber. "They're not clearing out Paradise Hill, are they?" he asked, surprised. His face shone with wetness.

Conrad shook his head. "I was down at Eddie's. I just came up here to—" To what? he thought. What had he expected? "I thought I might be able to help," he said at last.

Toronto leaned forward and stared through the windshield. "Well, unless you've got a private line up to heaven," he said, "I don't think there's a damn thing to be done." And then he looked over at Conrad and smiled sadly. "But maybe you do."

Conrad grimaced. Somehow his own private vision, Lemuel spreading his wings over Paradise Hill, seemed to have nothing to do with this exodus. If there were any kindness in the world, he thought, the rain would stop right now, and everybody would halt suddenly under a clearing sky, growing quiet as the sun stepped up overhead. Birds would resume their music, the wind would dwindle and die, and the river would sink, coldly brilliant, back to its familiar level. He thought of the Nile River basin, the Egyptian fellahin staggering into the breaches in the canals dug to irrigate the valley. He thought of the men standing shoulder to shoulder against the water, armed with torn-off doors and windows, bundles of cornstalks, pushing terrified livestock ahead of them, trying to block the tears in the levees. Every engineering student studied the Aswân High Dam, the world's most ambitious flood-control project, and every one of them understood how it held sway over forces of nature that before had seemed beyond control. There were dams, and then there were angels, Conrad thought. And if it was the business of angels to avert disaster, everybody could just go home right now.

Conrad folded his arms over the steering wheel, stared along with Toronto out into the rain. "What's happening up here?" he asked.

"People are moving stuff in," Toronto said. "The National Guard's bagging the river in town and up at the lake, but I don't think they really have much hope. The square is four inches deep already. It's just like a big bathtub, except there's no drain." He squinted into the rain. "I've never seen so much water," he said. "And there's no place for it all to go."

In the town below them, the streets were laid out in an uneven grid that accommodated rock outcroppings and ancient trees, marsh basins and the snaking tributaries of the river. Conrad closed his eyes a moment and tried to follow the course of the river, tried to recollect its path behind sheds and barns, through backyards and gardens. And then he remembered his own loft, his pigeons gathered there against their cages, trapped.

"There's too many old people in this town," Toronto said, interrupting Conrad's train of thought. He glanced over at Conrad. "Sorry," he said, smiling ruefully and lifting his hands in a slight shrug. Conrad realized how old he must seem to Toronto. No, not *seem*, he corrected himself. He *was* old.

"It's just that they move so slow, most of them," Toronto went on. "It makes me crazy just watching them. Half of them don't see what business it is of anybody's if they choose to stay right where they are, clinging to their credenzas. A lot of them lived through the last flood. You'd think they'd remember. But people hate to be pried away from their homes, don't they?"

Conrad didn't answer. He stared out through the dark half-moons cleared by his windshield wipers. An endless chain of people moved slowly toward the natatorium, the glass roof over the pool glowing with a green, subterranean light. Rose had liked to swim there, and sometimes Conrad had gone along to keep her company. He would take a book and settle himself in a plastic-webbed chair a foot or two from the pool's edge, the pages curling in the humid air. It was restful, watching other people exercise. He often nearly fell asleep, breathing in the smell of chlorine and something else, citrusy and sharp, like lime. Every now and then, glancing up from the page, he'd look up and watch Rose and two or three others quietly swimming their laps, their bodies flattened and distorted under the water like stained glass.

On the tarmac before him now, people carried suitcases and boxes, strange shapes bound in canvas and tied with rope or wrapped in blankets, all the things they thought to rescue. He watched a man and a woman carrying a birdcage between them, its dome covered with a flowered pillowcase. The woman, a rain hat crushed on her head, hesitated before Conrad's headlights and tried to lift the cloth cover. But the man, his mouth open in an expression of fear and anger, snatched at the cage, grabbed her arm, and hurried her along.

Conrad winced. "How do they decide what to save?"

"I don't know," Toronto said quietly. "All the wrong things, probably."

Conrad turned to look at him. "Your place all right?"

"Oh, we're high enough that unless this is the end of the world, we won't do anything more than see a lot of mud," Toronto said. "Stella's still at home with the kids. We took in a bunch of people who live below us. She's cooking something to bring up here later. Thank God for gas."

Conrad thought for a moment, then said, "I heard about Nolan."

Toronto looked over at him with a rueful smile and shook his head. "He's had a bad week." He leaned back against the seat. "First your letter showing up in the paper—Betty surprised me, you know, doing that, but I give her credit for it. She may worship him, and worship is usually blind, but she thought she was right and he was wrong, and she was willing to take a risk. For her, I guess it was the biggest risk she'd ever taken."

"Well, I'm grateful, I guess," Conrad said. "Surprised and grateful. A lot of people came by the house." He thought of the PS. Betty herself must have added it to his letter; it was a nice idea, he had to admit. He liked the idea of a garden planted at the cemetery in Rose's name.

He looked out at the dark parking lot, still massed with people. And then he thought again about Nolan. "Harrison Supplee said Nolan was up here this morning. Did you see him?"

Toronto nodded. "I tried to get him to go home," he said. "I think he had some kind of small stroke last night, up there in the bell tower. But he's so stubborn. 'Kenny,' he said to me. 'I haven't done anything for this town except put out a terrible newspaper for thirty years. And now I'm going to do something real.'

"And then, you know what he did?" Toronto laughed. "He put his arm around Betty, who'd been following him around like a worried mother hen, and he said, 'I know what I've got to lose now. I'm not going down without a fight.'" Toronto smiled. "You should have seen the look on her face."

He pushed his hands through his wet hair, wiped at his forehead. "Nolan's so *serious*. Almost dramatically serious. And this morning he was deadly serious. He's gone up to the dam. He wants to help, but I can't imagine he'll do anything other than get in the way." Toronto reached for the door handle.

"I think Harrison was grateful to him," Conrad said quickly. He didn't want Toronto to leave, not just yet. It suddenly seemed important to be clear about what Nolan had done. "He thinks Nolan woke everybody up," he offered.

"Well, he certainly tried," Toronto agreed. "You know," he said, leaning back against the seat, "I've never hated him like so many people do. He cares a lot about Laurel, about the people here. He just doesn't have a good way of showing it." Toronto kept his hand on the door handle but was quiet for a moment. "He took me bird-watching with him once," he said finally. "I'll never forget it. We went out near the fairgrounds for the Christmas count—you know, when all the bird-watchers go out and literally count all the birds they see, the different species, trying to track migratory patterns and so forth. You've probably done it yourself." He nodded at Conrad. "I've never been so cold in my life. It must have been ten below, anyway. But Nolan just kept on walking, no hat or anything, no gloves, and then at one point, in this little glade of pine trees, he stopped. He put his hand up like I should be quiet, and then he made this whistling noise, with his hands against his lips." Toronto put his fingers up to his mouth and gave a low whistle. "Like that, only I can't really do it the way he did. And then, out of nowhere, all these birds came fluttering down out of the trees, hundreds of them. I don't know how he even knew they were there. I just stepped back and watched, and the ground around him filled with birds standing there and looking up at him, like they were waiting for him to tell them what to do. It was one of the most amazing things I've ever seen."

Conrad watched Toronto's face, thought of the birds choking

the trees up at the lake. He thought Toronto was finished, but after a moment he spoke again.

"You know, he could have put out his arms and they would have lighted on his hands," Toronto said. "But he didn't. He just stayed there for a few minutes, as if he couldn't even see them. And then he turned around and walked back out of the glade. He could have had them feeding from his hands, but that wasn't it, wasn't what he wanted. I don't know if he knew what it was he *did* want, but whatever it was, he didn't find it there."

Toronto turned then and smiled at Conrad. "Since then, I've always had kind of a soft spot for him. He's not a mean man. Just sort of—scared to death all the time."

Conrad didn't say anything, but he thought of Nolan in his garden, wrestling with the idea of the improbable, angels and miracles and faith. Everybody's idea of what's extraordinary is different, he thought.

"And now," Toronto said, "I promised him I'd get pictures. I'm supposed to go up to the roof of the bank, shoot the water when it comes." He laughed. "Can you imagine a worse assignment?"

Conrad shook his head "No," he said. "I can't."

Toronto put his hand on Conrad's arm. "You should go on home," he said kindly. "Go on home and talk to that angel of yours. We could use him."

But Conrad was ashamed, though he knew Toronto was being considerate. He probably thinks I'm as useless as Nolan, he thought; wants to see I don't come to any harm or get in anybody's way. It wasn't any use protesting.

"Thanks, Kenny," he said then, putting his hands on the wheel. "You be careful."

Toronto slammed the door behind him and took off in a run toward his own car, dodging the people moving toward the natatorium. He ran beautifully, Conrad thought, like an athlete. His feet did not touch the ground.

CONRAD LIFTED HIS head when he heard shouting, saw the crowd of people before the truck halt and mill in confusion. A man in a long slicker shouldered through them suddenly, a limp figure—a girl or an old woman, Conrad couldn't be sure which—in his arms. Conrad's heart knocked irregularly within his chest. Someone's hurt, he thought. Someone's died.

It was the sight of the man carrying the still body that awoke in him a feeling of terror and dread, and he remembered an evening, so many years before, when he'd arrived at the Sparkses' door, let himself in, and called down the hall. He'd been in college at that point, and Adele, appearing at the door of the kitchen, had been surprised to see him. "We weren't expecting you, Connie," she'd said warmly. "You're home for the weekend?"

"Where's Rose?" he'd asked a few minutes later, after Adele had taken his coat, poured him a cup of tea, inquired about his studies.

"Oh—" Adele had looked around vaguely, as if her daughter might have been there just a moment before, as if she'd lost track of her for a second. "I think she's out walking."

Conrad had stood and looked out the kitchen window, the streetlights coming on, blooming like Chinese chrysanthemums, colored aureoles wavering around them.

"It's getting kind of dark," he said. "Maybe she went to the library? I could walk over there and meet her."

"Mmmm," Adele had murmured. "I'm sure she'll be back soon."

And so Conrad had hung around, drifting into the front parlor, where John and James were bent over their homework. He had pulled a chair up to the table, looked over the boys' shoulders, pointed out an error on James's math paper.

"Go mind your own business, *bird* boy," James had said, annoyed. "Go kiss my sister or something."

Well, I would like to, but I don't know where she is, Conrad had thought, standing, restlessly pacing the room before the long front windows.

An hour had gone by. Two. The family sat down to supper, Conrad pushing the food around on his plate.

"You growing a beard, Conrad?" John had asked him at one point, curious, and Conrad had been annoyed to be examined so closely. He felt hemmed in, under scrutiny.

"Shouldn't she be back by now?" he said at last, standing up and carrying his plate to the sink, lifting his arms while Adele tied an apron around his waist. "Where *is* she?"

"Everyone's entitled to get lost in their own thoughts sometimes, Conrad," she said gently. "I'm sure she's all right."

"But she's always here," Conrad objected.

"Not always," Adele said.

And Conrad had stopped at the way she'd said that. He thought of the Sparkses' home, so much larger and more comfortable than his parents' apartment. With its warren of basement rooms and its lofty attic, its branching hallways and narrow back stairs, the house was a world unto itself, perfectly able to sustain, he supposed, an entire lifetime within its walls. It had never occurred to him that Rose might find it confining, because he had never experienced anything other than a sense of liberation, verging on recklessness, there.

"I'm going up to the roof," he announced when the dishes were done. He felt rebuked somehow, chastened.

He climbed into the vestibule on the rooftop, opened the glass door, and stepped out under the stars. The white gravel glittered beneath his feet; the walls of Lemuel's pigeon loft glowed in their clean finish of white paint. The sky was clear; a silver half-moon hung cocked over his shoulder, sharp and motionless. A cool breeze blew in over the harbor, past the Statue of Liberty's uplifted white arm, and traveled across his face. Out over the water, the last of the Circle Line's ferries for the night turned gently in its own thick gray wake to chug back toward the docks.

Conrad walked to the edge of the roof, stared out over the dark street and the shadowy canyons of tarred rooftops. A few blocks away, he saw the orange glow of a fire, some building ablaze. A twisting column of bright, distant sparks rose in the air. The blue and yellow lights of the fire trucks revolved, spinning against walls. He could smell smoke.

And suddenly he knew Rose wasn't at the library, bent safely over a book in the deep hush of the reading room, her red coat spread out on the chair behind her, her fuzzy blue tam-o'-shanter resting on the floor at her feet by her book bag.

She was *out there,* one among the numberless masses of people hurrying through the streets, past storefronts, the windows lit with a shallow brightness, a deep essential darkness behind them. He thought of the park, with its concentric circles of stones and dark shrubbery, of the damp and fragrant arboretum, where orchids with pursed, weighty lips hung from the crooks of trees lit from beneath by the round eyes of floodlights.

He thought of the Marion Street Pigeon Exchange, the mumblers gathered in the back room under a bright light, making preparations for Saturday's race, the sale birds asleep in the front window in their dark cages, their heads sunk into their breasts. He thought of all that darkness and all the people closeted away behind their locked doors, the night taking shape in the form of tall shadows that stepped out lightly behind passersby, overtaking them, racing across the walls on the long, impossible legs of insects.

He looked over the city, its checkerboard of lights, the sprays of curving neon letters floating here and there in fantastic bouquets, the darting lines of cars' headlights. The light and dark formed a chaotic pattern, but the dark was, in the end, so much greater, so much more potent. And then he knew that she was lost. No, no, not lost; he tried to correct himself. Not *lost*. Just—out of reach.

He was back in the kitchen, his books spread out over the table, when she came home at last just after ten. He looked up when he heard the front door open and then close.

"Lemuel," he heard her call—she always called her parents by their first names—and then he lost her words as she passed into the front parlor, though he could still hear her tone, quick and excited.

"Conrad!" she said a minute later, sticking her head around the kitchen door and looking in at him.

Conrad affected a stretch. "Had a nice time?" he said, raising his eyebrows at her.

After a moment's hesitation, she advanced across the kitchen, bent over and kissed his cheek, put her arms around his neck. She smelled of the cold night air and something else, ashy and burnt. "I didn't know you were coming home."

"Thought I'd surprise everybody," he said, and then, despite himself, he extracted himself from her embrace and glanced at his watch, as if he'd been so engaged in his books that he'd lost track of time.

Rose stepped back away from him, began to undo the scarf from around her neck, a giant knitted affair like a python, her own creation. "I saw the most amazing thing tonight, Connie," she said, sitting down across from him and taking off her shoes, pulling up her knees to peel away her socks. Conrad watched the long fall of her hair slide over her cheek, a shining curtain of gold.

"There was a fire over on Lawrence Street. People had to jump from the third-story windows. Two children. And one woman jumped with a baby in her arms."

Conrad affected a yawn.

"I stayed to watch, the whole thing, till they had everybody out, everybody safe."

"That's nice," he offered finally.

Rose glanced up at him, slowly tucked her hair behind her ear. She gave him a hard look. "The last one out," she said carefully, "was a man. He was the one most afraid to jump. People were yelling up at him—'Jump! Jump!'—but for the longest time he wouldn't do it. He just kept standing there at the window, and every now and then he'd disappear for a moment, and then he'd be back again. You could see the flames in the room behind him."

"How exciting," Conrad said, but before the words were out of his mouth he regretted them, regretted them enormously.

Rose put her feet on the floor, looked away from Conrad. "He did jump finally," she said at last, after a long silence. "And then his mother, I guess she was his mother, came through the crowd, calling his name, 'Teddy! Oh Teddy!'"

Conrad listened to her voice telling the story, heard the woman's cry.

"I was standing right at the edge, by the tape line the police had put up. And then I saw that he wasn't so old after all. He was probably our age, maybe nineteen, maybe twenty. And he was an idiot. A real idiot, I mean, retarded, with a blubbery face. That's why he'd been so afraid. He didn't understand. He didn't understand that they'd catch him."

A silence fell between them. Rose reached up, began to braid her hair behind her head, her fingers moving deftly, making a quick, nervous chain. Conrad looked down at his books.

"I was just worried about you," he said at last quietly. "I went up

to the roof and looked out. I thought—I mean, I knew I *wouldn't*
—but I thought I'd see you, coming home, and—"

But he didn't finish. He didn't even know what he'd thought.
That he'd expected her to be there, waiting for him when he came
back? That he'd seen, for the first time, how she lived a life apart
from him? That he didn't have enough faith to be able to stand it,
the thought of her out in the world, away from him, her move-
ments untraceable, unknowable? That he might have lost her?
What had it been? All of those things, he knew. There didn't seem
any way to say all he felt, his shame and his relief, his fear and his
gratitude.

Rose was quiet a moment. "I couldn't leave until they were all
safe," she said, looking away from him. She shrugged lightly. "Not
that I could have done anything. No one could. The firemen
couldn't even get inside. But I had to see the end of it. I had to see
it all the way through."

Conrad nodded. "I know—" he began.

"I didn't even know you were *here*," she interrupted.

He nodded again, felt her looking at him. He heard her sigh.

"I would have been worried, too," she said then. "You'd be surprised, maybe, how much I worry about *you*."

He looked up at her. She smiled at him, and he felt a rush of
longing for her, imagined her gripping the yellow tape at the edge
of the fire, her face upturned to the boy in the window, wishing it
would all end well, wishing so hard that perhaps she had, just by
wanting it so much, made that boy jump, made him step out into
the smoky air, made his soft, weighty body slow as it sailed toward
earth, made him believe he would be saved.

HE PUT HIS head down on the steering wheel for a moment. There
was nothing to be done here now. Toronto was right. What had he
been thinking?

But maybe there was someone left, he thought then, almost with relief. Maybe there was someone who hadn't heard that the world could be a dangerous place, that it was filled with omens and warnings, flaming buildings and insidious disease and rising floodwaters. Maybe there was someone still asleep, still dreaming, in his bed.

For a second he thought of his pigeons. But it was only a second, a moment that was more like a memory. He heard the buffeting sound their wings made, pulling up into the air above Lemuel's rooftop. He saw them climb and then, having found the altitude they called home, steady their wings to proceed down the avenue of air between roof and cloud, land and sky, heaven and earth.

Conrad turned the truck, drove away from the natatorium down the hill toward the low streets, toward the river, toward the place he knew he'd come to at last.

Twelve

CONRAD TURNED UP the heat in the truck. A blast of wet, hot air flooded his ankles, burned across his jaw. He turned down Forest Street and headed for the square, but as he neared the granite wall of the bank, he saw that the water was already too high in that direction. Through a dim gap between the buildings ahead, he could see water spread over the lawn in the center of the square—a lake where no lake ought to be, its surface writhing under the falling rain. The bandstand floated there like a strange dream-ship, its canvas curtains ballooning in the wind.

He backed the truck up Forest to the Smile Market—its windows dark, its awning furled—and turned onto a side street, skirting the square and aiming for the residential part of town. Halfway down the block, through the disordering gusts of rain, he saw Lenore Wyatt hurrying toward her truck parked at the curb, the delivery boy, Burden, behind her with his arms full of boxes. Conrad saw Lenore recognize him, turn in astonishment to watch him drive past, Burden following her stare. Conrad made a gesture, a small, deliberate semaphore that said, It's all right. I know what I'm doing, and then he drove on.

Without lights anywhere, Laurel already looked strangely deserted. Here and there he passed people loading belongings into their cars, pulling away from their homes in steaming clouds of exhaust, glancing back through the rear window to see if they might have forgotten anything—a child or a dog left standing alone, abandoned.

Water ran in streams down the sides of the streets, fountaining up at storm drains blocked with leaves and branches, but it was mostly draining off still, down toward the square and the river itself. Conrad gripped the wheel tightly, peered through the windshield. With only one good eye, he was finding it increasingly hard to see in such heavy rain; he seemed to be driving into a solid wall of water, or to be underwater already, the dark shapes of trees wavering above him like distant reflections floating on the surface. He had cracked open the window of the truck but closed it now against the steady, harsh sound of the storm beating all around him. The wet air bleeding through the truck's vents smelled of things unearthed, and for a moment he was wildly claustrophobic, as if sodden leaves had been plastered over his nose and mouth.

At the corner of Jackson Street, under the dripping leaves of a maple tree, he caught sight of a young woman. She was struggling, a suitcase in one arm, two small children clinging to her neck. She was trying to force open her car door, which was slightly ajar, with her knee, but the suitcase was slipping from her grasp. Two other small bags, tipped over near her feet, lay on the sidewalk. Conrad braked the truck and got out, drew in a sharp breath against the force of the rain and the sour scent of wet wood, torn bark. The children—one not a year old yet, he judged—were wailing. The woman, her hair soaked and slicked over her cheeks, was clearly frantic.

He hurried toward them. "Please," he said. "Do you need help?"

The woman turned to him, her face surprised and alarmed. He supposed she had thought she was all alone, the last person left on the street. She hoisted the baby higher on her hip, stared at him a moment as if trying to weigh whether to trust him. "My mother," she said then, but to Conrad her voice sounded indistinct, and he had to lean toward her, peering at her mouth. "She's in the kitchen," the woman said, putting her hand over the baby's head. "In a wheelchair. Thank you."

Conrad looked toward the front door of the house. It stood partly open, the hallway behind it dark.

"In there?" he said stupidly.

"She's in a wheelchair," the woman repeated. "In the kitchen."

She dropped the suitcase and pulled the children roughly from her, forcing them into the front seat, though they tried to cling to her, tried to climb back out into her arms. "Sit down, Jared," she said to the baby. "Sit *down*."

Conrad backed away, hurrying up the path.

"To your left," the woman called after him, her voice high and fierce. "Left off the hall. She can't walk."

At the open door, Conrad paused a moment, then stepped over the sill onto a dirty tatter of carpet, which lay askew, crumpled at his feet.

"Fisher?"

He heard a thin voice. Through the gloom he took in the peeling wallpaper, a split of obscenely large, faded cabbage roses; behind the flowers the wall was papered in something older still, something yellowed with age—maps. Conrad stopped, drew near the paper, peered at it, and was startled to see a place he knew: the faded, concentric blue rings and ovals described the rising altitudes of the White Mountains, Mt. Abraham, his own Paradise Hill.

"Fisher?" The tone rose, quavering, fearful, echoing through the house as if it were empty, as if it had been stripped already of its possessions.

Conrad jumped. He stepped farther into the hall and saw a pile of boxes; clothes and books spilled out of them at the foot of the stairs.

"I'm here," he said into the darkness. "I'm coming."

He put his hand to the wall, jumped again when he saw his own image move across a round mirror, its surface a porthole, a well's black eye. He stepped to the doorway on his left and looked into the room. A candle, guttering in its saucer, threw a low, flickering light.

"Fisher?" The figure in the wheelchair turned suddenly at his entrance.

Conrad cleared his throat, took off his cap. He looked at the woman, an old tam pulled down over her hair, a coat bunched up around her in the seat. Two broomstick legs, bedroom slippers over the misshapen feet, scraped the floor. He cleared his throat again, and the woman's face registered alarm.

"I've come to help you," he said quickly then. "Your daughter—" He turned halfway and pointed to the door. "She asked me to help you."

"I'm waiting on Fisher," the woman said, querulous and shrill. She twisted her hands in her lap. Conrad saw she wore a night-dress, pale blue and tied at her throat with two thin cords, beneath her coat. "I'll wait," she said, and suddenly her voice sounded clearer, firmer. "I'll not go without him."

Conrad looked anxiously around him. Who was Fisher?

The woman looked up at him. "You've seen him? He knows I'm here?"

Conrad moved carefully then to stand beside her. He put his hands on the wheelchair, began to turn the chair slowly toward the doorway. The floor was sticky beneath his feet. A God's eye, made by a child from fraying bits of yarn, twisted slowly in the window over the sink.

"A tall man," the woman said, craning her head around to look up at Conrad. "Fisher is a tall man. Black hair, black as a crow."

"Yes, I—" Conrad started, and then thought that it was best just to keep going, bearing the woman before him out of the house, into the rain, into the car, out of harm's way. The dangerousness of his undertaking—racing against a river, a failing dam, the lake behind it—stuck suddenly in his throat; that, and the smell in the kitchen, something artificial and cloying, like spilled soap powder, or a tin of condensed milk opened long ago and left on a counter.

The woman in the chair breathed deeply, a long sigh. "I said I'd wait on him," she murmured. She leaned back against Conrad's knuckles, and he felt a sharp sympathy for her, for the untidy head, the lifeless legs, this woman left alone to wait in her dark kitchen. At the front door he stopped, took off his coat, and spread it carefully, tentlike, over the woman's head and shoulders, adjusting it so she could see. She sat quietly beneath his touch.

"It's raining very hard," he said gently to her. "But there's nothing to be frightened of."

At the curb the young woman hurried toward him. "Your coat!" She gestured at the car, ducking her head against the rain. "I can't take the chair," she said hurriedly. "The van picks her up, but the chair won't fit in the car." She bent down, peered into the old woman's face. "Mother? You're all right?"

"She's asking for Fisher," Conrad said then, through the steady, annihilating wash of the rain.

The young woman stood upright, pulled her coat against her throat, appealed to Conrad. "Can you lift her? Just into the car?"

But Conrad did not release the wheelchair's handles. "She's asking for Fisher," he repeated. It seemed to him that perhaps the young woman had not heard him, that he needed to tell her again.

"I'm sorry," the woman said then. "Please just help me. I didn't know how I was going to do it. I got called earlier, by her aide. I drove here right away. The children—" She gestured at the car.

Conrad didn't move. His head felt heavy.

"This is her house," she said more loudly, as though Conrad hadn't understood. "She's afraid to leave. She thinks my father's coming back."

Conrad stared at her.

"He passed," she said, and she had to raise her voice again to be heard through the rain, had to shout at him. "A long time ago."

Conrad bowed his head then, took in a deep breath against the force of the old woman's delusion. And then he stooped to reach beneath her, one arm snaking around her back, the other fitted under her legs. She smelled of unwashed sheets. And when he lifted her in his arms, he was amazed at her slight weight, the small head held upright, alert, on its thin neck, the hands reaching for his shoulders.

The young woman hurried to open the back door of the car. Conrad bent, the woman in his arms, to settle her gently in the seat, the rain pounding his back. Carefully he lifted his coat from her shoulders, slipped it from behind her.

"I'll tell him," he said, leaning close before he backed out, "where you are."

And she nodded, satisfied, reached out to touch his hand.

When he stood back up, the young woman was fumbling in her purse.

"No, no," Conrad said, backing off, hurrying into his coat, wiping his hand across his face.

The woman stopped, then held out her hand to him. "You came out of nowhere," she said, and Conrad thought of the maps papering the wall inside the old woman's house, the surprise of finding himself not in strange territory after all, but here where he belonged, at home, his own house marked at the top of Paradise Hill with a tiny black square. It was right there, on the map.

When the car pulled away from the curb, exhaust spewing from its tailpipe, its wheels sending up a plume of water, he saw that they had left the wheelchair behind on the curb, left the front door ajar. He hurried back up the short path, pushing the chair ahead of him. Inside he stopped uncertainly at the foot of the stairs, then pushed the chair carefully into the recess below the risers. He went into the kitchen and, bending over, blew out the candle on the table. The room filled with a swift and final darkness.

He walked back outside, pulling the door closed behind him. It was then that he realized he didn't know who these people were. Though he had thought he could recognize nearly every person on the street, Laurel being such a small town, he had never seen this family before.

HE DROVE SLOWLY, wet and shivering. He had not forgotten about the danger, about the lake with its restless cargo of black water lapping the rock edge, the old dam straining at its mortared seams. He sensed in one part of his mind that he ought to leave now, head uphill. But he couldn't tear himself away from the low streets and the empty houses; someone might still be left behind. It would be his fault, he thought, if someone were left behind.

He remembered his pigeons, and his heart wrenched against an image of the river spread over the meadow, trapping his birds, drowning them. He shook his head, spoke reassuringly to himself. They were on the second story; surely it hadn't reached that high. There's time, he comforted himself. Keep looking. I need to keep looking.

He passed the clotheslines of his neighbors, with their array of stiff trousers and drenched sheets, forgotten clothes dropped here and there on the lawns, a tiny pink sock belonging to a child, a patterned dress shriveling in the mud, the empty arms filling with water. He saw loose shutters beating the walls. He saw empty chairs on porches, some tethered to porch rails with baling twine, and bicycles resting against fences, chained tight. He saw doghouses trailing ropes, and swings winding and unwinding from the branches of trees in the unnatural wind. In the flower beds, the early fall phlox was blown to the ground, its flowers smashed like paper pulp. Here and there a child's toy lay in the street—a red bucket partly submerged, a ball spangled with gold stars, a sodden doll, one arm missing, its blue glass eyes staring heavenward into the rain.

Driving down Williams Street, he passed Harrison Supplee's house, foursquare and upright, white as a wedding cake, one of the five or six bigger houses in this part of town; most of Laurel's better addresses were up on the hill. The few grander houses down low were among the town's oldest, built by the original owner of the mill, who had spawned similar dwellings, purposeful and white, as dowries for each of his four daughters. A widow's walk, a folly, perched atop Harrison's house. The front door had been barred with a series of heavy two-by-fours nailed across the frame, over the knocker, which, as Conrad recalled, bore the shape of a branching tree, its trunk curved smoothly beneath your hand. How like Harrison, Conrad thought, to be prepared, to have barricaded his door. The wine red draperies in the front rooms were drawn.

He drove up and down the streets, staring through the windshield until his eyes ached, retracing his path, the same houses appearing over and over again. He turned down back alleys, now running with water and flotillas of wet leaves backed up like barges stuck in a canal. The water was rising. He could feel it under the tires of the truck, how the body shimmied now and again, rudderless for a second and then grinding, catching on higher ground.

And for a moment he understood how he could already be lost

in the flood, a tiny figure moving swiftly downriver, turning over and over, passing familiar storefronts and fences propped up here and there like signposts in a dream. He was carried past the dark windows of leaning buildings, past sloping gardens and toolsheds and deserted places where doors hung ajar at a crazy tilt, where windows gaped, blown out. He was borne into the darkness of the pine forest, where the river ran silent and swift, into the wavering meadows now become a wide sea, past May Brown's house, high on the hill above, its windows bright with a hot white light, and then past his own house, his arms reaching out as he was swept past his loft, his pigeons washing back and forth, wings limp, in the tide that ran through their roosts.

The smell of the river that bore him away—it was not clear and sweet but choked with green wood and torn root, with nail and fur and ripped bark; it filled his nose and eyes and mouth. And the sound of it—like Lemuel's organ, he thought, the rushing arpeggios and heaving wind, curtains blowing through the tall windows into the front parlor of the Sparkses' dusty brownstone, Lemuel himself bent over the instrument, his back shaking with joy. Where had he learned such joy? Wondrous Lemuel, now become an angel—he'd believed he could ascend on the wings of his birds into the blue ether, see the umbra of the earth itself cast into space. Of course he had preferred things built of stone, Conrad thought. The bigger the better. He had admired anything that would stand forever, cathedrals, the pyramids, the temples at Luxor, anything aimed at God's throne. That high.

And Rose, Lemuel's own flesh and blood, the girl with her mother's coloring, like the rose named 'Peace', pink and gold—she had lived and died over and over, her heart failing her sometimes for its very fullness, for the feeling of it branching within her like a tree, herself dispersed into the busy, material air of the world.

She had taken life slowly, a postulant to its tiny, significant miracles, tying her little bows of string around the sweet peas, snapping slender bamboo stakes to prop the lilies. She'd seen the eye of the potato sprouting like a fetus, seen a leaf unwinding, first light at its center, her eye to the perfect space there.

If Lemuel had ever imagined the end of the world, Conrad thought, it would have been biblical, like this, rocks and water moving in with a glacier's regal carriage. But Rose's ending—that would have been softer, kinder, he knew: the world's flooded surface strewn with seeds and budding branches, with the stripped bark of the birch, with pipsissewa, prince's pine, its pink blossoms scattered. It would have been a planting, a sowing.

And his? What was his ending? He found to his surprise that he could not imagine it at all, that he could see only what he remembered now of his life: the generous, high-ceilinged rooms of the Sparkses' house with their ornamental moldings; the white gravel rooftop glittering, a field of diamonds; the view from his French doors out into his flowering garden, down Paradise Hill; the wings of his pigeons, their tiny V shapes in the sky; the weight of Rose's round, girlish cheek, warm in his hand. He could remember, as he had once wished, only the precious things, now flying apart like beads on a snapped necklace.

Lemuel had been a master builder, had spent his life balancing rock in the air, a trick designed to delight, confound. Engineering was for the cautious, the skeptical, he had told Conrad, as if that were what he had always expected of him. Architecture, by contrast, was a faith. And Rose had been a gardener; that was her skill, the patient business of waiting and watching, of looking for the smallest signs.

And his? His had been the art of amazement, he knew now. Amazement at all that had filled his days, the brief calendar of his life.

HE STOPPED INSTINCTIVELY for the light at the corner of Williams Street and River Road. He stared ahead through the frantic arcs of the windshield wipers, drumming his fingers on the wheel, until he realized that the light was out, of course; it would never turn green and tell him it was safe to cross.

He gripped the top of the steering wheel as he turned onto River Road, steering around the water that splashed darkly here and there in waves over the top of the wall. On his right the river heaved over the edge of the bulwark in sudden cascades as far down the road as he could see, white froth foaming over the dark water. He thought of the boy with his finger in the dike, the boy who'd lain all night stiff with cold, his shoulder to the sea, until help arrived. Up ahead he made out the lights at Eddie's, the only lights anywhere, the white sign knocking back and forth wildly over the front door. He could hear the river, close now, a sound without intervals, a score without pause. He was frightened.

"Who's left?" he asked aloud, and his own voice sounded strange to him. He remembered standing on his fire escape when he was just a child, learning to train his first pigeons; he had called into the evening sky of the city, its wild, dramatic light. "Come home!" he had called after them, as if they would hear him and understand, his child's voice and the birds disappearing together into the setting sun, across the rooftops. "Come home!"

"Lemuel!" he shouted now, banging his palms against the steering wheel, startling himself. "Is anyone here? Tell me!"

And he thought he would be answered, that his voice, a distant signal, would be picked out from all the others, the angels in the fig tree, the strangers standing just to the side, heads conferring, wings stirring in the warm air. In her last moments Rose had spoken to them, to the gathering she saw ahead of her on the path. They had parted to let her pass, and she had nodded her head, murmuring. They had exchanged some words; he could tell by her intonation, her soft inflection, that hers were questions, that their answers pleased her. What had she said then? And would they hear him now? Surely they would hear him.

But as he pulled close to Eddie's, he saw with horror that Eddie's car was still parked around to the side of the low white building. The back door to the restaurant was ajar, a rectangle of light. Conrad pulled the truck over to the curb, took his hat from the seat beside him, and got out, staggering against the force of the wind. He ran to Eddie's car, his head bent, his feet sending up geysers of water, then cupped his hands and peered in through the black window, half expecting—hoping—to find him there, fumbling with his keys or slumped over the wheel, seized by a sudden, perilous need to sleep, a last rest. But the car was empty.

He turned and ran to the back door, stepped in over the chipped and peeling sill into the quiet kitchen.

"Eddie!"

There was no answer.

He walked quickly through the kitchen, past Eddie's cot, past a calendar stopped at a past time, months before, years before. He looked into the front room. The dishes had been stacked neatly in the wide sink, the griddle wiped clean. A single egg, white and pure, rested in the bowl of a spoon on the counter; oddly it struck Conrad that it was a trick, a balancing act, and he stared at it, waiting for it to fall and crack open, for a bird to struggle and rise from the shell.

Where was Eddie? And he thought of him, Eddie with his false leg, standing as he had done earlier that morning atop the bulwark, staring down into the river, its frenzied surface.

Conrad turned and ran back through the kitchen, back out into the rain, gasping against the cold, wet air.

He couldn't have gone far, he thought. Not crippled like that. Not with that leg.

He fought his way through the wind and the slashing rain out to the front of the building, turned, and faced down the long road. The dark buildings stretched along one side, their windows full of the flashing light of the storm; the river sped past on the other, the water jostling and swelling behind the wall.

And then, in the distance, through the rain, he made out a dark figure wobbling along the road away from him on a bicycle, veering sharply, unsteadily, around the water where it splashed over the wall in alarming breakers.

And after a second he could hear her.

"Dad!" she was calling. "Eddie Vaughan! Daddy!"

He started toward her, began to run. He came to the center of the road, ran crookedly down its white line.

"Hero!"

He yelled into the rain, but she didn't stop. He could hear her calling. Her voice came from all sides, the way it had bounced over the bowl-shaped hill of the cemetery, echoing against the mountains, coming back to her unanswered, nobody there but the dead. *Hello . . . Hello . . .*

"Eddie! Eddie Vaughan! *Daddy!*"

Conrad called her name then, over and over. He feared she would never hear him, but she must have at last, for when he thought he had no breath left in him, he saw her turn her head. She put out her leg and stopped the bicycle, planting her foot on the road. She turned uncertainly toward the sound of his voice.

When he reached her, he caught her arms in his hands, steadied her astride the bicycle. "Hero," he said, and found himself amazed that she was real, made of substance, the slight give of her ordinary flesh under his fingers, a smear of mud over her chin.

He looked at her face, the wet hair streaked over it, obscuring her expression.

"I looked for you," she said. "I went to your house."

He stared at her.

"I wanted you to help me," she said, and shook her head. He saw that she was crying. "I can't find Dad."

"What do you mean?" He glanced around. It was preposterous, he thought, that they should be standing here, that Eddie should have disappeared. He felt himself grow unreasonably angry.

He shook her. "His car," he shouted above the wind. "Why didn't he take his car?"

She looked up at him. Her wet face gleamed white, but her eyes were dark, full of fear and injury and pleading, and his own heart was breaking up inside him, a thousand assaults.

She held up a set of keys, clutched in her fist. "It won't start."

He stared at her. The car wouldn't *start*? And Conrad wanted to see it then, though some instinct told him that he was wrong. Please, he thought. Hadn't Eddie gone out the back door, the cash box under his arm, his hat pulled down over his head? Hadn't he gotten into the car, put the keys in the ignition? The engine had clicked, a small, final sound. Nothing.

Was that it? Or hadn't he even tried?

Conrad looked around wildly, gripped the girl's arms. He could see the river, its black surface roaring, nearly parallel with the top of the bulwark. He noticed, with an odd sensation of recognition, that someone had stuck a bouquet of plastic flowers—blue and yellow and pink, the dusty fake flowers Eddie kept in white vases on the tables—into a crack between the stones, like a shrine. He turned away from it.

"You've looked?" he asked then, wanting to be certain. "You've been looking?"

She nodded her head, turned, and searched with her eyes down the road away from them as if they might see him then, coming toward them through the rain.

She opened her mouth to speak, but at that instant a wave crested over the top of the wall near them, a sound like breaking ice, a dangerous thaw. Hero let out a cry, and Conrad pulled her back with him, his arm suddenly hot with a younger man's strength, biceps curled. He held her tight, but the tumult of stone cold water wrenched against his grip. The bicycle fell away soundlessly, fleeing in the wave's backwash, its silver spokes revolving. Conrad gasped. His mouth was full of water. He staggered, reached one hand pointlessly after his hat, which was swept away.

He shook his head, trying to catch his breath, and bent his face to look into hers. He stood nearly a foot taller than she, had to lean over to see her clearly. "We have to go," he shouted against the wall of sound. "We have to go. It's not safe."

But she protested. "My father," she said, trying to wrench free of him.

Conrad gripped her arms. He looked back over his shoulder at the river rising behind the bulwark, curiously ridged like the mountains themselves, crags sliding into crevasses, cliffs melting into foothills. He looked at the lights of the Four Leaf Clover Cafe, Kate's lucky place—four white walls and a blue door, the sign swinging madly.

She tried to pull away from him, but he held her tight.

He turned back to face her. "There isn't anyone left here," he said. "I'm sorry."

She looked down the road one last time, at the shapes the rain made, huge ships crossing dry land, their sails full of rain. And then she turned back to face him, slumped against him so that he could feel her full weight, the heavy weight of grief filling her veins. For a moment he wasn't sure he could support her. He was shaking.

And though it wasn't really any consolation at all, he knew he was right. There wasn't anyone left to be saved.

HE GOT HER into the truck, slammed the door, and then ran around to the other side and let himself in. She sat upright, staring through the windshield. From the seat behind him he retrieved a blanket, handed it to her. "Put that around yourself."

He backed out onto River Road and turned up the hill, driving as fast as he dared, up toward the natatorium, away from the river.

Could a man with a false leg, carrying an iron cash box, walk this far? Wouldn't someone have seen him, stopped, picked him up? But he'd been so tired. Conrad saw him then, standing behind his counter, handing over the four-leaf clover. Dispossessing himself. And Conrad remembered one evening not so long before, sitting alone on Paradise Hill under the graceful, shifting ceiling of his grape arbor, wanting to empty his own pockets, wanting to be done with it all.

He shook against a sudden chill, the cold slowing his pulse, confusing him.

Who was this girl? He glanced over at Hero, taking in the smooth, shallow curve of her cheek, pale as a statue's. Her hair was plastered down the side of her face, a loose bobby pin dangling. She reached up once, slowly, plucked away the strands from her mouth, and he saw that she was older than he had thought. Not really a girl at all anymore, though she had Eddie's blunt, childish chin, the blue, sincere eyes of a baby. She wore a man's rain jacket, dirty, with a worn corduroy collar, and Conrad realized with a shock that it was his own, cast off long ago, years before. He remembered Rose shaking it out, frowning at it, scurrying off to place it in a box somewhere, another donation for the impoverished. He recognized the buttons—brass, with a silver grommet in the center.

He glanced down at Hero's feet; her sneakers were gray, soaked with water. She wore a pair of old trousers, ripped at the knees; the flesh behind the tear was almost blue. He thought fleetingly of Rose's wicker sewing basket, the bright spools of colored thread, the needles lined up, shining in their velvet case, the orderly world of a prepared person.

He was pulling them away from the river, away from the sound of the river. He could hear it behind them, all the lowest tones of the scale released. He thought again of the lake, the dam, and Nolan. Was anyone still there, or had they given up at some signal from their foreman and fled away around the shoulder of the mountain, away from the course of the water? Was Nolan up there still, pointlessly dragging bags of sand to the dam, slipping on the slick rocks, tripping over the long fingers of tree roots that curled into the darkness? Was he falling into the water, his black coat billowing around him? Was Betty there, standing at the shore, trying to save him? Surely someone would have stopped him, Conrad thought. Someone would have seen that he wasn't fit, an old man armed only with the fever of his realization, his regret.

In the parking lot of the natatorium he stopped. Hero sat silently next to him. Staring at the bright square of the open doors, Conrad realized he had now almost completely lost the sight in his left eye. Harry had been afflicted for a time with a terrible condition, a detached retina, in which the world became riddled with tiny spots of emptiness. He'd had to lie facedown for three weeks after the eye was repaired. But this didn't feel like what Harry had described. This was more imprecise, he thought, a vanishing, the world pulled out from under his feet, flown to the rafters. He put his hand briefly to his face, saw the world go dark—or rather stream away, a vague shadow replacing the understood contours and perimeters of his world. He dropped his hand slowly. It rested on the seat between them. They said nothing.

Remembering, Conrad reached under his seat, withdrew the picture frame. "Here," he said, turning toward her; he wanted his voice to be gentle. "He gave me this."

Hero turned slowly in her seat, lifted her hands out from under the folds of the blanket, and took the picture from him.

"The *clover*," she said, and a little smile came over her mouth. It was amazing, Conrad thought, how it changed her whole face. It wasn't a face you expected to smile, he thought. A grave face. But it was, all the same, quite beautiful.

"He's not in there," she said then, looking up toward the natatorium.

"You don't know that," Conrad said. "You don't know that. Someone might have picked him up."

But he didn't move to open the door.

She shook her head.

Conrad looked out into the parking lot. It was empty except for the rows of parked cars and trucks. Everyone must be inside now, he thought. Everyone was safe. Eddie was somewhere. Safe. He turned to her. "Hero, this isn't really the time. Or the place—" He started to laugh, but it was a sound full of regret, all the regret of the last few months, since Rose had gone. "I have to say thank you, for what you've done for me. I want to say thank you."

She adjusted herself slightly, a barely perceptible movement next to him.

"It was all—delicious," he said. "It sustained me."

She didn't speak. He could feel an odd vibration beside him, Hero listening.

"My wife—" he began, then righted himself. "Rose—was so fond of you." He paused. "I guess you thought she would have liked that. You cooking for me, looking out for me."

And then Hero turned to him. "She told me," she said.

Conrad stared at her. "She told you," he repeated. "Before she died, she told you."

"No," Hero shook her head, and Conrad began to fly apart at the seams then, a wind blowing through him. The girl put out her hand, touched his arm. "Afterward," she said. "What you liked. She told me what you liked. How to do it."

Conrad stared at her, the blue eyes regarding him, the innocent eyes of an infant, so unlikely in her face. Trembling, he folded his hands over the steering wheel and brought his forehead down to rest upon them.

Rose had spoken to her, from the air over Hero's head, as the girl stood at the stove, waiting, poised. She had leaned down to guide her hand, touch the spoon. A pinch of this, a little of that. Thicken it with cornstarch, cream. Not so much salt. He likes chocolate. He likes meat. He likes sage dressing and cornmeal and buttermilk. He likes an orange peeled all in one piece, a helix. Clouds of steam had risen, the yeast of warm bread. Fat had sputtered in the pan. And over the meadows of the cemetery, over the long lawns with their statues of leaping boys and patient angels, over all the attitudes of the resting dead, over the grass and the earthworms and the knitting crickets, butterflies had risen in swarms, the flowers had opened, and the wind had made a heavenly music in the leaves. Rose loved him. Rose had spoken.

Thirteen

THEY SAT THERE in Conrad's truck, the memory of Rose's voice in their ears. His wife, leaning from the clouds, inclining toward him from what he vaguely thought of as a distant shoreline, had found a channel back to him, had seen that he was fed and cared for. And what had it been to Hero? He could not guess, except to believe that she had not been surprised, that her world had always been full of voices, the spokesmen of recrimination and doubt. Only there, on that lonely hillside, surrounded by grave markers, had the voices at last given way to cadences that were familiar and gentle, Rose's voice among them, prompting her toward a human kindness. In the great quiet of the cemetery, Hero had begun her recovery, tending her flowers, mowing the grass around the stones, watching the sun rise and set. In one part of his mind, Conrad still protested this—no one finds solace among the dead. How could the soul be cured in such a place? And yet he understood that Hero had found there the perfect asylum, found sanctuary among the voices of the past thrown across the washboard of the heavens, the conversation of angels. He had hated the ugliness of dying, the wasting pain, how from the first moment that he understood the incontrovertible path of Rose's illness, she was already beginning to be lost to him, though he held her hand tightly, though he made her speak to him, though he insisted, right to the very last moment, that she find him with her gaze, that she reply. He had protested the cruelty of random partings, children torn from their parents, spouses from each other, friends from friends. He had not understood, until now, that he could wish to believe in a different eternity, Rose taking up a permanent residence in the echoing corridors of his own heart. She would always wait there; she could speak to him still if only he would listen. Acts of imagination, Lemuel said, are man's answer to his own limitations, his yearning. Be limitless, he had said, arranging the pigeons on Conrad's arms, stepping back, his finger to his lips.

They sat there in Conrad's truck, each remembering the sound of Rose's voice. And then, from far away, from up on a ragged shelf of the mountains came another sound—the voice of the present, the distant roar of the dam at Lake Arthur tearing loose at last. There was a muffled explosion, the lapping of hushed wing beats. The birds waiting huddled in the trees above the lake rose into the air, a broad black cloak veering away into the sky, hurrying away. With a groaning bellow the lake broke free, poured in thick torrents down the riverbed, cracking the trunks of trees, lifting them by the roots, tearing away the oaks and the sumacs, the dogwoods and the poplars, the elders and the ash, carving away the earth, rearranging the known into the unknown, a white wake kicked up by a giant.

Conrad lifted his head from his folded hands at the sound, saw the double doors of the natatorium ahead of him darken with faces and figures, for they, too, had heard it, heard it over the tinny sound of the transistor radio, the inconsequential morning news echoing above the pool. Lenore Wyatt, her hand on Burden's sandy-haired head where he slept against her thigh, heard it. The Pleiades—a volunteer sandwich brigade, smooth-bladed knives poised over one hundred slices of soft white bread laid out side by side on an improvised plank table—they heard it, caught one anothers' eyes, and said wordlessly, Didn't you know it?

And they all, locked together—except for the old and infirm, who stayed behind, a teenage grandchild or a suffering spouse beside them holding their hands—came to the doors, stepped out cautiously into the rain, began flowing over the parking lot to the edge of the hillside, a river of witnesses, for a view down into town.

And it was just as Eddie had said, how they all stood there then, looking down at where they had been, where their lives had been lived. They tried to shake away the impossibility of it, the thing that was now just a memory, already growing old. How many steps to their front door? Hadn't there been a tree there by the path, a lilac bush planted one summer morning long ago? Where was the shed? The children's swings? The stone birdbath? The concrete griffin, hunched by the peonies? They would argue later —when entire buildings had been moved and streets had been rearranged like lines of string, after bridges had fallen and gaping vistas had opened where there had been none before—about these small things, the inconsequential order and placements, how it all had been. They fetched chairs and returned them to their neighbors, picked a sauceboat free from the mud, stepped on the tines of a buried fork, wept anew over lost photographs, certificates, jewelry, crying over what was funny and what was terrible—a piano listing in the town square, its ivory keys stripped, a wedding dress flying from a flagpole. How strange it was. Everything lost, nothing saved, three pigs found in the bank vault, a Boston whaler beached on the steps of the Congregational church, the mud that filled their houses now hardening to chalk. A wavering waterline ran around their walls, a memory of caution. Floors buckled, doors sprang from their hinges. At the town dump, on the windy mornings following the flood when people began cleaning out their houses, flocks of gulls and crows screamed over the detritus, circling high above the slow procession of cars and pickups with their rank loads of loss.

Conrad stood in the crowd at the top of the hill, felt the earth tremble under his feet, saw the explosion from the warehouse downriver where magnesium had been stored, the barrels now carried down the wide, churning current through the town, bursting into flames with the riveting phosphorescence of flashbulbs. It was impossible, Conrad thought, staring down at the rooftops far below him, black flecks of paper in a sea of frothing gray water. It was—impossible.

Standing on the hillside in the rain, they were strangely silent, though he could hear weeping from some, hear a child's high, protesting cry, hear the words "No, no." A man stood beside him, the retired mâitre d' from the hotel's dining room. Conrad glanced at him, saw he wore his medals from the war pinned limply over his chest. The man's hands hung loose beside him, emptied of weapons, palsied. Tears ran down his face.

And how strange, now, that a flood should be silent, Conrad thought, that he could hear nothing, that Rose's voice in Hero's ear should be the last thing he'd heard, the last thing he'd ever hear. He saw Rose sitting on the kitchen stool in their own house, a recipe book open on her lap, her glasses on her nose, reading aloud to him. The clock began to strike. "What?" he said aloud.

He'd lost her somewhere.

He turned in the crowd—after how long? how long did they all stand there watching?—to find himself embraced by Mignon, her head at his chest. "Oh, Conrad," she moaned softly, near his heart. And up behind her, gathering in close, were the other Pleiades, their hands linked.

He'd lost her somewhere.

They were turning, some of them, turning away now, coaxed

back indoors. The sky seemed to have disappeared, come apart, no longer rain falling but pieces of the upper story of the world itself, as if behind what they all thought of as the sky was something else, the necessary detritus from the moment of creation, not rock nor water nor rooting plant but shards of empty material, of nothingness. The air was thick, moist, both hot and cold.

"You're shaking," Mignon said. "Come inside."

But he'd lost her somewhere, he wanted to tell them. He'd lost the girl. Lost his wife. Lost her.

Someone put a blanket round his shoulders. He felt himself jostled along, his one good eye registering Henri's back in front of him, her wig righted now, patted into place, soaked dark at the edges. He felt the hot-air blowers of the natatorium, heard the hum of the generator, the steady whoosh of warm air, pumping like a heart. Someone pushed him gently onto a chaise longue at the edge of the pool. He heard the steady lap of water, a soft splashing. Someone passed a hand over his eyes.

"He's been out saving the world." It was Lenore. "I saw him, heading into town, oh, four, five hours ago."

"What was he doing? What on earth?"

"I think—he must have been looking for stragglers."

"Oh! Poor man. Who did he find?"

I've lost something, he thought.

"Burden, fetch him a coffee."

Conrad felt the cup being held to his lips, hot liquid in his mouth. He opened his eyes, looked out across the water, the bright, false blue of the pool, black lane lines wavering underneath.

And who was that, swimming? Making a steady crawl, enormous wings carving out scoops of water, throwing them high, a joyful sound, beads of brilliant water raining down. The swimmer turned his bright face to breathe. Conrad saw a grin spread out along his jaw, saw water siphon from his mouth like a fountain, saw the white hair, combed back, a goat's beard. Saw the eyes find him.

"Go home, Conrad."

He closed his eyes. He wasn't even surprised.

"It will be all right. They'll put it back together again. This is what happens. You'll see."

He opened his eyes again, saw the shape push itself from the water at the far side of the pool, shrink and quiver and transform itself into Rose's small, slender body, the neat waist cinched with a blue belt, her hair flicked back from her face. Her mouth opened, a flower. A sweet scent drifted across the water.

"Time now to go home, bird boy."

Home. Paradise Hill. Conrad tried to remember the view, saw it collect behind his closed eyes, each terraced garden one at a time, all the way down to his loft, all the flowers there opening to him. And then, with a wrench, he thought, My pigeons. Oh, Rose. He wanted to weep then, protesting a wrong that could not be righted, the river flowing through his loft, drowning his birds. Not them as well, he thought. Not my pigeons, too.

Maybe he should have gone home before he'd headed back into town, should have sprung the doors, set his birds free. But there hadn't been time. There'd been such an urgency, such responsibility. And now it was too late.

He forced himself to sit up, tried to compose himself against the weight of the grief, all his beautiful birds lost. I chose well, he tried to tell himself. I found Hero, drove her to safety. Still, his beautiful, innocent birds. Rose would have wept for him, the price he'd paid. Realizing this, he felt a small comfort. She would have understood.

He looked up, returned the coffee cup to Burden's freckled hand, his worried face hovering above.

"Thank you," he said. He looked around vaguely. "Thank you. I need to go home."

He stood, tried to prepare himself for what was to come. How many days would it be until the water withdrew, until he could get into the loft, bury his birds, the necessary business of what came afterward? He was so familiar with it, he thought, this aftermath. Suddenly he was so weary.

He patted his pockets, feeling that he had forgotten something. And then he remembered. Where *was* Hero?

He looked away from the circle of concerned women.

"Hero Vaughan," he said abruptly. "I had her with me. She was in the truck."

He saw Mignon glance at Henri.

"You have the girl?" Henri said.

"Well, I did." Conrad felt suddenly impatient. "I found her, down near Eddie's."

There was a silence. At last Mignon stepped forward, laid her small hand on his arm. "Conrad, they found Eddie. Harrison did. On the hill." Mignon's voice, full of that lilting Southern inflection. He turned to her, shocked.

"He'd had a heart attack, Conrad. He was walking up Forest."

Conrad looked at her numbly. A heart attack. But at least Eddie had tried, he thought. At least he hadn't jumped in the river. But how could it be? How could he have missed him? He'd driven that road a hundred times, looking and looking. He'd seen nobody. He hadn't seen Eddie, fallen by the curb, clutching his cash box, trying to make it to high ground. He shouldn't have left him there at the restaurant, Conrad thought, his heart seizing with guilt. And now Hero—

He looked around him. "I need to find her," he said, and broke free of them. And then he spun back. "And Nolan Peak?" he said. "Has anyone seen Nolan Peak?"

Mignon shook her head. "No," she said. "Nobody." And then she glanced up to the skylights.

"But look." She pointed.

And they all followed her gaze then, up to the roof, to the iron cross ties laid one against the other like swords, to the glass dormers high above. The rain had stopped, and a weak, sorrowful light shone down on their upturned faces.

CONRAD LOOKED FOR an hour, searching among all the people gathered in the natatorium. She seemed to have disappeared completely, with that strange habit of hers. He worried that someone had told her about her father, had taken her to him, his body already cooling in the basement of the hospital sixteen miles away. He stood outside the natatorium, watching the backs of people as they stood on the hillside in the gray light, looking down at their town.

At last, exhausted, he got in his truck and drove toward home, heading back on the roads that curved high above Laurel, coming back to Paradise Hill the long way. He was mindful, as he drove, of the world melting away beneath him, of the flood that washed through the low streets. He could hear it, a steady, muffled roar like the ocean, the intermittent, low sound of explosions, the wail of sirens.

He could think of nothing now except how cold he was, how much had been lost. He had not been able to save Eddie. His pigeons were gone. His mind ran forward and back. He worried about the girl. Someone *must* have told her. Where had she gone?

He pulled into his driveway and stopped the truck. He wanted to hear Rose's voice, Lemuel's voice. He strained toward the emptiness that lay ahead of him.

It's a trick, Lemuel had said. Close your eyes. But there was no trick to this, Conrad thought, closing the truck door, walking up the steps to his house. This is the habit of the survivor, one foot before the other, the hard work of continuing on. The new light that fell from the clearing sky was pale, apologetic, tender; not bright, he thought, not like the light at the end of the tunnel under the Sleeping Giant, the same day winking ahead after a passage through the dark. This was a different world altogether, nothing like the one he had left behind.

Once I thought I could not live a day without her, not an hour, he thought, stopping at his door. And yet here I am.

He opened his door, walked quietly down the hall to the kitchen, postponing the trip he would have to make, the moment when he would stand on his highest terrace, look down at his flooded loft. He stripped off his wet shirt, rubbed himself dry with Rose's apron, which hung over the doorknob of the pantry. I have so many things to take care of now, he thought, shaking, trying to find in himself some core of will. He rummaged in the pile of laundry on the floor, found a dry shirt. His hands fumbled with the buttons. I have to bury my birds, help my neighbors, he thought. Someone has to see to the girl. I have to see to the girl. She has no father now, no mother. Someone has to help her.

Hold my hand, Rose, he wanted to say as he left the kitchen.

He passed through the house and out to his terrace, moved to the low stone wall to look down and meet the black mirror of water there lapping the roof of his loft. He was already filled with the sadness of such a loss, the cold business of what came afterward, the unforgivable permanence of continuing on in a place made forever strange by the absence of what you loved. He thought of his garden, of how his footfalls, Rose's, had left a faint and resilient mark over each part of it, a random, uninterpretable path. He thought of the angel's great feet, Lemuel's feet planted before him. He thought that for a man who had had an uneventful life, he had in this last week been given enough mystery. He had entered it, walked into it, as through a door in the air itself. He had wandered there, weaving among the visions of his past and his future, and now was passing, slowly as the minute hand of a clock marching round the hour, back into the present. He would wrap his birds in white sheets and bury them beneath the birches, he thought, where the motion of the leaves was the motion of flight itself. He was amazed that he thought of this, that he had acquired the aptitude of the survivor, this instinct for what was right. The sun will rise and set each day from now until the end, he thought, and he made himself look down.

She loved you. Rose loves you.

He shook his head, put his hands on the wall.

A late summer bumblebee rose offended from the stones, zigzagged away into the soft air, a tiny black dirigible. He followed it with his eyes as it gradually lost altitude, sailed down the hill on steps of air, toward his loft.

Look. Look again. For above the tomb of water, on the tiled roof of his loft, was not nothing, not a space where something should have been, but a miracle, the white wings themselves, the dance of his birds, not lost, not drowned, but freed and clinging to the roof, to home, to what they knew. All around them the river had risen over the meadow, had rushed through the doors of the loft, had climbed to its curved roof. But his birds were safe.

He put his hands on the rough stone, climbed to the top of the wall. He stood there until his heart registered a perfect, mysterious balance, its chambers swelling. And then he threw back his white head, raised his arms, and held his face to the clearing wind.

From the roof below, they saw him and rose to meet him, circled his head in a crown of flashing light, came and lined themselves along his outstretched arms, white feathers billowing, taking on air, poised for flight. Wings.

Epilogue

SOMETIMES, NEAR THE end of his life, he was not sure whether he lived in the past or the present. They could not save his eye—central artery occlusion, they said, caused by a small blockage in his heart, a clot breaking free at last and traveling up to his eye.

Mignon or Hero or May Brown drove him around for weeks until he got used to the sensation of navigating the world with only one eye. Lenore came over and cleaned the house, Burden carrying loads of trash out to the truck, months of rubbish. Conrad taught Hero to feed the pigeons. Eventually he learned to adjust to the feeling of imbalance. He acquired a cane. He started to take the truck out again himself, Mignon sitting placidly beside him for company, but he did not drive once the sun had set. He took the steps down to his pigeon loft slowly, one stair at a time.

Gradually the two states—his life with Rose, his life afterward—lost the line of demarcation between them, a chalk stripe that faded gracefully over time. Sometimes he thought he was on the Sparkses' rooftop, would see Lemuel spread-eagled beside the balustrade, the city lights below winking in the darkness, the wind in his hair, his pigeons rising around him. Sometimes he saw Adele turning from the stove, a long-handled spoon in her hand, her eyes laughing at him. Sometimes he thought he was with Rose, sitting on the bed in his socks and undershorts while she undressed at night, a brush in her hand. He spoke to her, to Lemuel. He would stop before a plant, reach his fingers toward its petals, and the name of it would come to him, Rose's voice in his ear. Honesty.

Veronica. Forget-me-not. His garden grew wild, more overgrown each season, volunteer wildflowers sowing themselves in the rich earth. Birds did most of his planting now, and deer most of his harvesting.

Sometimes, sitting by Rose's marker at the cemetery on the long summer afternoons, he would start as Hero's shadow fell across the grass at his feet. "Come inside," she would say, leaning down, offering her arm, the sun behind her. Hi Roller, who never liked to be far from her, would circle their heads as they walked across the grass toward Hero's cottage through the falling light. There on the worn linoleum floor, the little terrier would lie still, watching the pigeon eat from the dog's supper bowl, and Hero would laugh.

It pleased Conrad to have made her this gift, to have given her a homing pigeon. The cemetery always seemed a lonely place to him, though he felt happier knowing there was a lost pigeon who called it home now along with Hero, a bird who came when she whistled, dipping through the dusk, its wing mended, its single eye fixed on Hero's roof. Hero might fix Conrad dinner, drive him home later under the domed sky massed with stars. He never confused her with anyone, though. He always seemed to know her.

Sometimes he asked her to tell him again about how she had come to his door the day of the flood. Finding no one there, she had run around to the back of the house, looked down into the meadow, and seen the water crawling toward the loft. She had run down the slick, stony steps, two, three at a time, had flung open all the doors, had urged the pigeons skyward, into the rain, waving her arms. They didn't want to leave, she told him. Of course, he thought. They're homing pigeons. Where would they have gone?

What he remembered of the months after the flood was the sound of industry, of Laurel being rebuilt. From high on Paradise

Hill, he could hear the grinding sound of the heavy trucks bringing lumber to Laurel, the steady ring of hammers, the buzz of chain saws. He saw facades resurrected, saw new gardens laid out with string, saw bricks laid one atop the next, mortar spread between them. A new flag flew from the pole in the square; a second plaque was added to the wall of the bank, six inches higher than the old one.

One evening he went to the Congregational church for an exhibit of the photographs Toronto had taken from the roof of the bank. He passed before the pictures, amazed at the strangeness of walking now where water had once buckled the pews and submerged the marble altar. Staring with his one eye at a picture of the bandstand, torn loose from its moorings and spinning crazily in the center of the flooded square, he suffered a moment of severe imbalance, staggered back, and found himself supported by Toronto.

"Steady," he said, and tightened his grip on Conrad's arm.

The Pleiades planned an after-the-flood party for the town, served up hot dogs and hamburgers and chicken from grills set up on the town square. Some people, the young people, danced, and Conrad took a turn or two inside the bandstand, now resettled on its old foundation, with May Brown.

No one rebuilt Eddie's, though. Harrison Supplee arranged with the city authorities to have the site turned into a tiny park, with a sundial at its center and two benches and an American flag. The grass there was studded with clover.

There was a wedding held in his own garden, Nolan's shaking hand placed atop Betty Barteleme's. Betty wore pale blue, a sequined jacket that made her look, Mignon said, leaning toward Conrad with her hand over her mouth, like the body of a great silver fish. The Pleiades catered the affair from their own kitchens.

Betty gave Nolan a bound volume of his columns, "From Peak's Beak"; Conrad had gilded the lettering on the leather cover. Nolan gave Toronto the *Aegis*—"Have fun," he said sarcastically—and Betty a ring with an opal at its center, a tiny, bright eye. He wore violets in his lapel, and Conrad pushed his wheelchair to the makeshift altar set up in the arbor.

Nolan had suffered one stroke after another, four in all, though Betty believed it was the cold that had caused them, not his effort to brace the dam. How very cold he had been that afternoon, carried back to her on the shore where she waited, her own lips growing blue. It was some young man, she never knew who, who had pulled Nolan from the water where he sat, a surprised expression on his face, not three feet from the bank, unable to move. He could talk, though he didn't much anymore, and when he ate, food dribbled from the corner of his mouth. He wore his bow tie, held Betty's hand. He smiled in a lopsided way at the well-wishers who came before him and held out their hands to him or touched his knee. He always remembered ringing the bells, the perfect sensation of weightlessness as he'd clung to the ropes.

Sometimes, kneeling in the garden at Mt. Olive, near the double helix of rosebushes planted by the Pleiades in Rose's name, Conrad thought he saw Rose walking toward him through the flowers, a bouquet in her hands, her white dress fluttering around her.

And he would try to sit up straighter then, try to show her his good side. "How sweet you are, bird boy," she would say tenderly, coming to stand before him, reaching her hand to his cheek. "How I love you." And he would try to smile at her through his tears.

"The view," he would say to her, trying to distract her from his sorrow, seeing the fingernail moon rise early in the still-blue sky. "Look at the sky, the swallows."

And then he would be home again, just as if a curtain had been pulled aside. He was home in his own garden, flowers pulsing behind his eyelids, home in their bedroom with its silvering mirrors. He would be kneeling by her bed in those final moments, a flutter of wings around them, his pigeons lifting skyward. "What did you say? Rose! What did you say?"

For she would be going, she would be on her way. And he heard her then at last, heard the final words that had eluded him all this time.

"Paradise," she said, and lifted her hand.

"Look, Conrad," she said. "Look at the view from Paradise Hill."